EIGHT MILLION MINUTES

Samantha Kay

Copyright © 2024 Samantha Kay

First published in 2024

The right of Samantha Kay to be identified as author of this work has been asserted by her in accordance with the Copyright, Designs and Patents Act 1988.

All characters and events in this publication, other than those clearly in the public domain, are fictitious, and any resemblance to real persons, living or dead, is purely coincidental.

All rights reserved.

No part of this publication may be reproduced, stored in a retrieval system, or transmitted, in any form or by any means, without the prior permission in writing of the publisher, nor be otherwise circulated in any form of binding or cover other than that in which it is published and without a similar condition including this condition being imposed on the subsequent purchaser.

A CIP catalogue record for this book is available from the British Library.

Cover design by Samantha Kay ©2024

*For Katrina and Bruce. Loyal friends
with the purest hearts.*

SAMANTHA KAY

Also by Samantha Kay

Found

Good People

You're A Dream To Me

SAMANTHA KAY

PROLOGUE

It was all so romantic.

The crackling fire, the champagne, the piano playing a gentle melody in the background.

Even the weather had received the memo. The biting cold outside had finally broken into a flurry of snowflakes landing softly on the windowpane beside them. With lovely full bellies and smiles on their faces, Abbie and Jason clinked their glasses together and each took a sip. Then Jason kissed Abbie on the lips before snuggling in even closer.

Finally, *finally,* it was just the two of them, in total privacy. Somewhere that wasn't the store cupboard or the fire exit by the stairwell, or inside the car. After six long months of sneaking around, they were free to kiss, hold hands and have sex as loudly as they liked - at least until 10.30 a.m. tomorrow, when they'd have to check out and pick up their separate lives again.

Abbie felt sad at the prospect, but willed

herself not to feel down. For months she'd worried that their affair was nothing more than stolen moments in the Tesco car park after work, but this weekend Jason had finally proved himself. She could hardly bear to think how much all this extravagance was setting him back, but surely this was the kind of perk that came from dating an older man. After all, no nineteen-year-old boy her own age - could have afforded a stay in a place as nice as this.

'I'm so happy,' said Jason, looking into her eyes, lovingly pushing a loose strand of blonde hair behind her ear.

Abbie smiled, but before she could respond, their moment of bliss was interrupted by the sound of a baby crying.

'Who brings a baby to a place like this?' protested Jason.

While he scanned their surroundings, trying to locate the jarring noise, Abbie noticed a distressed-looking woman walk into the lounge area. She was accompanied by two young children - a toddler, a boy, maybe two years of age, standing closely next to her and the screaming baby held in her arms.

'Oh fuck!' exclaimed Jason, horror etched on to his face. 'How did you—'

'Find you? You left the email confirmation on your laptop, you fucking piece of shit!' shouted the woman, charging towards them, tears pooling in her eyes.

Suddenly, a tryst in the store cupboard didn't seem so bad after all, thought Abbie. At least in the store cupboard their liaisons stayed solely between themselves, and the spare toilet rolls. Amongst the boxes of plastic cups, and paper towels Abbie could convince herself that Jason's wife and kids didn't really exist. That they were no more real than characters from a novel she had read, or a TV show she had watched. But here, in the opulence of the fancy hotel lounge she'd waited so long to enjoy, they were as real as the nose on her face, as was the destruction and heartache she had caused.

'Here, you want my husband, you can have everything that comes with him,' wept Kelly, thrusting her now-hysterical baby into Abbie's arms and propelling her son in the direction of Jason. 'Enjoy your weekend,' she managed, before fleeing the lounge.

'Kelly, wait, wait!'

Jason ran after his wife, leaving Abbie holding his red-faced, distressed baby, while a rather confused toddler stood next to her, not knowing whether to follow his arguing parents or stay with his sibling.

'Hi,' said Abbie.

The little boy smiled back, then yawned. It was well past his bedtime. Embarrassed by the scene, Abbie tried in vain to soothe Jason's baby.

True, dating an older man had its perks, she thought, but it also came with a fair amount of unwanted baggage.

CHAPTER 1

ABBIE

It stinks in here. Of damp and cigarettes, along with the subtle hint of dustbins. I watch as Hamza the letting agent forces open the window, doing what he can to freshen the air around us.

'It hasn't been lived in for a while,' he coughs. 'Just needs ventilating, see?'

With the window open, the noise of the traffic outside has increased tenfold, bringing with it the added smell of cooking oil.

'It's really small . . . and it needs quite a lot of work,' I say, eyeing up a small hole in the wall. 'And is it normal to have the bed that close to the oven?' Fully aware the answer is no.

Hamza shrugs and I can tell he's trying his hardest not to roll his eyes.

'Look, Mrs Turner, it's a flat, in London, with great transport links, all to yourself and the rent is well within budget. You'll have to try and overlook the damp.'

'So, you agree that it does smell of damp.'

Hamza sighs, but otherwise stays silent.

He knows as well as I do that this place is an utter dump and I wonder if he feels any shame for having brought me here. I let out a loud frustrated breath, feeling no need to disguise my disappointment. Then I take one last hopeless look around. I gingerly open the door to the tiny bathroom again, in the vain hope I'll discover a secret pathway to a magical utopia, containing a shiny clean apartment.

As I open the door, a large moth flies out and the door handle comes off in my hand.

'It's OK, just slip that back on,' Hamza says carelessly.

I do as he says and place the loose handle back in its slot. The sad fact is, Hamza is right. As miserable and ugly as this place is, it's one of the best we've viewed so far.

There was the flat above the pet shop, which really wasn't as cute as it sounds, the whole place reeking of urine. Then there was the 'renovated' squat in all its original crack-den chic, followed by the former weed factory. It might have been a strong contender, with its countless plug sockets and top-notch installation, had it not been for the shifty-looking neighbours.

It's safe to say, in the cold harsh light of day, the fresh new start planned in my head is starting to look a little bleak. It appears that if I want a new life without Jason, a damp-smelling flat with a nicotine-stained ceiling is as good as it's going to get, at least until a divorce settlement when I can buy a flat of my own.

'OK, I'll definitely give it a think,' I tell Hamza, swallowing down my resentment.

'All right, but don't take too long about it. A place like this, at this kind of price, could be snapped up by the end of the day.'

Hamza's words are followed by a loud bang. We both jump and turn to see that the dirty and dilapidated window blind has fallen off, crashing straight onto the cold hard floor. I glance at the suicidal blind and walk out. No words are necessary.

Feeling more than a little glum, I walk back along the road, eventually arriving outside *Daisy's*, where I immediately start to feel better. This is my business: a giftshop-cum-tearoom situated on the corner of a once thriving, now dying high street. I peer through the large front window at the display of fancy candles and reed diffusers, along with sparkly photo-frames, gift cards and a whole array of shiny trinkets to tempt the customers. The other half of the shop floor consists of five tables, where tea, coffee and a varied selection of cakes and pastries are served and enjoyed. The shop really is my pride and joy. Never in my wildest dreams did I imagine that one day I would own my own business, but I did it. Little old me.

However, as is the norm nowadays, the

tables remain empty, as does the entire shop, except of course for the sight of Molly slumped behind the counter.

Her face is invisible below a head of half-black and half-blonde hair, her focus so obviously fused down on her phone rather than on the shop.

Infuriated by the sight, I march towards the entrance. The small bell above the door tinkles on my entry, but there's no reaction from Molly. I step inside and let out a loud cough, making my presence known.

'Excuse me?' I snap.

Molly's body shoots up in fright, her phone falling clumsily onto the hard floor with a loud clank.

'The phone - again!' I explode. 'Molly, how many times do I need to tell you! What if I'd been a customer? What if I'd tried to steal something?' It's time to assert my authority.

Molly ducks behind the counter to retrieve her phone, before quickly popping back up again. She looks flustered, anxiously pushing her large framed glasses back on her face.

'I know, I know. I'm sorry. I just needed a moment to check all the details for tomorrow's protest.'

At twenty years old, politics student Molly is only two years older than Harry, my eldest step-child. Molly is lazy, tardy and has an awful lot of outspoken opinions for somebody whose

EIGHT MILLION MINUTES

life experience doesn't exceed beyond a year's stint handing out skates at a roller disco. But despite all her shortcomings she's trustworthy, creates a good rapport with the customers and, crucially, is willing to work for minimum wage every weekend.

I swiftly make my way behind the counter, asking, 'God, what is it this time? Fighting for the rights of misshapen carrots?'

'Ha, you're so funny. It's a march to Downing Street if you must know. Socialists Against Capitalism.'

'Erm, isn't that kind of a given? Like, vegans against cannibalism.' I pick up the unopened post from under the counter and start sifting through it.

'And what did *your* generation ever do to change the world? Join Facebook?' Molly asks snarkily.

I grimace at the final demand from the electricity company and place the post back under the counter where I had found it, hoping that by the time I look again, it might just disappear.

'When I was your age, I was busy supporting my now husband in a custody battle whilst living in the smallest flat known to man,' I reply with an air of arrogance, implying how incredibly mature and grown up I was at Molly's age.

'Good to see your life is going full circle

SAMANTHA KAY

then.'

I laugh inwardly, unable to hit back with a witticism of my own.

'How was this one?' Molly wants to know.

I tell the truth. 'Not great,' I sigh, 'but certainly not the worst. It's only the next road along, so it would have been perfect.'

So far, Molly is the only person I've confided in regarding my plan to leave Jason. As my employee and an unbiased outsider, she makes a safe soundboard for all my problems.

'I don't get it,' she says, puzzled. 'You say you practically live alone already. Why not continue to do that in a beautiful home, rather than some crappy flat?'

She does make a good point. My marital home is beautiful, and our holidays are exotic, but what does any of it count for if it's mostly experienced alone? For the past few years, being married to Jason is like being single, but with none of the benefits. When at home I'm largely alone, and even on holiday Jason will be glued to his phone or laptop, stepping out of restaurants to take calls or leaving me alone by the hotel pool for hours while he disappears to the room or the foyer to seek a better WIFI reception.

The time I spend alone at home stretches like a prison sentence. Often the only thing breaking the loneliness is when my step-kids Harry and Ellie swing by, but these days their visits are rare and their company nothing short of agony.

I'm over longing for Jason to be more present. If I'm going to be alone, I'd rather do it on my own terms without the complications of married life holding me back.

I look into Molly's youthful face and remember a time when I too had no idea of all the complexities adulthood had in store. Too kind to quash all of her world-changing hopes, I smile sweetly and change the subject.

'You making tea?' I ask, moving away from the counter, keen to take a moment to enjoy something warm, in the hope the lunch-time crowd descends soon.

'Yeah, about that: are you sure this tea is responsibly sourced? Because I have some doubts,' Molly announces.

I stare at her blankly. Unable to offer any kind of answer to her question I shrug my shoulders, truly struggling to give a shit.

Getting the message, she says sheepishly, 'I'll look into it another time.'

'Good idea.' And turning on my heels, I head to the Ladies to freshen up.

JASON

Gerald is something else. A retired hedge-fund manager in his mid-seventies, he's of slight build and a gentle disposition, softly spoken, and has always walked at a slow and steady pace, an aura of calm and serenity encompassing him.

But behind the wheel of a Supercar, the man is an absolute monster.

I hang on with all my might to the door handle as Gerald whizzes the yellow McLaren 600LT around the test track. He laughs and whoops with absolute glee like a child at the fair as I swallow hard, fearful I might vomit all over the interior, which will do little to secure the sale.

Finally, and not a moment too soon, Gerald slows the car down until we make a complete stop.

I unclip my seatbelt and stagger out of my seat. I rest my arm on the roof and lower my head into my hand, just until it stops spinning, feeling too sick to worry about saving face.

'What's up, Jase? You getting soft in your old age?' Gerald taunts me, easing himself from the car, still giggling like a naughty schoolboy.

'Gerald. You are an animal,' I wheeze, unable to believe that someone as mild-mannered as him can wreak such havoc on the track. Eventually I feel well enough to hold my head up unaided and to join Gerald in a slow walk around the vehicle.

They say there are no friends in business, and although that may be true, I'd say my relationship with Gerald is as close as one gets. I owe a lot of my early success to him.

Once a humble car mechanic, I tried my luck as a car salesman shortly after I finished my apprenticeship. Working at a Toyota showroom in Ilford, I soon became the top salesman in my region. Some years later, it was at that very showroom I fell madly in love with the new pretty blonde on the service desk, which certainly wasn't a part of my plan. I was a married man with two small children and never would have thought myself the type to put everything on the line, but the heart wants what it wants.

Bruised and broken from a lengthy divorce and bitter custody battle, I didn't have much else to lose. But with Abbie by my side, she made me believe we could achieve anything together. I took the plunge and started my own business, buying and selling high-end cars. It was a risky move, but it paid off – big style. This year, my business, *Turner's*, celebrates its eighth successful year in the trade.

It was way back in that very first year that I met Gerald.

He could have bought a car from any of the big high-end dealers, but he took a punt on me, a desperate chancer, trying his best. Maybe he saw something of himself in me, who knows, but we hit it off. He recommended me to some friends and word soon spread.

Situated in Epping, just off the M11, *Turner's* employs a total of sixteen people, and is bursting at the seams with Supercars worth more than some people's homes. My site even boasts its very own test track (kind of). A neighbouring private airfield lets us use their land from time to time for test drives - a lovely perk for our customers and something that distinguishes us from the competition.

So far, Gerald has purchased a total of four cars from me. A Porsche, two Ferraris and a Lamborghini, and I have a feeling the McLaren might well be lucky number five!

'She really is something, Jase. I think this might well be the most beautiful thing I've ever seen,' Gerald tells me, admiring the car's elegance and poise.

'Don't let Suzie hear you say that, she'll get jealous,' I joke, referring to Gerald's fiancée, a Hungarian thirty-something who's just secured the position of potential wife number four.

'Honestly Jase, I love her so much.' Gerald is clutching at his chest, looking gooey-eyed.

I've met Suzie a few of times. Most recently at a car event a month or so ago. Other than sporting an enormous set of fake knockers, I struggled to uncover any other endearing qualities, but she makes Gerald happy, so . . .

'Suzie, yes, she's a lovely girl.' I nod.

'No, not Suzie, the car!' Gerald says impatiently.

I laugh and shake my head. I should have known better. The number of times Gerald has been married and divorced is a subject of great fascination to me. My one divorce was stressful and costly enough, let alone three, and I find it strange that to Gerald, wives are so . . . disposable. I love my wife. Everything I do is for her. The very idea of replacing her is unthinkable.

'All right, Lewis Hamilton, let's get inside and talk some numbers,' I say, just as the dark clouds above us begin to spit rain.

CHAPTER 2

ABBIE

Between the failed flat search and Molly's lecture on government austerity, I decide to break with tradition and call it a day early, leaving Molly to close up on her own.

As I pull my red Mini Cooper onto the driveway, I turn off the ignition and take a moment to admire our home. We moved here about five years ago, and our detached five-bedroom mock-Tudor house is a measure of just how far we've come. However, lovely as it is, it's not quite where we want to be. We live in Gidea Park, an area where East London meets Essex, a mere two miles away from Jason's ex-wife and kids. We could live in a quieter street in a nicer area with cleaner air, but while the kids are still in school, Jason was adamant we should be near them. Because that's what happens when you pinch someone else's husband - you're forever held to ransom by their ex-wife and kids!

The traditional exterior of our house, with its black beams and red-brick walls, is in stark contrast to the very modern interior: a total renovation that took two years and cost many thousands of pounds. Two smart bay trees stand to attention either side of the black-painted front door, and pink rose bushes bloom under the front windows in the summer, adding a dash of country charm to our little corner of the world.

The very idea of leaving such luxury certainly fills me with a great sense of sadness. But what is the point of having a two-car garage (housing Jason's Lamborghini Huracan as well as a red Ferrari 488), three ensuite bathrooms and a state-of-the-art kitchen if it's part of an existence that is lived practically alone?

When I insert my key in the front door, I'm surprised to find that it's already unlocked. I look back at the drive, confirming that Jason's 'everyday' car - a silver Jaguar F Pace - is nowhere to be seen. Maybe I forgot to lock the door this morning? It's unlike me, but not unheard of.

I open the door and step inside, but when I go to tap in the code for the alarm, it has already been deactivated. Strange. I'm sure I set it this morning. The cleaner hasn't been today, to the best of my knowledge, and it certainly isn't like Jason to pop home during the day, and even less like him to leave the alarm deactivated and the front door unlocked.

Stepping into the light and airy hallway, I'm met by the love of my life, Daisy, pitter-patting her little paws on the wooden floor towards me. Daisy is our rescue tabby cat and the inspiration behind the name of my business. Welcoming me with a little chirpy meow of happiness, she weaves herself in between my legs. It's then I hear a noise.

Someone is in this house.

My heart hammers inside my chest. There's no sign of a disturbance, but I can most certainly hear sounds coming from the front room. With my door keys held in my hand like a tiny sword, I creep towards the front room. I can hear a voice, that of a man. He isn't speaking loudly, it's more of a groan, implying that he isn't alone. I feel my hand begin to shake, my heart beating so fast I'm worried it might actually give out.

I approach the front room and very gingerly peer around the open doorway, letting out a yelp of absolute horror at the sight greeting me.

In her hand Ellie is holding the biggest willy I have ever seen, that of a teenage boy, lying back on my sofa with his school trousers pulled down to his ankles. Ellie is kneeling on the floor beside him, her bra on full display. On hearing my yelp, the pair scramble from their positions as I spin around, wishing to unsee the ungodly sight of my teenage stepdaughter issuing a blow job in the living room.

'Why are you home early?' screams Ellie.

'Oh, I'm *so* sorry for interrupting!' I scream

back. I decide to remove myself from the situation I unwillingly find myself in and storm towards the kitchen, leaving Ellie and her 'friend' to gather themselves together.

Unsure what exactly to do with myself, I'm now standing in the kitchen waiting for the kettle to boil. Soon afterwards, I hear the front door open and close. Assuming the pair have skedaddled, I breathe a sigh of relief, then am further startled by the appearance of Ellie, who is standing before me fully clothed, back in her school uniform. I must admit, I'm impressed by her boldness. If I were in Ellie's shoes I would have fled as fast as my feet could carry me.

We stand either side of the breakfast bar and stare blankly at one another, neither quite knowing what to say.

Ellie very much resembles a younger version of her mother. She's pretty, with long thick fair hair and blue eyes which currently emit their usual expression of disdain. Ellie is certainly no longer a child. Her figure displays maturity and curves, but the awkward fidgeting of her hands and the panic in her eyes reveal her for the juvenile she still is.

'Dad said I was allowed to bring people over,' she blurts out in her typically snotty tone.

'Did he also say it was OK to have sex in the front room?' I shoot back.

Ellie doesn't respond. She pouts, her fidgeting hands now in overdrive.

'Can I just ask why you didn't use your bedroom?' I say, unable to understand Ellie's risky choice of location.

'There's no lock on my door and usually no one's home.' Her voice is small, her eyes on the floor.

I know I should follow up with the obligatory parental questions, such as: How long has this kind of thing been taking place? Are you using protection? Are you fully consenting?

But I don't go there, not sure I can stomach the answers.

'Anyway, I'm not doing anything wrong. I'm sixteen,' she says defiantly.

'And how old is *he*?' I ask, realising I didn't even look at the boy's face, all my attention drawn directly to his erect penis.

'Well, he's not thirty and married,' Ellie sneers, disdain oozing from her tone.

I shake my head, annoyed with myself for thinking we could have a single conversation that didn't sour within minutes.

Ellie was a mere baby when I met Jason and when our affair was exposed. She's too young to remember a time when her father and I weren't together. When Ellie was little, we enjoyed an easy and relaxed rapport but over the last three years, things have become strained. The once sweet and considerate little girl who loved nothing more than dancing around to Taylor Swift songs with me has been ravaged

EIGHT MILLION MINUTES

by hormones and stuck in an almighty strop. Her company is often unbearable, her filthy moods more often than not fired straight in my direction.

With the help of her mother, Ellie has been well versed on all the controversial facts.

I'm the reason her parents aren't together.

I'm the reason Jason was a stranger during the first few years of her life.

And right now, *I'm* the reason her routine roll-about in the front room has ended early.

'So rude - and there was me thinking we didn't need to bother your dad with this,' I say, keen to show her who's boss in my own home.

'You're not gonna tell him?' Ellie's cockiness suddenly morphs into sheer panic.

'No, I'm not - *you* are. Right now. Let's give him a call.' I pick up my phone from the counter and swipe the screen.

'No, no, please! Please don't!' Ellie rushes round to my side of the breakfast bar, clumsily knocking into one of the bar stools, eager to stop me doing the unthinkable. She makes a grab for my phone, but I'm too fast, swiping it away and holding it above my head. Ellie jumps to reach the phone in my hand but can't quite manage it.

I decide to run away, darting as fast as I can out of the kitchen, but Ellie is hot on my heels. I make it only as far as the lounge doorway before I feel Ellie wrap her arms around my waist and rugby tackle me to the floor. Taken aback by

SAMANTHA KAY

quite how strong she is, I'm unable to wriggle free as she straddles me, using all her body weight to pin me down. With my phone squished somewhere between the two of us, Ellie starts to tickle me all over. I begin to laugh, impressed at the lengths she is prepared to go to, for Jason not to find out about her escapades.

Although I struggle, she continues to tickle me into submission.

I hear a dull thud as my phone drops on the floor. I manage to grab hold of it, while trying in vain to bat Ellie's hands away, but it's no use. Unable to withstand the torture for a second longer, I cave.

'Stop, Ellie, stop! Please! All right, I'm not gonna tell him!' I shout through hysterical laughter.

'Promise! Promise you won't tell him.'

'I promise!'

Ellie releases me, looking relieved, if a little dishevelled from our tussle.

'Just don't let me catch you at it in the front room again or I'll change my mind,' I say, still trying to catch my breath, standing up from the floor and straightening myself up.

'Where are we supposed to go?' asks Ellie, sweeping her long hair from her face, huffing loudly.

'I'm sure you'll figure something out,' I say, offering unwilling allegiance. Then I make my way back into the kitchen and head towards the freshly boiled kettle to make a cup of tea.

'You staying to see Dad?' I call, opening the cupboard above where the mugs are kept.

'No. He'll be ages,' mumbles Ellie, just loud enough for me to hear. 'I'm going home.'

With that, I reach down just one mug and am secretly relieved that within seconds I hear the sound of the front door close.

Happy as I am to see the back of Ellie, it makes me sad to think how difficult our relationship has become. I had secretly looked forward to the day my step-kids would have grown older. To a time when they'd see me as less of a wicked step-mother and we could enjoy a relationship that was more in the way of a friendship. Unfortunately, it seems such a dynamic is further away than I'd hoped. Maybe even impossible.

*

Sitting at the kitchen breakfast bar with my laptop open, my finger hovers over the 'pay now' button on the electricity suppliers' website. Having put off paying the bill for weeks, I'm worried there isn't enough money in the business account to cover the cost. The truth is, I know I should have wound down *Daisy's* a while back. Business has been slow for ages, but I just can't bear to admit defeat. The shop is my baby, my project I built from nothing – kind of. It all came together through a combination of hard work and a little help in the form of an unexpected inheritance.

Years ago, when Jason and I first got together, our early relationship had few cheerleaders, but no one was more disapproving than my parents. In fact, they were so angry and embarrassed by my choices, they decided to cut off all contact with me.

Fortunately, the same could not be said for my ever-loving grandfather. Difficult and cantankerous as he could be to others, to me, Pops; my mother's father, was the sweetest, kindest man in the world. Shocked by my parents' cruelty, he refused to turn his back on me. I'd visit him regularly, giving him company and a listening ear to whatever gripe he had that week, and he would welcome me with open arms and tea on tap.

As the years passed, the tensions between me and my parents gradually eased. That is - until Pops sadly passed away.

As a show of love and appreciation for the time I'd given him, Pops left me a substantial sum of money in his will. My parents were angry and suspicious, believing they were entitled to every penny he had owned, accusing me of 'stealing' the money from under them. In short, the old tensions were reignited, harsh words were exchanged and we haven't spoken since. Not a single telephone call, birthday or Christmas card has been exchanged in years.

Wanting the money left to me to be used

in a meaningful way, I opened *Daisy's* in Pops honour, and as a big 'Up Yours' gesture of defiance to my parents. So, despite the current financial challenges with the business, to throw in the towel now would feel like a betrayal of him and of myself. And after all, the shop has suffered tough times before and it's always come through the other side.

Taking a deep breath, I hit the pay button, hoping for the best. Then I close the page, causing the page behind to reveal itself - a property website listing rental flats that I know I'll struggle to afford on my own.

Not wishing to depress myself further, I close the property page too, causing the desktop picture to glare back at me. Taken eleven years ago on our wedding day. Jason and I smile brightly into the camera, our arms wrapped around one another, dressed in our wedding attire and looking a picture of happiness.

Aside from a greater sprinkling of salt and pepper in his short dark hair, Jason has hardly changed at all. The lines under his blue eyes have become a little deeper, but like a fine wine, he's improving with age, even if his belly is looking a little fuller these days.

Sighing, I cast my mind back to our wedding day and everything we'd had to overcome to reach that point: Jason's divorce and the custody battle, as well as the disapproval of our relationship from just about everyone. Our wedding wasn't a grand affair, we couldn't afford for it to be - but simply to make our relationship official meant the world to both of us.

I remember how happy we were in our tiny first flat with our empty bank accounts. We would budget all week just to be able to afford a takeaway on a Friday night and we'd go to bed early in the winter as a means to save on the heating bill.

Indeed, our home today is everything we could ever have dreamed of, but with just me in it, the whole place feels soulless.

These days, living with Jason is much like the beginning of our relationship, taking me back to a time when I had to endure sharing him with someone else. Except this time, instead of sharing him with Kelly, I'm sharing him with the bloody showroom. It comes before everyone and everything. It's as if the showroom's feelings are going to be hurt if Jason should leave before seven in the evening or ask someone else to lock up for a change. In the meantime, the kids and I are offered scraps of his time in between working and work-related events.

Originally, I had thought that setting up my own business might bring us closer together, as something we now had in common – but it hasn't worked out that way. While *Turner's* has gone on to thrive year on year, my profits have slowly dwindled to nothing. The worst thing is, I can't even bring myself to talk to Jason about

EIGHT MILLION MINUTES

it, humiliated that I couldn't make a better go of things.

I take a look around our large silent kitchen. It has all the mod-cons we could ever dream of, from a state-of-the-art coffee machine to a huge black Smart fridge that connects to our phones. The screen on the door will tell you what's inside, because simply opening the door is *so* last century.

It's undeniable that Jason has provided us with a very comfortable lifestyle. This in some ways makes it even harder - because how could a person with a bright green Lamborghini in their garage possibly have anything to complain about? Outwardly, we live an enviable lifestyle, but the reality is somewhat different...

A few months ago, for my birthday, Jason bought us tickets for a West End show, just the two of us. Like any good mistress playing second fiddle to his wife (the showroom), I was delighted for the opportunity to spend some time together. He promised we'd get there early, have some dinner, then go on to the show, but a meeting with his marketing company ran over. Not only was he too late to grab dinner with me, but he also missed the entire show.

Undeterred and wanting to make a point, I went alone. I sat in the stalls like an absolute loser, and cried silently when the house lights went down. It was without doubt the saddest and most alone I've ever felt in my entire life.

30

SAMANTHA KAY

Naturally, Jason grovelled an apology, but I didn't speak to him for a whole week.

That was the straw that broke the camel's back.

My husband provides. He would never lay a hand on me. He's good and kind, incredibly handsome and really very charming, but the life we have *isn't the one I want.*

I catch sight of the dinner I've made Jason sitting on the kitchen counter waiting for him under a sheet of tinfoil. Another mealtime missed, another night spent alone. I let out a deep sigh and just as I'm about to close the laptop, I hear the sound of the front door opening. I look at the time on my watch. It's half past six, a good three hours earlier than he would usually return home, and I feel my insides skip a little. Excited that he's home, I wonder if he's sensed everything I'm feeling.

Is it really time to end everything we've built together? Is there still something between us worth saving?

I wait with bated breath, when finally, Jason enters the kitchen.

'Hey! You're home early,' I say, pleased to see him.

'Yeah, my laptop at work is knackered. The whole thing shut down and wouldn't restart. I need to get a new one,' he says, gravitating towards his dinner on the counter. He looks tired, stressed. Dressed in his usual work attire of smart shirt and trousers.

Jason lifts the foil from the plate to reveal a cold portion of chilli con carne and rice.

'Oh well, as much as that sucks it's nice to have you home early for a change,' I say sweetly and I mean it. I miss him being home. I miss the person I used to eat dinner with each night, and fall asleep with in front of the TV. I even miss the person who'd leave their dirty socks on the floor and who would never put the toilet seat back down. I wish with all my heart that he would be present again like he used to be, before *Turner's* came before everything else.

He smiles a handsome smile back at me, before walking to the drawer next to the oven, opening it and pulling out a fork.

'Did you have a good day?' he asks, taking a large bite of chilli from his fork, then walking towards me, kissing me on the lips with his mouth full.

'It was OK. Ellie was here earlier.'

'Really?' Jason is surprised. He knows it's unlike Ellie to come by unless she wants something, usually money.

'Yeah, she . . . just wanted to grab something from her room. I met her boyfriend too,' I add, unable to suppress a wicked smile.

'Ellie, has a boyfriend?' Jason echoes, eyebrows raised.

I ponder for a second, debating with myself how much I should divulge.

'He seemed nice enough – a bit shy, reserved,' I lie.

'He didn't go to her room, did he?' I can't quite make out if Jason is angry or just being protective, or maybe both.

'Oh no, they were only here for all of five minutes.'

A look of relief sweeps across his face.

'Anyway, Molly was telling me about some thriller movie she watched and I thought we could . . .' I begin to say, trailing off as I watch Jason pull his phone from his trouser pocket and swipe through it, completely ignoring me.

'OK,' he mumbles with his mouth full, his eyes glued to the tiny screen in his hand.

'So, maybe we can watch it?' I try, knowing full well Jason hasn't listened to a word that has come out of my mouth.

'Watch what?'

'The film. You know, since you're home early,' I suggest, feeling hopeful, if a little pathetic.

'Er, yeah, maybe.' He slips his phone back into his pocket, places the fork onto his plate and makes to leave the kitchen.

'Where are you going?' I ask.

'I told you - the work laptop went dark on me. I've still got stuff to finish so I'm gonna use my old one upstairs. Thanks for dinner.' With that, Jason and his chilli leave the kitchen and disappear upstairs.

Alone once again, I sit in stunned silence, annoyed with myself for expecting anything more from him. I look back down at my own laptop and, ignoring our happy smiling wedding picture, I reopen a webpage and begin my flat search once again, not caring whether or not I can afford the rent.

JASON

Sitting in my office in almost complete darkness, I'd barely noticed the early evening drift into night. The only light in the room is coming from the glaring laptop screen on the desk. It hadn't occurred to me to stand up and turn on the light. I take a look at my watch. It's 9.30 p.m. I rub my tired eyes, stretch my arms above my head, yawn and decide to call it a night.

My home office is pretty uninspiring. It's small and cluttered and mainly functions as a graveyard for old phones and general junk that we can't bring ourselves to throw away, but the space meets all my work needs well enough. I finally close the laptop and leave the office, heading down the landing to the bedroom. I can hear the TV is still on and I'm glad, hoping it's a sign that Abbie is still awake.

'Sorry I took so long,' I say, going inside. 'We can still watch that f—' But as I secretly suspected, Abbie is sound asleep in bed, the TV remote held loosely in her hand. I take gentle hold of the remote and point it towards the television on the wall to turn it off, plunging the room into darkness.

I look down at Abbie and feel a stab of regret that I didn't wrap up work sooner. I struggle to remember the last time we watched TV together on a weeknight. It's not uncommon for me to return home after Abbie has fallen asleep. On the odd occasion she is awake, by the time I have eaten and showered, the best part of the evening has passed and before we know it, it's morning all over again.

She looks beautiful asleep, without a scrap of make-up and her blonde hair tumbled on top of her head. I love the stripped-down version of her, a version only I get to see. I lean down and tenderly kiss her forehead. She stirs a little, a soft moan releasing itself from her mouth. As always, I'm hopeful she might wake up, but she doesn't. And then she rolls over, her body facing away from me.

I remember a time when Abbie couldn't sleep without me. If I wasn't next to her, she couldn't fully relax until we were together again. Now it seems my absence is something Abbie is fully accustomed to.

I wander over to the chest of drawers where I place down my phone and empty my pockets of my wallet and a small pack of chewing gum, before finally removing my watch. It's a heavy thing, a TAG Heuer. Simple enough in its style, with a steel strap and a blue face. In the darkness of the silent bedroom I wince in the knowledge that my everyday watch is the equivalent of several months' rent in the first home Abbie and I shared together.

I remember it well. A tiny flat with noisy plumbing and dodgy electrics that used to trip *every time* we dared to use the microwave. The place would be freezing in the winter and barbaric in the summer, open windows and electric fans making no difference to the stifling conditions. The happiest day of my life wasn't the birth of my kids, or my wedding day (first or second), but the day I could finally afford to move myself and the woman I so dearly love out of that hell-hole. True, my divorce and child support payments were crippling, but eventually, things became easier.

Between us, Abbie and I had worked hard and saved enough to put down a deposit on a modest home we could finally call our own. It did us proud until things really picked up with *Turner's* and we eventually moved to our current abode, a place so big and shiny I nearly pinch myself every time I step through the front door.

I look over at Abbie once again, sleeping peacefully without a care in the world. It's certainly not easy spending so much time apart, but if this is the price I have to pay for the life we each deserve, then so be it.

I need a shower and, not wanting to wake Abbie, I decide against using the ensuite, and instead make my way to the guest bathroom along the hall.

*

Stepping into the shower, I let the hot water cascade down my body, feeling the most relaxed I have all day. I reach for the bottle of body wash, snapping open the lid and squeezing some into my hands. Starting at the top and working my way down, I wash away all the sweat and toil from another long day. Absent-mindedly, I whistle along out of tune to The Human League's 'Don't You Want Me' playing through the bathroom speakers as I lather my chest, under-arms and then my stomach, paying no great attention to my evening routine.

My hands head south, reaching the more intimate parts of myself – and that's when I feel something out of the ordinary.

I stand still, unsure whether I've just imagined it.

I put my hands back where they were, and there it is: on the bottom of my left testicle is a lump. It's not a large lump, maybe the size of a pea, but it's most certainly there, a very real, small lump.

I look down at myself, lifting my penis to get a full view of things. Nothing looks untoward. There's no redness, swelling or pain to speak of, but the lump is stubbornly there. A rush of panic sweeps in, and even in the heat of the steamy bathroom, the blood in my veins runs cold.

I quickly rinse my body clean of frothy

SAMANTHA KAY

body wash, turn off the shower and hop out. Wrapping myself in a fluffy white towel, I place a hand each side of the bathroom sink and stand perfectly still, as if someone's hit my pause button, yet all the while my mind is frantic.

I know I'm not getting any younger, but surely, I can't be skidding headfirst towards the grave just yet.

I've still got so much living to do. Walking Ellie down the aisle, becoming a grandfather. Retiring into the sunset with Abbie, our twilight years to be spent aboard cruise ships circling the Caribbean and sipping colourful cocktails . . .

I can feel myself starting to panic again. Still standing at the sink, I turn on the tap and splash my face with water, hoping the sensation will calm me down. It doesn't.

I pace the bathroom and force myself to rationalise. Now is not the time to catastrophise. It's just a lump, a small lump that wasn't there yesterday, so who's to say it will still be there tomorrow?

I slip on a fresh pair of boxers, turn off the bathroom light and in the darkness tiptoe back down the hallway to our bedroom. I slide into bed beside Abbie, settle on my side and lovingly gaze at her.

Should I wake her?

No.

There's every possibility the lump won't be there tomorrow. After all, it could just be a spot,

EIGHT MILLION MINUTES

or an insect bite, or a reaction to a new brand of washing powder . . . the possibilities are endless.

So no, it really wouldn't make any sense to wake Abbie and worry her. With that, I roll onto my back, close my eyes and will myself to relax.

Tomorrow is a new day. Everything will be better in the morning, it always is.

CHAPTER 3

JASON

I have not slept.

Not a wink.

It's 6 a.m. I'm standing before the bathroom mirror, cock and balls in hand, and I can confirm that the lump is still there. It's no bigger, still small, but a sleepless night of sickening worry has done nothing to shrink it. With my boxers down by my ankles, I shuffle ever closer towards the floor-length mirror next to the shower and take a long hard look at everything. I squint and peer at myself, desperately trying to see something, anything that might give me some answers.

Nothing.

I shuffle closer still, until I'm practically at one with the bloody glass, when my inspection is interrupted by a loud yelp of horror.

'Jesus, what are you doing?'

I hurriedly pull up my underwear as Abbie clutches her chest in fright in the bathroom doorway.

'Sorry, did I wake you?' I splutter.

'No, I thought you'd left for work already.' She pulls down her pyjama bottoms and sits on the toilet. 'What are you still doing here?' she asks, it being common practise for me to have left for work before Abbie wakes each morning.

'I er, didn't sleep well. I think I might be coming down with something,' I reply as Abbie yawns and the sound of her peeing trickles into the toilet bowl.

I go to the sink and turn on the tap. Having already sprayed myself with deodorant and brushed my teeth, I splash my face with water. My morning wash routine is now complete.

'Is it something . . . *down there*?' Abbie asked sheepishly, pointing towards my nether regions.

'No, no. I'm just feeling a bit peaky.' I react defensively, hurriedly drying my face then leaving the bathroom in a hurry to get dressed before Abbie can interrogate me any further.

Later, dressed and ready for work, I stand in the kitchen waiting by the coffee machine as it fills my large travel mug. Abbie patters barefoot into the kitchen, still dressed in her pyjamas and her hair clipped messily on top of her head.

'You taking the laptop for a walk?' she asks jokingly, pointing towards my old laptop next to the coffee machine.

'Yeah, I told you, the work one's up the

creek.'

'You want some brekkie?' she asks sweetly.

'No, thanks. I need to get to work.' I say, willing the coffee machine to go faster.

'I can make you some eggs - dippy ones with soldiers,' Abbie offers, trying to tempt me, her simple offering irritating me.

I'm dying of cancer, and she wants to talk to me about dippy eggs!

'No, it's fine,' I say tightly. 'I've got a meeting. I need to go.'

'But if you're not feeling well, maybe you should have something. Coffee alone really isn't the breakfast of champions you think it is.' And she starts pulling the bread from the cupboard above her head.

I roll my eyes, bored at forever being lectured on my eating habits.

'I'm fine. Really. It was just a bad night,' I snap, my tone a little harsher than intended.

There's a silence between us, the only sound the chugging of the coffee machine. It's taking bloody ages. All I want to do is get out of this bloody kitchen and sit in my car alone and cry. Abbie is looking at me searchingly. She knows that something is wrong, and I'm annoyed with myself for losing control, for giving myself away.

'Are you worried about something? Is that why you didn't sleep?' Abbie asks, knowing it's out of character for me not to sleep. Usually, I'm out for the count the second my head hits the pillow.

'I'm fine,' I tell her, trying to sound less stressed. 'Honestly. I'm probably just a bit rundown.' Thank God the coffee machine finally finishes filling my mug. I screw on the lid, ready to flee.

'I can ring the doctor for you if you like,' Abbie offers. 'If I ring at eight they can book you a same-day appointment.'

'Abbie, will you leave me alone! I told you, *I'm fine!*' I shout. At the end of my tether, I grab the laptop from the work surface and storm out of the kitchen without looking back.

*

I've been sitting alone in my car for the past hour and a half. The first hour of which was spent sobbing. Pulled into a corner of a large supermarket car park, I allowed myself to break down behind the steering wheel. It felt rather cathartic at first. Opening the floodgates, giving all my worry and angst an outlet. But then a supermarket worker spotted me.

On seeing my tear-stained face and devastated expression she started to come over, looking concerned. Feverishly, I turned on the ignition and got myself out of there before she had a chance to intervene.

Now, I've just pulled into my designated parking space outside the showroom.
The clock on the dashboard reads 7.57 a.m.

Abbie's words about the doctor replay in my head. I'm struggling to remember the last time I visited a doctor, having always prided myself on being a pillar of strength and in unfailing good health. Right now, however, I feel vulnerable and afraid, the feeling unusual and most unwelcome.

My mind has been spinning for hours, every thought more catastrophic than the last, but I'm trying to be calm and rational. I have life and health insurance. I've made a will and have no bad debts. My house is well and truly in order, that much I'm confident about, but what about all the things I might not live to see, all the things that might never be?

Will I live long enough to see Harry graduate university, or even see Ellie finish school? I'm worried about all the things I'm yet to teach my kids. Neither of them know how to change a car tyre or so much as a light bulb. And what about Abbie?

I had a whole life before her - but she's known nothing but us. Will she ever recover from her grief and adjust to life without me? Will Harry and Ellie continue to keep in touch with her, or will she be left alone, with nobody. Pottering around the house with nothing but the memories of the life we once shared.

The very idea renders me terrified.

I glance at the time again. 7.59 a.m.

Frightened as I am, I know I have to make every attempt to survive, if not for myself then for those I love. My trembling hand reaches for my mobile phone and I search for the number of our local GP. Summoning all my courage, I tap the dial button.

The phone rings twice before it's answered with a recorded message, notifying me to hold as I'm already fifth in the queue, GP appointments being as sought-after as tickets for the Rolling Stones. The music plays for what feels like an eternity as the numbers in the queue slowly dwindle.

By ten past eight, I still haven't spoken to anyone. But just as I'm about to give up hope, there's an answer.

'Grove Surgery,' announces an uninterested female voice.

'Hi, I would like to book a doctor's appointment please?'

'What's the problem?'

Stunned by the question, I fall silent.

'Hello?' says the receptionist, checking I'm still there.

'Yes, hi. I'd like to book an appointment,' I repeat, choosing to ignore the question.

'OK, and what seems to be the problem?' the receptionist also repeats, like a robot unable to differ from her programmed script.

'Are you a doctor?' I ask, already sure of the answer.

'No sir, but I can't book you in if you don't tell me the problem.'

I don't want to be rude, but I am becoming increasingly aggravated by the interrogation.

'Can't you just book the appointment and I'll discuss the issue with the doctor?'

'No. It speeds up the process if you tell us.'

'But I don't want to tell you.'

'Then I can't book you an appointment, sir.'

'But I need to see a doctor.' I'm ashamed of the note of desperation in my voice, unable to understand why this process needs to be so painful.

'Sir, I've got a lot of people waiting, if you can't tell me—'

'I have a lump. On my ball! Is that enough information for you!' I snap.

'How long has it been there?' the receptionist asks calmly, completely unfazed by my outburst.

'Does it matter?' I say, sure I've embarrassed myself quite enough.

'How long, sir?'

'I noticed it last night.'

'Any pain, swelling, redness or discharge?'

I ponder for a moment, half-wondering if I should say yes to all of the above if it means I would be seen quicker.

'No,' I sigh, not wanting to tempt fate.

'One of the doctors can see you today. I have an appointment at five-thirty this evening.'

'Fine. I'll take it.'

The receptionist takes some further details to confirm the appointment. As she taps away on her keyboard, I suddenly remember that tonight is Harry's sixth-form art show. I promised him I'd go . . . but what's more important? My life, or Harry's ceramics?

I know I should negotiate a different time, but I also know that if I do, I'll more than likely lose my nerve.

'That's all booked, we'll see you today at five-thirty,' confirms the receptionist.

'Thank you. Bye.'

As the call ends, I breathe a sigh of relief. I've made it over the first hurdle. Before I step out of the car, I set a reminder for a few hours' time, to message Abbie, asking if she'll step in for me at the art show. I'll just tell her I've been held up at work. A believable enough excuse.

ABBIE

I. Am. Fuming.

Marching through the school corridors, I curse Jason under my breath as I head towards Harry's big art show. Ordinarily I take a keen interest in the lives of my step-kids. Over the years I've sat through many a swimming lesson, dance recital and theatrical production involving small children singing musical classics out of tune, and for the most part I've enjoyed it, watching Ellie and Harry's different interests come and go, witnessing them evolve and their confidence grow.

But one thing I definitely don't enjoy, something I've never grown used to, is the presence of Jason's ex-wife - Kelly.

I follow the signs to the art department and feel my stomach tie itself into knots. Jason knows how difficult I find it, dealing with Kelly minus him in tow, and personally I think it a new low that he should insist I attend this art show alone. His work taking priority *yet again*.

Eventually I reach the school's art studio and I'm greeted by a male teacher with long scraggy hair, bad teeth and a gold hooped earring that makes him look like a pirate.

'Hi. I'm looking for Harry Turner,' I say with a forced smile.

'I believe he's somewhere over there.' The pirate points to the far corner of the room.

Amongst a small crowd of teenagers and parents, standing silently in front of a large black and white portrait of a human eye, I spot Harry. Tall and broad, my eighteen-year-old stepson is a good-looking young man with dark hair, Jason's blue eyes - and all the personality of a house brick.

The last few years have seen a once sweet little boy morph into an awkward teenager, totally lacking any of his father's charm and charisma. Both Jason and I are hoping that Harry's pending university experience will help to bring him out of his shell.

I make my way over to him, secretly wondering how long I have to endure it here.

'Hiya Harry.' As I wrap my arms around him, Harry displays all the emotion and warmth of an ironing board, keeping his own arms firmly by his side.

'Where's Dad?' he asks as I release him from our awkward embrace.

'He got held up at work. But I'm here,' I chirp, aware that my presence is a crappy consolation prize.

Harry continues to look ahead with a blank expression. I turn to the portrait of the human eye. It's a large drawing, sketched entirely in pencil but meticulously detailed, so much so it could have passed for a photograph.

'Wow, this is amazing. You're so talented,' I gush, peering into the picture's iris, absorbing all its detail.

'It's not mine,' mumbles Harry.

'Oh, sorry,' I utter, wrong-footed, abruptly moving away from the drawing.

'These are.' On the tall desk in front of us, Harry limply points to a small safari of ceramic animals, including a giraffe, an elephant and a hippo, as well as some decorative pottery.

'Oh, well, these are lovely.' I pick one up to take a closer look. They're cute, even if the giraffe does seem to have one leg shorter than the other three.

'Harry!' calls the teacher with the pirate earring, waving his hand to beckon him over.

Harry immediately abandons me, hurrying off towards him without offering a 'Won't be a minute' or a 'See you soon.' My heart then sinks further when I see Kelly approaching. Dressed smartly in a knee-length black dress and white blazer, she is holding a small white cup and saucer and wearing a disingenuous smile.

Kelly is pretty enough. She has shoulder-length fair hair and a decent figure. She's always well put together and there really is no denying that she has very good skin. But there's a hardness to her that never seems to soften, at least not around me.

Nervous and alone, I place the wonky giraffe down on the table, careful not to let it topple over.

'Hi,' says Kelly, taking her place beside me.

'Hiya.' I feel distinctly under-dressed next to her in my ripped blue jeans and a white T-shirt.

Standing side by side, neither of us engage in any further pleasantries, as is usual. No doubt it had been naïve of me to think we'd ever become 'gal pals', engaging in coffee mornings and exchanging friendly gossip, but it's sad that things have always remained quite so strained. I bite down on my lip and look around the room, wishing to spot a distraction or reason to leave this woman's side.

'Where's my husband?' she demands, taking a sinister slurp from her cup.

I suppress the urge to groan. Kelly's snarky attitude reflected in the way Ellie speaks to me these days.

'I can't account for *your* husband, Kelly, but mine's been held up at work.' I find it laughable that after all these years, Kelly still takes such pleasure in undermining our relationship.

'So, he sent you as his stand-in, did he,' she sneers.

'No. I want to be here. To support Harry.' I catch sight of the clock on the wall and am disappointed to see that barely ten minutes have passed since my arrival and I dread to think how much longer I'll have to endure Kelly's company.

'The kids tell me he's always working late,' she says sweetly, then comes in for the kill. 'I remember when he used to tell *me* he was working late. Turned out he was having an affair.'

After delivering this, Kelly smiles smugly. To the outside observer, we may look like friends engaging in nothing more than easy chit chat, but I can already feel my insides boiling over, the sensation a common one when in her presence. I control myself, since if I respond to that remark, no good will come of it.

'Well . . .' I shrug. A tense silence ensues, leaving me hopeful the difficult conversation between us might now be over. I wish she would just walk away! But Kelly is far from finished.

'You weren't much older than Harry, were you, when you started sleeping with my husband?'

I shake my head in despair. I might have known this conversation would escalate. How very wrong I was, to think she would leave me alone now.

'What's your point?' I ask, unable to understand what Kelly is hoping to gain exactly.

'Just saying. Not sure how I'd feel, you know, *as a parent*, if I discovered that my teenage daughter was out there sleeping with God knows who.'

Tempted as I am, I refrain from outing Ellie. I promised I wouldn't tell on her, and although to do so would give me such intense pleasure, I'm a woman of my word.

'How are your parents?' Kelly then asks, taking another loud slurp from her cup.

I close my eyes and inhale a deep breath as Kelly lands her fatal blow.

There's really no response I can offer that won't end in some kind of emotional outburst. Determined to retain some dignity, I decide to remove myself from the situation.

'Excuse me,' I say brusquely, wanting to be as far away from this horrible woman as possible.

As I make to brush past her there's a clink of crockery, the sound instantly followed by a wet, warm sensation landing on my chest. I release a loud yelp and freeze in shock. I look down at my white T-shirt, now stained with a large brown patch causing the material to become see-through. Fortunately, the liquid isn't hot enough to burn my skin, but the smell of coffee is strong and already making my skin feel sticky.

The room falls silent, everyone's eyes upon me.

I look up at Kelly, who is grinning openly at my discomfort.

'You did that on purpose!' I cry out, so angry I'm afraid I might burst into tears right

SAMANTHA KAY

here in the art department.

'Of course I didn't,' she protests, but her expression of satisfaction shows differently. She is enjoying every second of my humiliation.

For years, I've endured Kelly's insults, partly because I believed I deserved them, and partly because I was determined to keep some level of peace. Being a homewrecker is hard enough, without publicly sparring with the scorned ex-wife. But right now, as I stand in a school art studio for a child who isn't even my own, my T-shirt ruined and reeking of instant coffee, I know the days of putting up with her are over. Once I leave Jason, I'll gladly leave Kelly behind too. And so, it seems logical to me that there's no longer any reason to keep a dignified silence.

'You know what, Kelly? I might not be perfect, but at least I'm not an *absolute cunt*,' I say loudly and proudly, wiping the smile straight from her stupid face.

Much to my delight, I hear a couple of shocked gasps, confirming that all present heard my words, including the scruffy-looking teacher. But my triumph is short-lived, since when I begin to stalk out of the room, I catch sight of Harry. I give him a small pained smile and a wave that he doesn't reciprocate.

Red-faced and teary, I march back down the school corridor the same way I came. Despite how upset I feel, there's a new spring in my step.

I'm feeling more determined than ever to make a fresh start. Away from Jason, his intolerable children and his *absolute cunt* of an ex-wife.

JASON

Sitting on a soft cushioned chair with suspicious stains, I try to recall the last time I felt quite so nervous. I arrived ten minutes early for my GP appointment and so far I've been left waiting a further thirty. The wait has done nothing for my nerves. Now I'm the only person waiting to be seen, the other few patients having slowly worked their way through the surgery ahead of me.

I can't stop my hands from fidgeting. My mouth is dry, my chest so tight I'm starting to worry I could self-induce a heart attack. I can almost hear my thumping heart. If cancer doesn't kill me, the worry alone will. Suddenly, the voice of the receptionist snaps me out of my worried trance.

'Mr Turner?' Through the Perspex glass the female receptionist limply points towards the door to the left of where I'm sitting. 'Dr Moghul's ready for you.'

I nod my thanks. Trying my best to calm my nerves, I walk over to the door, gingerly pushing it open. On the other side of the door sits a large middle-aged Asian man.

'Hello.' Dr Moghul greets me, without looking away from his computer screen.

'Hi,' I reply, closing the door behind me and sitting down on the other side of the large desk.

'How are you?' Dr Moghul enquires, still looking at his screen, the light reflecting on his spectacles.

'Yeah, good, thank you,' I manage to say, absorbing the sight of the doctor's thick moustache and the stain on the lapel of his suit jacket.

'So, how can I help you today?' he asks, taking only a fleeting look away from the screen in my direction, his chubby fingers still tapping the keyboard.

'I found a . . . lump last night,' I say quietly.

'Where?'

'On my . . . testicle,' I whisper, painfully forcing the words from my mouth.

'On your scrotum,' nods Dr Moghul, correcting me. 'I see. Please go behind the screen and remove your trousers and underwear.'

The moment I've been dreading is now upon me. I stand up and walk slowly to the other end of the small room as if I'm about to face a firing squad then go behind the screen and reluctantly unbutton my trousers.

'When was the last time you had a prostate exam?' the doctor asks.

'I'm not sure I've ever had one,' I tell him as I pull down my trousers, my underwear sweeping along with them.

Standing in my socks, naked from the waist down and feeling ridiculous, I hear the snap of a rubber glove and turn to see Dr Moghul standing next to me, applying a generous amount of lubricant to his gloved-up index finger.

My eyes widen in horror.

'Lie down on the bed on your left side, please.'

Too afraid to argue, I do as I'm told.

Feeling violated, in no time at all, I am tucking my shirt back into my trousers, slipping on my shoes and going back to my seat. Today is the first time I've had my genitalia handled by another man and I can confirm without any hesitation that I didn't like it one bit.

'You'll be pleased to know your prostate feels perfectly fine,' Dr Moghul informs me cheerfully. Having removed his rubber gloves and washed his hands, his attention is firmly back on his computer screen as he taps away on his keyboard, seemingly focused and relaxed.

Unable to wait a second longer, I dig deep inside myself and ask the question I've been waiting all day to hear the answer to.

'And the lump on my . . . Is it . . . is it cancer?'

'It could be any number of things,' Dr Moghul shrugs. He gives no further information, and the only sound in the room is coming from the tap of his fingers and his heavy breathing

I feel disappointed. What an anti-climax. Naturally, I didn't want to hear that I was dying, but I want - *need* - some kind of explanation.

'But, is it something I need to worry about?' I ask desperately.

'I'm going to refer you on to a urologist and for some blood tests,' the doctor says matter-of-factly, giving nothing away.

'Can't you tell me anything?' I protest, starting to lose my patience.

'Not at this stage,' Dr Moghul replies, as the sound of his printer kicks in.

'Then what was the point of coming here?' I burst out, my frustration needing an outlet.

Perfectly calm, Dr Moghul retrieves the document from the printer, picks up a pen and begins to tick off some boxes on the sheet of paper.

'Mr Turner, the first step - was to come here. All the answers you need will be with you soon enough.' Finally, and for the first time since I stepped into the room, he looks me in the eye and gives me the paper.

'Now, you'll need to hand this in when you have your bloods done, and you'll be sent a letter in the post with an appointment to see a urologist.'

'How long will I have to wait for an appointment?' I ask, desperate to have an answer to something.

Dr Moghul shrugs, unable to give any kind of reassurance on wait times.

'Brilliant,' I say, standing from my chair. 'Well, thanks for all your help.'

With a strong air of sarcasm, I as good as snatch the paper from the doctor's hand and without even a polite thank you or goodbye; leave the room, not feeling an ounce lighter from my woes.

*

It's almost 7 p.m. and for the second night in a row I'm home earlier than usual, thanks to my GP appointment. Feeling severely out of sorts I leave my shoes at the door and let my feet lead me through the house and up the stairs. Arriving at the landing, I can hear that the TV in the bedroom is on, the faint light seeping from the doorway, and I feel happy that Abbie is still awake, as it's still early. I want to see her, I'm desperate to be near her. I want to hold her in my arms and smell her hair and kiss her skin. I want to feel the comfort of her body against my own.

I step into the bedroom and there she is. My Abbie. Sitting up in bed, tucked under the covers and already wrapped in her pink fluffy robe, holding a cup of tea and watching trash on the TV, Daisy curled up next to her. It is the most wonderful sight I could ever wish to see.

'Hiya.'

'Hi.' Like Dr Moghul, Abbie barely looks at

me. As I'd feared, she's angry with me for missing Harry's art show and she has every right to be.

Feeling guilty and emotionally exhausted, I plonk myself down on the bed and wrap an arm around her. I gently kiss her cheek, keeping my face close to hers, hoping we can quickly iron out the tension.

'I'm sorry I missed the show.'

'Don't apologise to *me*. Harry was the one that wanted you there,' hisses Abbie. She's not just annoyed, it turns out; she's furious.

'I know, I'll call him tomorrow.'

'I hope it was worth it. Whatever you stood him up for.'

I'm not entirely sure it was, but I choose not to say anything, not wanting to transfer any unnecessary worry to Abbie, even if it means having to be in her bad books. I rest my head on her shoulder, wanting to be close to her.

'How was the show?' I ask with some hesitation.

'Fine.'

I'm fully aware that 'fine' implies the exact opposite, and there's no doubt in my mind that Abbie's foul mood is likely to be Kelly's doing, but I can't deal with another Kelly drama. Not tonight.

Feeling remorseful, and keen to make myself feel a little better, I let my hand wander inside Abbie's robe. I caress her stomach and her hips. I nuzzle my face into the nape of her neck and tenderly kiss the skin behind her ear . . . and that's when I feel her pull away. Without saying a word, she climbs out of the bed and storms into the ensuite bathroom, slamming the bathroom door so hard I'm sure I feel the house shake as Daisy leaps off the bed and runs away to find somewhere safe to hide.

Randy and rejected, I sit alone. I rub my tired head, knowing all is not well. Feeling too tired for a row, I climb from the bed and make my way to the bathroom down the hall, wanting nothing more than to draw a line under the most difficult of days.

CHAPTER 4

ABBIE

It's been almost a week since the art show coffee incident. Although my initial rage has subsided, I still feel out of sorts. I never did tell Jason what happened on that evening, but as usual, he's scarcely been around, and even when he is he seems withdrawn and generally more grumpy than usual.

Today, however, has been a good day - so far. We opened early, at eight, and *Daisy's* has seen a steady flow of hungry customers with many a pastry sold, keeping the till ringing and Molly busy.

'That will be six pounds exactly, please,' I say, as another happy customer purchases a cappuccino and a *pain au chocolat*. As she riffles through her purse to find her bank card, I hear my mobile phone vibrating under the counter, sneak a peek and see it's Hamza the estate agent calling.

To date, my search for a home of my own

has not proved fruitful and Hamza is as good as useless. Still, with no Plan B in mind, I figure it's in my best interest to hear what he has to say.

'Apologies,' I tell the customer, 'but I need to take this. Molly, would you mind finishing up with this lady, please?'

As Molly abandons wiping the tables and takes over serving, I step out into the area behind the shop floor and swipe my phone to answer.

'Mrs Turner? Hi. How are you today?'

'Yeah, all good, thank you, Hamza.'

'Have you had a chance to look at the email I sent you?' he demands, an unusual sense of urgency in his voice.

'No, sorry, I've been working and—'

'It's here, Mrs Turner, finally. *It's here!*'

'What is?'

'The perfect property,' he says excitedly. 'Great location, ridiculously cheap, newly and fully renovated.'

'Right,' I say, failing to match Hamza's enthusiasm. I've had too many disappointments from him in the past and now don't believe a word he says.

'Look, we can't delay. This place will be gone by the end of the day, I can guarantee it. Can you view it now?'

I sigh. After all, this guy used the exact same line when convincing me to view the flat with no windows. Not one window, not a single one. Not even in the bathroom.

'Not really. I'm working. I can meet you at, say, half five?'

'Nah, it'll be long gone by then. Meet me there *now*. It's only fifteen minutes' walk from your shop. The details are on the email. I'll see you there shortly.' And he hangs up.

Hamza's track record being what it is, I'm still not convinced this viewing could be any better than the others. I check my watch. It's 10 a.m. The breakfast rush is nearly over. No doubt I'll be able to view the property and return before the lunch-time rush begins. I don't have anything to lose, and so I grab my handbag and ready myself to leave.

*

'So, what do you think?' asks Hamza, looking frightfully proud of himself.

I gaze around the flat in awe. It's stunning. We are standing in the living room, where the sun beams through the large floor-to-ceiling window, filling the whole area with a warm and hopeful glow.

As stated, the whole flat is newly renovated. Everything is so clean and shiny. There are no holes in any of the walls, no mysterious smells or stains. The outlook from the window is nothing special, merely a view of the car park and the block of flats opposite, but that doesn't matter. The area seems quiet and safe, and within walking distance from the shop. It's perfect, and I can see me and Daisy being very happy here.

Naturally, the space is small after the kind of opulence I've enjoyed over the past few years, but it's way more spacious than any of the other dodgy properties I've seen so far, with a bathroom and kitchen all newly fitted and never used.

'I love it,' I announce, walking over to the chrome dimmer switch, pressing it and playing with the dial, confirming that the lights are in safe working order.

'Why is the rent so cheap?' I ask, certain that a place this nice and large should carry a price tag well outside my budget.

'A man died here,' says Hamza, his voice a little sheepish.

'Oh, like, an old man?' I say assumingly.

He coughs.

'Sorry, I tell a lie. Two men. They were murdered.'

'*What?* You're not serious?' My voice is high-pitched in shock.

'Deadly. No pun intended. A man was stabbed in the neck in here, and another found in pieces in the hallway. I believe there was axe damage to the floorboards. A lot of blood *everywhere*. Hence the full refurb,' explains Hamza. We're both now standing in the hallway, as he gestures with his hands to show where the body would have been, like some kind of twisted tour guide.

'The bodies were here for a week or so before the other residents began to complain about the smell. The place has been standing empty for a while. The owner is desperate to get someone back in here. Hence the low price.'

I stand open-mouthed and horrified, trying to process all the grisly details.

'A whole week? Didn't anyone hear anything?' I ask faintly, unable to comprehend such a gruesome set of circumstances.

'Top quality soundproofing, Mrs Turner. And well, dead bodies are notoriously quiet.' Hamza is sniggering at his own joke. I don't find anything funny in the story; in fact, I feel a little queasy.

He suddenly notices my expression and says hastily, 'Look, I know the history is less than ideal. But it's within budget. If you like what you see, Mrs Turner, we could make it happen by the end of the day. What do you say?' urges Hamza, trying to bring me around and remind me of what's important.

I let my feet guide me back into the living room. It smells of fresh paint and new carpet. A stark contrast from the damp and cigarette aroma I've become familiar with. The flat is everything I could dream of and is by far the very best property I've viewed. Recent experience has taught me that places such as this are few and far between. It's dog eat dog out there in the world of rentals, and there's no room for squeamishness about two dead bodies. If I can't overlook it, a hundred other people will, and I'll be left viewing some tiny dive with no flushing toilet.

The time is now. I can't let an opportunity this good slip through my fingers.

'I'll take it,' I say, reaching out to shake Hamza's hand.

'Fantastic!' he roars, shaking my hand with such enthusiasm, I'm a little worried it might just fall off.

JASON

I'm sat in another waiting room, forcing myself to relax, but at least this time there are no suspicious stains on the chairs. With a cup of coffee in one hand and my mobile phone in the other, I read through some work emails, trying to make good use of my time.

It's been almost a week since my initial visit to the GP. That was when I took the decision to make a claim on my private health insurance. After a couple of phone calls and some rigorous form-filling, I've managed to bypass the NHS backlog and have secured myself an appointment with a urologist at a local private clinic that not only provides comfy seating but also an array of complimentary hot beverages. Blood tests and a scan were caried out at record speed over the past few days and now, ready or not, I'm here to learn the results.

I'm trying my best to concentrate all my nervous energy into my emails when a text message from my parts man pops up. The replacement petrol cap he ordered from Germany has arrived for a customer's car, but it's the wrong one. I let out an irritated groan, this being the kind of headache I go above and

SAMANTHA KAY

beyond to avoid. I'll need to contact the customer and notify them of the delay, but first I'm keen to fire off my frustrations to the supplier. However, before I can begin, I am interrupted by the calling of my name.

'Jason Turner?'

I look up from my phone and see a young black

male doctor, much around my own age, smiling warmly. With no choice but to abandon work, I get up and shake his hand.

'Mr Turner. Hi, I'm Mr Grant. Good to meet you. We're just down here.' He leads me along the corridor towards his consulting room.

It's been a mere ten minutes since I arrived here, and already I'm stood naked from the waist down with my testicles being fondled by another man for the second time this week. Trying to relax, I focus all my attention onto the small white sink in the corner, while Mr Grant has a feel around, umm-ing and ahh-ing to himself.

Finally, he pulls away from my genitalia and tells me, 'OK, get yourself dressed, Mr Turner, and we'll have a chat.' He pulls off his blue vinyl exam gloves and disposes of them in the large bin next to the bed. Then he rolls down the sleeves of his clean white shirt and leaves me alone to get decent.

Fully clothed, I take a seat at Mr Grant's large desk, bracing myself for what he's about to say. At this point, I just pray that whatever might be revealed will at the very least bring me a step closer to a solution.

'Right, Mr Turner, I've had a look at your blood-test results, and based on everything I've just seen, I can confirm that you have nothing at all to worry about.' Mr Grant's words are followed by a reassuring smile.

I sit still, as if all the air has been sucked out of me, unable to believe that in just a few seconds, days and nights full of worry and anguish can be extinguished so quickly.

'Really? Are you sure?' I splutter.

Mr Grant nods, tells me, 'Cancer markers typically show up in a blood test. Although you have nothing to worry about there, your cholesterol is a little high, which is not unusual for a man of your age, but even so I'm going to write you a prescription for statins. I think it's important you try and bring that down. Also, your vitamin D is a little low, but there are some over-the-counter supplements you can take for that. I'll write those down for you.' Mr Grant locates his notepad and pulls a pen from his smart shirt pocket.

'But the lump. If it's not cancer, then what is it?' I ask, unable to park all the questions still whizzing around my mind.

'It's an epididymal cyst. A fluid-filled lump. Rather common and will likely disappear on its own.'

I'm ashamed to admit I feel a little deflated, disappointed even. For days I've psyched myself up to expect the worst. I was ready to discuss chemo, biopsies, scans, life expectancy. Now it's as if all my nervous energy has nowhere to go.

'Are you absolutely sure it's not cancer?' I persist. 'Might it be worth getting a second opinion or—'

Mr Grant holds up his hand, keen to end my rambling.

'Mr Turner, I've seen a fair share of cancer in my career. Trust me when I say you're going to live. Of course, if you do notice any changes such as swelling or pain, by all means come back and we'll take another look. But right now, like I said, you have absolutely nothing to worry about.' Mr Grant tears the sheet of paper from his pad and hands it to me, before turning his attention back to his PC to arrange my prescription.

Finally, I allow myself to breathe a sigh of relief. *I'm not dying.* Unlike so many others, I'm allowed to leave this place with the great privilege of being able to carry on with my life. I smile to myself, dizzy with gratitude.

ABBIE

Mas works in his family's kebab shop across the street. He's a twenty-one-year-old student studying Business and Economics. He has an olive complexion, thick, glossy black hair and a playful, charming smile. True, he carries with him the faint aroma of onion, but otherwise, I can't list any negative qualities.

On the days Molly works, I struggle to get rid of him. He fancies the pants off her. He's a good-looking boy with prospects, and sometimes they seem to engage in an easy and flirty rapport. However, time and time again, Molly so cruelly gives him the brush-off. I feel sorry for the kid, but while he's here buying up my stale pastries, who am I to interfere?

Mas usually starts work around the time we close, often making him our very last customer of the day. Having served him a large coffee and an eleven-hour-old croissant, he delays his exit, chatting to Molly as she wipes the tables. I take great pleasure in eavesdropping on their conversations while I cash up.

'My uni's hosting a board-game night tomorrow. Want to come?' says Mas, full of

SAMANTHA KAY

enthusiasm.

'Why would I do that?' Molly replies, rolling her eyes.

'I remember you saying you like to play Monopoly.'

'I play it with my family at Christmas to please them.'

'Ah, me and my husband used to play Monopoly *all the time*,' I break in. 'When we had no money and couldn't afford to go anywhere, we'd play Monopoly.' And I feel nostalgic, remembering a simpler time.

'See? Who doesn't love a board game. You said you were really good at it. We could team up, be the champions and win free shots,' Mas says, taking a sip from his coffee, Molly's rejection doing nothing to dampen his sprits.

'Yeah, like I'm gonna take part in any activity that encourages a toxic capitalist culture. Buying up properties, bleeding the less fortunate dry and humiliating them into bankruptcy,' snaps Molly, at which point it's my turn to roll my eyes. Molly really does have a skill for sucking the fun out of absolutely everything with her political lectures.

'Unless it's with your family at Christmas?' quips Mas. I'm pretty sure he senses how ridiculous she's being, but it doesn't seem to put him off.

Ignoring him and tossing her hair, Molly lifts a chair, placing it on top of the table.

'Well, if you change your mind, let me know. I hear there's gonna be a giant Jenga - and who doesn't love Jenga! Thanks for the coffee, Abbie,' Mas says politely, and heads for the door.

'You're welcome. Have a good night Mas.'

Molly walks him to the door, closes it behind him, locks it and tuns the sign to *Closed*.

'Why are you always so mean to him?' I want to know.

'I'm not,' she protests, screwing up her face.

'And weren't you just complaining how you have no plans for tomorrow night?'

But before Molly has a chance to respond, my phone begins to ring and vibrate on the counter. It's Hamza calling. It's been a mere six hours since I viewed my dream flat, and a mere five hours since we put in an official offer to pay the full amount of rent, no haggling. I wasn't able to go a penny over the asking price, which I'm sure won't make me the most desirable of tenants, but I tried. Positive that Hamza is calling with bad news, I'm ready to get the rejection over with as soon as possible. I abandon cashing up and my conversation with Molly and swipe my phone to answer.

'Hello.'

'Mrs Turner . . .' begins Hamza, pausing for what I assume to be dramatic effect, but I can't take the suspense a second longer.

'It's a no, isn't it?'

'They said yes!' He says it with such glee, he could have fooled me into believing I'd won the lottery.

'No way!' My words are followed by a cry of delight.

'Yes, way, Mrs Turner! We did it! We just need to sort out the deposit and the paperwork – we can do all of that tomorrow.'

I can hardly take it in. In fact, I feel a little lightheaded. Finally, it's happening. I've climbed the first step on the ladder of a brand-new life and oh, how overwhelming it feels.

'Wow, it's all moving so fast.' I find I am gripping the shop counter, needing to steady myself.

'If you say so.' Says Hamza, not quite sharing the same sentiment. 'Like I said, we'll start on all the official stuff in the morning,' Hamza says. 'But I'll get a reply over to them right now.'

'OK, great. Thanks so much, Hamza.' I end the call, aware that my voice is wobbly.

Molly is looking a little confused, having witnessed my emotions switch between excitement and bewilderment within seconds.

'My offer to rent the flat was accepted,' I tell her, still a bit disbelieving.

'Ah, that's great news!' squeals Molly, throwing down her cloth on the table and leaping behind the counter. She grabs hold of my hands and we both jump up and down like two giggling children.

As we celebrate, I can't help thinking that now the moment I've waited months for is finally here, in truth I feel conflicted.

My marriage is over.

I feel profoundly sad. After everything Jason and I have been through
together, I never could have imagined that one day it would end like this. But end it has. I mustn't lose sight of why I'm doing this. I want more than Jason can give me. I want a partnership, a real husband, not an absent one. I want a friend I can share my life with, not the illusion of one.

I'll tell Jason tonight. When he arrives home from work at nine, possibly ten o'clock tonight, I'll tell him. This life, this strange unsatisfactory existence we have isn't working for me anymore. I'm moving on, to a new life . . . without him.

I continue to jump around with Molly, trying to disguise my sadness, the tears falling from my eyes easily mistaken for ones of joy.

CHAPTER 5

JASON

On leaving the hospital, I swing by the chemist and drop in my prescription. It's busy in there, so I walk out again, not wishing to hang around. I'll head back tomorrow to collect the tablets I need to lower my cholesterol and the supplements to elevate my vitamin D. It's a lovely evening so I think to hell with the routine, and decide to come home instead of going back to work.

I walk through our front door and practically float through the house, feeling lighter than air, elated to be home and healthy. I can't wait to see Abbie and hold her tight, relieved that my days with her aren't numbered after all.

Not used to being home so early, I potter around in the kitchen, at a loose end, not quite knowing how to fill the time until Abbie returns home. I take a peek at the screen on the fridge door, checking out what's inside. I contemplate making a romantic dinner for us both, but soon abandon that idea. I'll treat us to a take-away, or better yet, maybe I'll book us a table somewhere nice, somewhere special. But first things first, I need a coffee.

Over at the coffee machine, I catch sight of Abbie's laptop, sitting closed on the breakfast bar counter where it usually lives. It's only now I remember the wrong part arriving from Germany. In all the goings-on with the consultant earlier I never did respond to the issue, and it's imperative that I do so.

My own laptop is still at work. I know I can use my phone to write an email, but I always opt for a full-size keyboard where possible since my stubby fingers always cause me to mistype on the tiny touch screen. I know Abbie won't mind. She's a business owner like me, and she would want me to be able to complete whatever work I need to get done in the most convenient way possible.

With nothing else to do, I'll make myself a coffee then finish off some work before Abbie arrives home, thereby making excellent use of my free time. A couple of minutes later, with a steaming cup of coffee and a newfound zest for life, I pull out a bar stool and take a seat at the kitchen breakfast bar. I open up Abbie's laptop and type in her password Mr5Turn3r! We both have full access to each other's passwords and PINs. It's just marital convenience.

The laptop instantly springs to life, and it's clear that Abbie hasn't closed down any of her pages, which I always tell her she should do. It's not good for the life of your laptop not to shut things down properly. As I am thinking this, I notice the open page staring back at me: it's the webpage of a property rental site.

Surprised, I tilt my head to one side and scroll down a page advertising small one-bed flats for renting. Thank heavens, I think, that that stage of our lives is well and truly behind us. Not giving the site a second thought, I minimise the page, revealing the one behind it, that of Abbie's email account. I notice a couple of unread messages, one a circular from Ticketmaster and the other an email from Hamza@Ashfordproperties – the subject line reading *Offer Accepted.*

I stare hard at the email. I know *Daisy's* has been struggling. I wonder if maybe Abbie has finally made the heartbreaking decision to throw in the towel and sell the shop? However, it's odd that she hasn't run such an important decision by me. We're married, we're a team. Why wouldn't she tell me?

I guess I can't deny how absent I've been of late. Maybe she wanted to, but I just haven't been around enough, or she didn't know how to break the news.

I know it's wrong to snoop, but if my wife's livelihood is in trouble, surely, I have a duty to try and ease whatever suffering she might be experiencing. With curiosity finally getting the better of me, I click into the email.

Dear Mrs Turner,

I write to confirm that your offer for the full rental price on the property Flat 3, Howard Court has been accepted by the landlord.

Please excuse the informality of this email. An official acceptance letter will be processed in the morning.

Kind regards,

Hamza Islam

Dumbfounded, I re-read the email several times, unable to make head nor tail of it. Why would Abbie be renting a flat? And if so, why hasn't she told me anything about it?

Desperately needing answers, I click out of the email and see on the main page a whole list of emails from this Hamza guy. I read one at a time, each one containing a similar correspondence to the last, with links and pictures of various properties. They are all small, cramped flats, and all demand ridiculously expensive monthly rents. It's then, on maybe the fifth or sixth email I open, that everything becomes abundantly clear.

A response from Hamza reads: *OK, feedback received.*

I scroll down the message from Abbie to which Hamza had replied.

This one is lovely, but it's way out of my price range. I'm leaving my husband and moving in alone. There'll be no need for an extra bedroom if it comes at such a huge expense.

My mouth drops open. There it is. In black and white, all the answers I need. Frozen in shock, I stare at the words on the screen, unable to comprehend what's happening, or what has already happened as the case may be. This whole saga I've uncovered, of Abbie planning some kind of escape from me, has come as a massive shock. I had no clue, not a single suspicion.

I thought we were happy!

I thought we were in love.

I click out of the email and return to the property webpage behind it. I scroll through it, each property more depressing than the last. Small, rundown hovels, yet seemingly a better alternative to living with me. The knowledge of what Abbie has secretly been up to is making me feel nauseous. I don't want my wife living in some kind of pit. She should be living here, with me, in the lap of luxury I created for us.

It's then I hear the front door open then close, and I'm catapulted back to the present. Hurriedly, I close Abbie's laptop and push it away as if to distance myself from the awful truth it has just revealed to me.

'Hiya' says Abbie, breezing into the kitchen. 'You're home early?' she says, as if it were a question.

'Yeah.' I get down unsteadily from the bar stool, feeling dazed, as if I've just received a punch to the face. 'Did you have a good day?' I enquire, trying my best to look and sound normal.

'Yeah, you?' asks Abbie, placing her handbag down next to her laptop on the breakfast bar and throwing her keys inside.

'Yeah. Same old.' And then I pour an almost full cup of coffee down the sink, unable to stomach it, and say, 'I was thinking we could go out for dinner tonight or get a take-away, if you fancy it?'

I look up from the sink and over at Abbie. She's wearing a bottle-green knee-length dress, well fitted and showing just a smidge of cleavage. Her blonde hair is thrown into a loose and stylish ponytail. She's utterly beautiful.

'No, I can't say I do. Actually, there's something I need to talk to you about,' Abbie tells me, standing straight with an assertiveness that implies she means business and I know, with every fibre of my being, that what she's about to say will
blow my whole world apart.

All I can think about in this very moment is how much I love her. I've loved Abbie more than I've ever loved anyone. I've given her so much and sacrificed everything for her, and I'm prepared to do whatever it takes to stop her walking out of the door.

'Jason, I—'

'I have cancer,' I blurt out, my words

stopping Abbie dead in her tracks.

Her eyebrows furrow and she shakes her head gently, letting out a small laugh of disbelief.

'What?'

'I have cancer,' I repeat, my voice serious.

'How? Where? I mean . . . what?' chokes Abbie, struggling to string her words together.

I clear my throat. I can see the shock in her eyes and all her confidence melting away. I've played this very moment out in my head multiple times over the past week. Terrified of having to tell my beloved wife that our time together is potentially now reaching the saddest of endings.

Merely an hour ago, I was giddy with joy to be given the all clear. However, now it seems the very worst of outcomes might be the exact tool I need to save my marriage.

'Testicular,' I mumble, staring at the floor, unable to look Abbie in the eye, worried she might be able to see through me.

'How long have you known?' she says as tears begin to spring into her pretty blue eyes.

'I found a lump last week. Got the results about an hour ago. That's why I missed the art show last week, because I went to see the GP.' Unexpectedly, out of nowhere I feel my own eyes begin to fill with tears. After a week of not knowing and genuine fear, my own emotions are finally catching up on me and I'm grateful for the timing. My tears making for a believable performance.

'Why didn't you say something? I would have come with you,' says Abbie, breaking down and starting to sob. She joins me at the kitchen sink and wraps her arms tightly around me. I bury my head in her shoulder and allow myself to cry out all my fears and frustrations.

'I didn't want to worry you. I need you, Abbie. I love you,' I say, sobbing uncontrollably.

Eventually, I'm the first to pull away. I wipe my face with the heel of my hand and look at Abbie, her face is flushed, her eyes are red and puffy and her make-up is smudged and smeared halfway down her cheeks. It's such a relief. There's no denying she still cares and I'm satisfied I've done enough. However, I'm keen to test the waters, just to be sure.

'What did you want to tell me?' I ask, rubbing the back of my neck, trying to reclaim some composure.

Abbie stands silently, taking a second to process my question. She reaches for some kitchen roll, pulling off a sheet and wiping her eyes, but for every tear she wipes away, a new one appears.

'Nothing,' she says, her voice shaky. 'It wasn't important.'

'It's OK, tell me,' I push, curious to hear her answer.

'It's just the er . . . the speaker in my car. It's crackling. Quite a lot,' Abbie stutters.

I wonder if what she's said is even true. I drove her car last week and everything seemed fine. But that's beside the point.

'OK, I'll take it to work. Get it looked at,' I reassure her. Then I let out a long, deep breath of relief, assured my work here is well and truly done.

My wife isn't leaving me, at least not today.

ABBIE

Submerged in a tub of fluffy bubbles, I hold my breath and slide my entire body under the water where I allow myself to cry, the water silencing my sobs. *Is this what the universe thought to give me? Is this really what we deserve?*

I'm genuinely worried I brought all this upon us both. It's a punishment.

I wished so hard and for so long for things to be different, for a change in our marriage. But cancer . . . I might have wanted out of my marriage, but I never wanted Jason taken from me, for him to be stolen by some incurable disease. I never wanted him to suffer.

Struggling for breath I push myself back up to the surface, sweeping my hands over my face and hair. I feel lightheaded. The heat and steam of the bathroom are doing little to aid the dense pressure in my head. A few short hours ago everything seemed so straightforward. I was moving on to a new and exciting destination, but now it's as if the shutters have been slammed down in my face.

Suddenly there's so much to do. So much to think about.

Jason needs me. How can I abandon him now? He'll need treatment. He'll need help. Practical, loving help. What will happen to the showroom? And how on earth are we going to break the news to Harry and Ellie?

I feel my chest tighten as sobs begin to rise up again, the sadness physically taking over my body. I submerge myself back under the water and continue to silently cry alone.

*

Later, dressed in my pjs and feeling a little fresher, I emerge from the ensuite and enter the bedroom. Jason is lying in bed. He's bare-chested, one arm tucked behind his head, his focus on the phone in his other hand, the TV showing a football match and talking to itself in the background. To the ignorant observer, Jason doesn't look to have a care in the world. How can someone seemingly so at ease and relaxed have so much going on under the surface?

But then again, that's typical Jason. He's an expert at bottling everything up, not letting anyone in. Stoically ploughing through his troubles, proudly never asking for help. But this is different. This isn't about issues with his tax returns or dealing with a difficult ex-wife. This is much more important, much more serious than any of that. It's life or death.

I need to be here and do everything I can for him.

Jason looks up from his phone and smiles

at me, pulling back the duvet, inviting me to join him under the covers.

'What do you want to watch?' he asks, placing down his phone and granting me his full attention.

'Shouldn't we talk about stuff?' I ask, settling myself down beside him.

'What stuff?'

'Cancer stuff. Like - what have the doctors said? When do you start treatment?'

Jason sighs, making it clear he doesn't want to have this conversation.

'I know you don't want to talk about it—'

'They haven't said anything yet.' He sounds abrupt, which is typical of him when he's stressed about something. I don't let it put me off.

'They must have told you something. Do you need an operation? Are you going to have chemo?' I am pushing for answers to my many questions.

'The doctors told me they are going to be in touch. They need to organise a treatment plan. It all takes time.'

'How much time? You have cancer - isn't time of the essence?' I can feel myself beginning to panic. Jason's blasé attitude is worrying me.

'Look, if I've not heard in a couple of days, I'll chase them up,' he says, picking up the TV remote, ready to end the conversation.

'OK, well, I should be there with you

at your next appointment. I want to hear everything they have to say.' I'm well aware that Jason can't be relied upon to tell me everything. He's a master at burying his head in the sand.

'Oh, all right then, if you really want to,' he agrees, albeit rather reluctantly, flicking through the TV channels.

'Can I see it?' I ask, my voice small, not sure of the response I'll receive.

'See what?' he asks absent-mindedly.

'The lump. Is it big? Does it hurt?' I want to fully understand everything we're dealing with.

Finally, he meets my eyes, saying, 'No, it's not big or painful. There's not really anything to see. It's more . . .' He trails off.

'*What?*' I ask, desperate for him to be open with me.

Releasing a small sigh, Jason gently takes my hand in his. He guides it under the covers and into his boxer shorts. After a few seconds of shuffling around, I can feel it. On his left testicle, there's a small hard lump.

I remove my hand. The physical presence of the lump has made everything real. We sit up and look at each other.

'Are you scared?'

He closes his eyes. 'No,' he says.

'I am,' I whisper – terrified, in fact.

Jason looks at me and I finally see him soften. 'Please don't be sad,' he says sympathetically, and he wraps me in his arms.

Freshly showered, he smells all yummy and clean.

'It's because I'm worried. That's a normal way to feel. Sorry I'm not a robot like you,' I say, and try to laugh, swallowing down my tears, feeling safe in his embrace.

Jason releases me from our cuddle. He looks into my eyes and runs a hand through my hair.

'Abbie, look, it's just . . . it's been a long day. A lot has happened and it's not going to be solved here and now.' And he kisses my lips.

'I know.' I nod in agreement, willing to ease up on the Q&A - for now at least.

Jason kisses me again, caressing my skin. Our kissing quickly becomes more passionate and before I know it, my pyjamas are on the floor. Jason slides himself down the bed, bends my knees and plants his face between my legs. I close my eyes, my breathing becoming heavy, enjoying the sensation of his mouth on me. This really is the complete opposite of what I had expected from this evening. I imagined shouting, tears, us sleeping in separate rooms. I pictured Jason on his knees, begging me not to leave him. Instead, here I am on my back, allowing us to use sex as a distraction to a much bigger set of problems . . .

CHAPTER 6

JASON

What on earth was I thinking?

It goes without saying, I might have bitten off more than I can chew.

Aided by nothing other than black coffee and sheer panic, I've spent the entire morning huddled in my office with the door closed, searching online for (what else), testicular cancer! It did occur to me that I should search for a psychologist while I'm at it, but one thing at a time.

The amount of information that I find online is overwhelming, to say the least. I've been scribbling things down in my work notebook. Amongst the list of tasks I need to follow up today at *Turner's* I've made notes on all my research: treatments, side-effects, timescales, life expectancy, charities, fundraising ideas.

Now, I rub my tired face and lean back on my chair, silently mouthing the words: *What the fuck is wrong with me!* I need to come clean, to tell Abbie it was all a big mistake. I'll pretend that they got my results mixed up with some other poor sod's. Happens all the time, far more than the system care to admit.

But then what?

Abbie will leave me. She'll go ahead with renting that flat, and I'll be back to square one. No, I can't take that risk. I refer back to my notes. Amongst a recipe for coffee cake - those Macmillan cake and coffee mornings do look like fun - I discovered that the standard treatment for stage one testicular cancer is an orchiectomy. In translation – ball removal. That might be difficult to fake. Abbie will notice that both of mine are still present, and having a healthy one removed might be taking things a tad too far.

I did, however, find some very useful information regarding chemo pills. Patients take them at home. I can do that! Although it says here that chemo pills aren't generally used to treat testicular cancer, but 'generally' doesn't mean never, does it? Maybe I should have gone down the prostate cancer route, but it's too late for that. I've crossed the Rubicon with testicles, so testicles it'll have to be.

I know - I'll start taking those cholesterol pills and the ones for vitamin D. They can be my chemo pills. Sorted. But as I scroll through the webpage, I learn that there are side-effects from the chemo pills. Flu-like symptoms, nausea, vomiting. I can do that! I once faked a stomach ache so well, I secured a whole week off school and was only a hair's breadth away from having

SAMANTHA KAY

my appendix removed. I'm not keen on the idea of taking time away from the showroom, but if that is what I need to do to save my marriage, then so be it.

There's a knock on my door. I look up from my scribbling and see my top salesman and second-in-command Dean, looking smart and alert, dressed sharply in a crisp white shirt and navy-blue trousers. I like Dean. He exudes an air of confidence and competence. Through the glass wall, I see that he's standing beside Gerald.

'Hey boss, you have a visitor,' Dean announces on opening my door.

I close my notebook, stand up and welcome the newcomer into my office. 'Gerald, lovely to see you!'

We shake hands before I sit back at my desk and Gerald takes a seat opposite.

'I hope you don't mind me dropping in unannounced,' I hear Gerald say as my attention drifts back to my laptop screen. Ah, it says here that not all chemo treatment results in hair loss . . . perfect. I never would suit the skinhead look.

'Jason?'

I hear my name and my head jerks up. I look at Gerald a little startled, having momentarily forgotten he was there.

'The McLaren - how's she getting on? May I see her? I can't wait to take her home,' Gerald says, a gleeful smile spread across his face.

95

I sit with my mouth open.

'The McLaren,' I echo, blinking hard. 'Yes, of course.' To give myself time, I start to search through my desk papers, racking my brain to recall the latest update.

'Yes, I er . . . believe the plates are being sorted today. No, sorry, tomorrow.' I open my notebook to quickly jot down the words *no hair loss*, before closing it again. I glance up and smile at Gerald, trying to seem cool and in control, but he's looking a little concerned. I know I'm not behaving normally.

'Everything all right?' he asks.

'Yes, of course,' I reply, pulling myself together and adding, 'I assure you that all is well, and she'll be ready for you to drive home in a couple of days.'

'Not the car. I meant you. You seem a little . . . distracted.'

I grimace, annoyed with myself. The very last thing I ever want to do is seem unprofessional, especially in front of a customer as important as Gerald.

'I'm fine,' I say. 'Sorry. There's just a lot going on at the moment.'

'With work?'

'Always, but no, work is fine. Business is good – great, in fact.' But my tone is lacking in positivity as I rest my chin in my hand.

Gerald searches my face before issuing me with a knowing smile. 'I know that look. If only we could chop ourselves in half, eh. Give as much at home as we do to the business,' he says warmly, withholding any judgement.

'Yes. If only,' I agree, my words followed by a deep sigh.

'How bad is it? Has she got herself lawyered up yet?'

I'm not sure how much vulnerability I should display in front of a customer, but it's an honest question from a decent and pragmatic man. Maybe it won't kill me to creak open the door on the matter. If nothing else, I'm sure Gerald has a good divorce lawyer on speed dial, should I need one.

'Not quite. I think I might have bought myself some time, but honestly, I don't know what to do. I have no idea how this is all going to play out,' I admit, my forlorn state difficult to hide.

'Try not to worry. If you think you've managed to buy some time, that's good. You can still turn things around,' Gerald says kindly, his words full of wisdom.

'I just have this horrible feeling she's already made up her mind.'

'She probably just wants to be seen, to know that she matters as much to you as all this.' Gerald gestures through the glass walls at the array of shiny Supercars.

'Of course she matters. All this is for her - why can't she see that?' I massage my aching head, frustration and plain old sadness starting to consume me. I stare down at my desk, not wanting Gerald to see quite how upset I am.

'To be fair, I might not be the best person to offer advice on this. If I had all the answers I wouldn't be engaged to Anne of Cleves right now, would I?' Gerald says with a smile.

His words break the tension and make me laugh.

'But you're happy with your lot, aren't you?' I question, having always assumed Gerald was rather ecstatic with the way his playboy lifestyle has panned out.

'I'm not *un*happy. But I'm no fool. I know my relationship is merely transactional. I get to wake up beside a beauty young enough to be my daughter and in exchange, she's treated to designer handbags. And it's fine, because the alternative would be a rather lonely existence.' He stares thoughtfully into the distance, and for the first time in all the years I've known him, I sense a strong feeling of regret.

'But what I'd give to wake up next to Catherine of Aragon again,' he goes on. 'To have that kind of connection with somebody. Someone who has been there all the way through. Someone who helped you build your success and would still be there should the empire fall, that's what you want in your old age. Not someone who thinks *North by Northwest* is a Kimya West album.'

I'm pretty sure he means Kanye West, but I choose not to correct him. Gerald's right. As enviable as his lifestyle might seem to others, as far as I'm concerned my future is with Abbie, and it always will be.

'But how? How do I make her change her mind?' I ask, a slight desperation in my voice. Pretend cancer might have bought me some crucial time, but I'm not sure it's a strong enough glue to hold everything together for ever.

'She fell in love with you once before, and you can make her love you again. Maybe cast your mind back to a simpler time - that's what I'd do,' Gerald says after thinking about it.

I nod. *A simpler time.* Sounds good. I suppress the urge to write that down in my notebook.

'So . . . this car, can I see her?' asks Gerald, slapping his knees and rubbing his hands together in excitement.

'Of course.' I jump up from my seat. 'Come on, she's with valeting. Let's go and say hello.' As I lead Gerald out of the office and through the showroom, I notice that I'm feeling mildly better than I did half an hour ago.

ABBIE

I made my way into work, opened the shutters and sat myself down at one of the tables. After ten or so minutes of further deliberation, I finally took the plunge to call Hamza and deliver the devastating news – that I will have to pull out of the flat because my husband is ill.

'I'm so sorry, Hamza. I feel as if I've let you down,' I say, sorry to have wasted everyone's time and effort, including my own.

'Not at all, Mrs Turner. These things happen. And again, I'm so very sorry to hear about your husband.'

'But if things change, which they may well do, you'll be the first person I come to.' I'm keen to show something in the way of loyalty, wanting to prove that I'm not a complete and utter time-waster.

'Well, there's really no need to restrict yourself. There are plenty of other letting agents out there.' Subtlety is not one of Hamza's strong points it seems.

We end the call, just as I hear a tapping on the glass. I look up and see Molly at the door waiting to be let in.

SAMANTHA KAY

'Morning,' I greet her as I open the door, flipping the sign from *Closed* to *Open*.

'Morning!' she chirps, thrusting a small white envelope at me.

'What's this?' I ask.

'Just a little something to celebrate your good news.'

I rip open the envelope and pull out a bright and shiny card. It's one that we sell here. I wonder if Molly actually paid for this card, but not wanting to ruin the moment I decide not to challenge her. *Congratulations* is spelled out in gold writing on the front, surrounded by multi-coloured stars and butterflies. I open the card, and inside is a little keyring with a small house charm attached to it. It has a mint-green wall, a pink roof and a tiny pink front door. The message inside the card reads:

Congratulations on your fresh new start!
So happy for you. Love, Molly x

I feel my eyes fill with tears.

Less than twenty-four hours ago, everything was within my grasp. A life away from Jason, his intolerable children and cunty ex-wife, but now it's as if everything has been snatched away. As if the universe is forcing me to reconsider what's important. Cancer stalling my plans and trapping me.

'Oh Molly, that's so kind,' I manage to say, staring hard at the tiny house charm. 'But you really shouldn't have.' I feel myself choke up, unable to quite believe my own bad luck.

'Not at all. I'm so happy for you, Abbie.' Molly pulls me in for a hug and it's then, in the embrace of a fellow human being, that I can't hold it together any longer, and I break down.

Molly is alarmed and immediately releases me. 'Oh God –why are you crying?' she says, displaying mild disgust.

'I had to pull out of the flat,' I tell her, struggling to get my words out between sobs.

'Why? What happened? You were so happy about it yesterday.'

Eventually I manage to calm down just enough to explain. 'It's Jason. He . . . he has cancer.'

Molly's mouth drops open and her eyes widen. 'Oh shit. That's bad.'

'Yeah. Testicular.'

'How bad is it?'

'We don't really know yet. He only found out yesterday.' I sniff loudly and wipe my eyes with the back of my hand, trying not to damage my make-up.

'Wow - that is such terrible timing.'

'I know. He told me as soon as I got home. I never even got to talk to him about moving out, about the flat.'

'Right...why not?'

'Because he has cancer.'

'Yeah, but I still don't get why that means

you can't leave.'

Molly's nonchalant attitude towards something so incredibly serious is irritating me greatly.

'*Because he has cancer.* Molly, am I speaking a different language or something? My husband has just been diagnosed with cancer! He needs treatment, he'll need a lot of help,' I say through gritted teeth, trying not to lose my temper.

'But is there a reason why you can't still help him from your own place?' Molly insists, tilting her head to one side in the annoying way she does when I try to explain the benefits of capitalism.

'You know, last week weren't you the one asking me why I should leave a beautiful home for some crappy one!'

'Yeah, when you were looking at forking out to move into a converted crack house. But you found a great place. I don't understand why you have to give that up because Jason got some bad news yesterday.' She speaks as if Jason's diagnosis is a minor inconvenience on a par with a spilled cup of coffee.

My feelings get the better of me and I can no longer hold my tongue.

'Oh my God! You know what, Molly, you are such a child!' I explode. 'You have all these outspoken views, but you literally know *nothing* about life and how to be a fucking grown-up! Jason is my husband, not the boy from the kebab shop that I give the run-around to! He needs me right now, and *I* need to be there for him!' Tears are streaming from my eyes again, and I know I may have gone too far, but I meant every single word.

Molly looks at me through the thick lenses of her glasses and I can't tell if she's shocked by my outburst, or quite simply disappointed by my choices.

'You know what, Abbie? You're right. I really don't understand any of this. So why don't you take five and I'll make you a tea using one of your *irresponsibly* sourced tea bags,' she replies, with only the slightest hint of aggression. She puts away her bag and jacket then very kindly makes her neurotic boss a cup of tea.

CHAPTER 7

JASON

'Cast your mind back to a simpler time,' Gerald said.

I assume by a 'simpler time' he means the early stages of Abbie and my relationship. For me, the stand-out memory of that time was how we had no money. In fact, we were flat broke. I remember our electricity cutting out at the most inconvenient of times, usually just before the cliff-hanger of whatever show we were watching on our tiny TV, or in the middle of cooking dinner, or while Abbie was blow-drying her hair. Sometimes it was due to the flat's dodgy wiring, but usually it was because the meter had run out.

Another bad memory is the rows I used to have with Kelly about me being able to see the kids, whom I missed so much, before we reached an arrangement that worked for us all. What's more, our arguments were usually carried out via our separate solicitors, resulting in hefty bills.

However, despite all the hardships, as I cast my mind back over the sixteen years that

Abbie and I have spent together, I do recall a lot of great times too.

I remember how good we were at making our own fun. For instance, we created our own nightclub. We called it *Jabbie's* - our names combined. We even made a sign out of cardboard and glitter and on a Saturday night we'd hang it above our kitchen door. We'd turn the lights down and the music up, and dance around the flat like lunatics whilst drinking cheap booze. Sometimes we'd invite friends over to join us, and once I was allowed to see the kids again, we even started involving them. Their song choices were questionable, but the starry effect from Ellie's special nightlight really helped capture the atmosphere we were after.

Another memory that comes to mind is the number of trips we made to the local park. We'd take the kids, letting them run around and go on the climbing frame, pushing them on the swings . . . but I also remember all the times we'd go there without them. Abbie and I would walk around the duck pond, sit down on a bench, huddle together and share a bag of chips.

I just wish I knew what Abbie is searching for exactly, or why she's suddenly so unhappy.

The first signs of spring are finally breaking through. The evenings are staying lighter a little longer, the temperature is less brutal.

Proud of the fact that I'm able to offer

Abbie more than a bag of chips on a park bench these days, this evening I left work early, picked up my prescription and am ready to start operation 'Wooing My Wife Back'. As I pull up outside *Daisy's* my heart sinks to see only one table being used. True, it is late in the day, but even so, it's a sad sight to behold.

I turn off the ignition and pick up the small paper bag containing my medication. I want to check that everything is there: one box of cholesterol pills, and one box of vitamin D pills. Annoyingly, the box has *Vitamin D* printed across it in massive letters. I was hoping to palm those off as anti-sickness pills. I make a mental note to purchase another pill bottle to transfer them to. Maybe while I'm at it, I'll get myself one of those day-of-the-week pill organisers that my grandmother used to have. Just the sight of one of those always gave me an eerie fear of illness. Yes, I'll do that tomorrow, order a pill organiser, some bottles and some labels . . . Actually, I might have some labels at work, I'll check.

But right now, I can't afford to get lost in the details. I have bigger fish to fry. I open the glove box and shove the small paper bag of medication inside, out of sight. Then I jump out of the car, and head towards the shop.

When I open the door, the small bell above it jingles. **The last customer passes me by on his way out.** Abbie is behind the counter, cleaning out the big coffee machine. She looks up.

'What are you doing here?' she asks, looking surprised.

'Charming,' I reply.

'You know what I mean. It's not like you to come by, especially not at this time. Is something wrong?' says Abbie, assuming there must be some new world-ending development, and I feel a little guilty for putting that very notion into her mind.

'No, no, nothing new. Can't a man surprise his wife with spontaneous dinner plans once in a while?' I say with what I hope is a charming smile.

But my patter doesn't have the desired effect.

'I'm not really dressed for dinner,' Abbie says, 'and I smell like coffee and I still need to cash up and close the shop.'

Like the true salesman I am, I don't let her lack of enthusiasm deter me.

'Well, we both have to eat,' I point out reasonably. 'It doesn't have to be anywhere fancy. Anyway, where's Molly? Can't she close up?'

'She has an afternoon lecture,' Abbie mutters, turning her attention back to the coffee machine.

'Oh, that's a shame.'

'No, it's not. Before she left, I had to endure a long lecture on how the milk we use is destroying the environment. Cows are going to be the death of us all, according to her.'

'Sounds thrilling. Well, I'm here now. I'll help you close up.'

Abbie gasps. 'My hero!' she says sarcastically, clutching her chest. She tosses a cloth to me, and then the multi-surface spray cleaner. 'You can start wiping the tables - and make sure you do them properly. I'll be checking.'

'Yes, boss,' I say, issuing a salute, happy to accept my orders.

It's been a long time since I took part in manual labour, but I must admit there's a sense of satisfaction in completing the tasks put to me. Every table has been wiped clean, the chairs placed on top, and I've just finished mopping the floor. With my shirt-sleeves rolled up I glance around and feel proud of myself. Then I make my way back round the counter with my mop and bucket.

I think Abbie may be in the toilet, so I loiter for a moment, not quite knowing what to do with the mop and bucket. That's when I catch sight of the few objects placed on the shelf under the counter. There are all the usual things you'd expect to see, like cleaning cloths and sprays, spare piles of napkins and paper bags, as well as some opened post.

It's the post which piques my interest, and I'm itching to pick it up and read it. But it's wrong to snoop, and so I force myself to look away. I can now hear Abbie moving around out the back. No doubt she'll come in at any moment.

Try as I may, my curiosity gets the better of me. With one hand holding the mop, I use the other to poke at the pile of letters. I tilt my head as the pile moves slightly, giving me a better view - and that's when I see large red writing at the top of an envelope. It reads: *FINAL NOTICE.*

I wince. I know business has been slow, but Abbie never told me things were this bad. I poke at the pile a little more, the letters fanning apart slightly, and I see a card. I glance behind me - still no sign of Abbie - and gently pull the card towards me. It's upside down, but I can see it reads *Congratulations* across the front. I manage to open it up and, squinting, I read the message inside.

Congratulations on your fresh new start!

A sudden loud tapping on the door startles me so much that I let go of my mop, which falls to the floor with a clank. A young guy with black floppy hair is standing outside *Daisy's*, holding a large brown-paper bag. I hastily fold the card and put it back on the pile before heading over to the door and opening it.

'Sorry, mate, we're closed,' I say.

'Hiya, Mas.' Abbie appears behind me, all smiles, seemingly in familiar company. 'Thank you so much. How much do I owe you?' she asks, reaching out to take the bag.

'Nothing. Dad said it's on the house. He's really grateful to you for sorting out Mum's birthday gift for him.'

'He didn't need to do that. But tell him thank you.'

'Will do. Have a good night, Abbie,' the young guy says, issuing a small wave and a friendly smile at us both.

'And you, Mas.' Abbie closes the door behind her and relocks it with one hand, cradling the large bag in her other arm.

'What's that?' I ask.

'This is our dinner. I ordered you a chicken sheesh with chips and hummus.'

'Oh really? I had something a little nicer in mind.' I'm a bit deflated, unsure whether a takeaway kebab is going to be enough to win my way back into my wife's affections.

'I know. But I'm tired and hungry, so this'll do just fine. Put a couple of chairs round a table and I'll grab some plates.'

'But I just cleaned the tables,' I protest.

'And a mighty good job you did, too. Don't worry, I'll help you clear up after,' she says with a sweet smile, thrusting the paper bag at me.

And so we devour our food sitting at a table in a snug corner of the shop, and I realise this is probably the longest time I've spent at *Daisy's* in years. I feel ashamed not to have taken a greater interest in things.

'How's business?' I ask with my mouth full.

'Brilliant. In fact, Richard Branson called only yesterday - he wants to invest!' Abbie mumbles, licking garlic mayo from her fingers, as it oozes out of the pitta between her hands.

'Seriously, how are things?' I push again.

'I don't want to talk about work. I want to talk about you. Did you chase the doctor?'

'No.'

Abbie lets out a frustrated huff, but before she has a chance to go into one of her lectures, I jump right back in.

'I didn't need to. *They* called *me*.'

Abbie looks at me wide-eyed, waiting for me to follow on, to tell her the latest.

Instead, I take another bite from my food, making her wait.

'Well - what did they say?' she demands, her patience wearing thin.

I swallow. 'They want me to start treatment next week.'

'What kind of treatment?'

'Chemo. But they can give me chemo in pill form. I take a course of pills at home, then they'll follow up from there.'

I look at Abbie and I can see the panic in her eyes. She licks her lips anxiously in the way she does when she's trying not to cry.

'I read online that they usually remove the testicle first,' she says, her voice choked.

It's quite likely that Abbie and I have been researching the exact same information online.

Having seen this coming, I've mentally prepared myself for this.

'Yeah, I read that too. But the doctor said that's old information now. It seems that for the type of cancer I have, they don't need to go down that route. The pills should do the trick.' I'm impressed by my delivery and level of conviction.

'It's gonna be okay.' I reach for her hand, gently taking it in mine, trying to offer reassurance.

'I know . . . I was just thinking about Molly - her aunt that passed away last year, the one with breast cancer.' Abbie says this in a manner that implies she's told me about this previously, which she probably has, but I have zero recollection of Molly's cancer-riddled aunt. I nod my head anyway.

'She had those chemo pills. Apparently the side-effects were pretty brutal.'

'I know. The doctor talked me through it. But it'll be worth it.'

'I hope so. Look, Jason, when are we going to tell Harry and Ellie?' Poor Abbie looks so downcast. But I don't want the kids to know – definitely not. My plan does not include upsetting them and their world.

'I wasn't going to tell them anything. I don't want to scare them.' I say firmly. My so-called cancer is merely a means to an end to save my marriage, and there is absolutely no need to

EIGHT MILLION MINUTES

involve the entire family.

'I know. But they're not babies. They're going to wonder why you're not at work, why you're suddenly so ill.'

She's right. If my performance is going to be convincing enough for Abbie to stay, it can't possibly go unnoticed by the kids. I feel a wave of panic sweep through me, fearful that the magnitude of this exercise is already snowballing beyond my control.

'Can that be a tomorrow problem?' I ask sincerely, knowing I'll need time to think through all the logistics.

To my relief Abbie nods in reluctant agreement before saying, 'I'll need to speak to Molly tomorrow about taking some time off. I expect I'll have to shut the shop.'

'Why would you do that?'

'Someone needs to look after you.'

Oh no. Flattered as I am, the last thing I want is for Abbie to put her livelihood on the line.

'Can't Molly still run things while you're away?'

'Not really, as she's only part-time. She has uni, remember. Anyway, it'll probably save me money to stay closed.'

Abbie looks stressed and utterly defeated, and I berate myself for not noticing before how greatly she's been struggling.

'How long has it been this bad?' I ask gently, unsure if I should mention the final

114

demand under the counter.

'A while,' Abbie tells me, looking forlornly into her kebab, which she puts down on her plate.

'What if you let Molly go? Is that an option?'

'I've thought about it, but to be honest it wouldn't change anything. Firing her won't make up the losses, and I like having her here. It means I'm not tied to this place all the time, if I need to run an errand or something.'

An errand like looking for a new place to live, I think bitterly to myself.

'Why haven't you spoken to me about this sooner?' I ask, although I know it's my fault for not being interested enough to notice what has been going on with her business.

'Why do you think? You're never around! Honestly, when was the last time you and I spent any real time together?'

I bite my tongue, delighted in the knowledge that our recent holiday to Barbados was time and money well spent!

'I know, and I'm sorry. I want that to change, I really do.' I say, keen to keep on track with the small amount of progress I'm making, terrified Abbie's going to mention the flat and her plans to leave me.

Instead, she sighs, and after a few seconds of silence she brings us back to my situation. 'So, how long is a round of chemo pills? A week? Two weeks?'

'I don't want to talk about cancer anymore.'

'We can't *not* talk about it.' And Abbie takes a huge bite from her kebab, leaving behind a large blob of garlic mayo by her mouth.

'Yes, we can.' I pick up a napkin and delicately wipe the mayo from her face.
'I'm in the middle of a delicious dinner with my beautiful wife, and I want nothing more than to gaze at you while you tell me all about your day.'

Abbie smiles at me from across the small table - a genuine loving smile that fills me with confidence that everything is going to be OK. With that, I continue to work through my kebab, while Abbie tells me all about her day.

CHAPTER 8

ABBIE

It's early on a Sunday evening and, in a break from the usual routine, we're getting ready to pick up Harry and Ellie who will be joining us for a meal at our favourite Chinese. Despite the obvious strain of the cancer diagnosis, the past week has gone well. Jason's been super-attentive and positive, and it's been nice - unexpected, but nice.

Standing in the bathroom, I take one last look at my unsmiling reflection in the mirror above the sink. Unbeknownst to the kids, Jason is scheduled to start his first round of chemo pills tomorrow. With neither of us really sure what to expect from the coming weeks, Jason was keen for us to spend some time together as a family. I, on the other hand, could happily have done without it.

My Sunday evenings are usually spent lounging around in a tracksuit catching up on my soaps, while Jason pretends to switch off but in reality barely looks up from his phone. Oh well, I suppose that if Jason is prepared to break the habit of a lifetime and put in some effort with the family, I should follow suit.

'I'm ready,' I call to Jason, walking downstairs and gravitating towards the kitchen where I've left my phone and handbag. I find him sitting on one of the stools at the breakfast bar, dressed and ready to go. Assuming he's engrossed in his phone, when I get a little closer I'm surprised to see him huddled over a colourful plastic pill organiser and a small selection of medication.

'What are you doing?' I ask.

'I just wanted to sort out my pills for tomorrow.'

I'd always assumed that a cancer diagnosis in the family meant an endless drama-filled process. Emotional hospital appointments with understanding consultants delivering mind-boggling information on treatments and side-effects. However, with us it's been quite the opposite. Jason had all the initial contact with the doctor without my knowing, and in the interests of speed, follow-ups regarding his treatment have been done over the phone.

Initially I was worried not to be more involved. Jason doesn't always pay great attention to mundane instructions and often relies on me to do all the listening, but to my surprise, he's taken to this with the utmost seriousness.

'Isn't it just two pills a day?' I ask, sure his prescription didn't consist of as many pills as first feared. He'll take one chemo pill along with one anti-sickness pill to help with the unpleasant side-effects for the next week. Then there's to be a week's break, then another week of pills, then . . . we'll see. Hopefully he'll be cured. If he's not, we start all over again.

'Yeah. But the doctor said it's really important to take them properly and not forget what you've taken,' Jason explains, 'so...' He opens a small white and orange box, pulling from it a foil sachet of pills.

'Do you need any help?' I ask.

'If you like.' He pulls out the bar stool next to him, gesturing for me to take a seat. He hands me the foil sachet. I snap a small white oval-shaped pill from the foil and hand it to him. Jason dutifully drops it into the orange section of the pill organiser labelled *Monday*. Then he picks up the small brown bottle next to him on the counter. Twisting the top off, he pours a small number of pills into his hand.

'These are the anti-sickness pills,' he says solemnly. 'They should help take the edge off. I hope they work.' He drops one into each compartment.

'Are you worried about tomorrow?' I ask, snapping a second pill from the foil and handing it to him.

Jason shrugs and places the pill into the yellow *Tuesday* compartment.

He seems a little down, his sombre mood concerning me. A scary health diagnosis combined with the fact that my husband is emotionally constipated when it comes to discussing his feelings could potentially be a recipe for disaster.

'You can talk about it, you know. Whatever you're worried about,' I suggest carefully, snapping a third pill.

'I dunno . . .' he sighs, unable to look at me.

'What? Tell me what's bothering you,' I prod, urging him to open up.

He reaches out his hand for the third pill. I hand it to him.

'I don't want you seeing me sick,' he mutters, keeping his focus on the organiser.

I laugh. 'Jason, it's been sixteen years,' I scoff. 'We've seen each other sick before.'

'Yeah, bugs and colds and stuff. Never anything serious. Never anything like this.'

Finally, he looks at me. There's a sadness in his eyes, a worry; a level of vulnerability I don't think I've ever witnessed from him before, and I feel horrible.

I imagine the scene if I'd left. Him sitting here alone. Sorting out his medication, feeling scared, not knowing what the future has in store. Not having anyone to turn to.

I look down at the foil sachet, hoping to hide my own guilty conscience.

'What if the treatment doesn't work and I get *really* sick?' he bursts out. 'What if I don't get better?'

'Then I'll be here with you,' I say simply.

'Promise?'

I take hold of his strong hand in mine. 'Of course. We're a team, aren't we?' I smile.

He smiles back, his display of vulnerability not at all like him - and oddly, it's a little bit of a turn-on.

'Anyway, stop catastrophising,' I order him. 'Let's just cross one bridge at a time, eh?'

'I love you.' He says, is voice quiet and sincere.

'I love you too,' I tell him, looking down at his hand in mine, wondering how feelings that were once so pure and simple, became so complex. Then I let go and hand him the fourth pill, keen to finish our task.

*

Running slightly behind schedule, the four of us take our seats at a round table in the middle of the large busy restaurant. A friendly waiter hands us all a menu before hurrying away again.

When official custody arrangements were put in place some years ago, Harry and Ellie's visits worked like clockwork. They would stay with us every other weekend, one-half term a year and two weeks in the summer holidays.

Now the kids are older, the legal arrangements no longer apply, and these days friends and other interests take much greater precedence in their lives over boring old dad and their wicked stepmother. By which I mean that we hardly see Harry at all, but Ellie usually swings by when she wants something, or when she wants to get away from her mother, or to issue blow jobs in our living room.

With Jason making the decision not to tell the kids about his diagnosis, the reason for our impromptu dinner has aroused their suspicions. Personally, I think the kids are old enough to handle the truth, however harsh it might be, but Jason disagreed, keen to keep things under wraps for now.

'Why are we here?' groans Harry, crooking his neck to look down at the menu on the table, it being far too much effort to pick it up.

'I'm glad you asked, son. This place is what's called a restaurant. We order food, they bring it, and then we eat,' Jason replies with a smug smile.

'I mean why are we here tonight? It's no one's birthday,' moans Harry, making it abundantly clear that he'd rather be anywhere else but here - and he's not the only one. A few short days ago, I was of the belief that family meals spent dragging out small talk with the two most ungrateful children on the face of the earth were long behind me, but no such luck!

'Why do we need a reason to spend some time together?' shrugs Jason.

'Is one of you dying?' asks Ellie, issuing me a snarky side eye while spinning the turntable in the centre of the table.

I look at Jason, who looks up from his phone and over at me. I wait for Jason to reply.

'No,' he says after a pause.

'Is Nana dying?' Ellie is obviously still unconvinced that our family get-together does not have an ulterior motive.

'Not as far as I know,' says Jason, focusing on his menu.

'Are you getting divorced?' mumbles Harry.

I fix my focus on my own menu, feeling beyond awkward, but strangely impressed at how intuitive Harry and Ellie actually are.

'No one is dying. No one is getting divorced,' Jason says firmly, and I think how nice it must be to live in a world where everything is so efficiently glazed over for you.

'What time do you think we'll be done?' whines Ellie, echoing my own thoughts.

'We've not even ordered drinks yet.' Jason is beginning to show his frustration.

'Why, you got somewhere to be?' I ask, trying to soften the atmosphere.

'I told Grace I'd see her tonight,' says Ellie, picking up her phone, her fingers frantically tapping away.

'In that case you should have told Grace you had plans with your family tonight.' Jason swipes Ellie's phone from her and places it beneath his own on the table, sneaking a peek at his own screen as he does so.

'Is this about when you called mum a cunt?' Harry blurts out, still trying to suss the reason for our outing, just as the waiter swings by our table with a basket of prawn crackers.

Mortified, Jason kicks Harry under the table. 'Watch your language! We're in public.'

'That didn't stop Abbie,' Harry sniggers, undeterred.

'What's he talking about?' demands Jason, starting to lose his cool.

'Anyone want to share a chow mein?' I interrupt, casually picking up a prawn cracker and taking a bite.

'Abbie. She called Mum a cunt,' Ellie happily informs her father before reaching for two prawn crackers and I'm disappointed but not surprised to learn that any alliance between myself and Ellie is purely one-sided.

Jason looks as if he's about to blow a gasket, unhappy with the language coming from his children's mouths.

'Can we all please stop saying the word cunt at the dinner table! When was this?'

'At my art show after Mum spilt coffee on her,' Harry informs him.

'If no one wants to share a chow mein I'm

happy just with a rice.' I say, wondering if to order chow mein and a rice would be too much food, more than happy to disengage from this conversation.

'Why didn't you tell me?' asks Jason, locking eyes with me from across the table.

'I dunno.' I shrug, reaching for another prawn cracker. 'It wasn't that important.' In all seriousness, in light of more recent issues, that is absolutely true, but I know how protective Jason is and how much he hates being kept out of the loop.

'Or maybe it's because you're never around,' interjects Ellie.

'That's true. If you'd bothered to come to my art show, you'd have known about it,' Harry accuses him, showing some obvious resentment for his dad's no-show.

'You know what, you're right. You're all right.' Jason sounds choked, fidgeting with his chopsticks on the table. The kids and I look at each other, half-wondering if Jason's about to cry. 'That's why I wanted us to have this meal together as a family. It's important we try and spend more time with each other.' Sure enough, his eyes are a little teary-looking.

'Are you sure you're not dying?' Ellie frowns.

'I'm sure.'

'So can I still go to Grace's after?'

'No, you cannot. You have school

tomorrow.'

'So, the chow mein?' I repeat, losing the will to live.

'I'll share one with you, Abbie,' says Harry, just as the waiter returns to our table, ready to take our order.

JASON

Having dropped Harry and Ellie back at their mum's house, I'm driving home with Abbie. The revelation from dinner has left me feeling a bit shaken up. Three big things have happened: Abbie has been rowing with Kelly, Abbie has been planning to leave me, and Abbie's business is failing – *and I'd had no idea about any of this.* I'd been totally in the dark, with not a clue, not a single notion that anything was wrong.

No wonder she wants to leave me.

I dread to think what else has been going on without my knowing.

Is Ellie having sex with her boyfriend? Does Harry have a drug habit?

Who knows! Certainly not me.

'Am I an awful person?' I mutter over the sound of Blondie playing on the radio.

'What? Of course you're not.' Abbie says, and as convincing as her response is, I'm not sure I believe her.

'I'm gonna die. I'm gonna die and on my headstone it's going to read: *Jason, nice guy, but not around much,*' I say bitterly, hitting the brakes hard, my reaction to the red light a little delayed.

127

EIGHT MILLION MINUTES

'You're not going to die,' Abbie says.

'We're *all* going to die, Abbie. And that is definitely what they'll say about me. You included.'

'OK, well - whose fault is that?'

'Oh cheers! Don't try and humour me or anything.' I sulk, frustrated at how quickly Abbie's sympathy evaporated.

'Why are you trying to pick a fight?' she snaps back as the traffic-light turns green and I pull away.

'I'm not. I'm sorry. I just feel like I'm missing everything.' By which, I don't mean *missing out* but missing the obvious signs that all is not well with the woman I love, and it bothers me. It bothers me very much.

'Then maybe, you need to change up your work-homelife balance,' Abbie informs me, the undertone of resentment not going unnoticed.

With no idea of what to say, I choose not to respond. When I glance at Abbie, my heart wants to burst, and it pains me that I can't seem to read her anymore. After a prolonged silence filled by nothing other than Elton John's 'Rocket Man', I decide to say something before we make it home.

'I do it for us, you know,' I try to explain, indicating left into our road. 'So that things can be better. So that we don't have to live in some tiny flat with no money. I don't ever want us to go back to that. Do you?' I'm actually dreading her answer, unable to understand what it is she wants these days.

'Of course I don't,' she sighs, and I feel an overwhelming sense of relief.

I pull the car onto our drive, turn off the engine and the music from the radio stops. We each release our seatbelts but neither of us makes a move to leave the vehicle. I think we both have some kind of silent understanding that our business isn't quite finished here.

'You're a good person,' Abbie says, looking at me with the kind of affection one would show a stray kitten.

I grimace; still not sure I believe her.

She turns in her seat and takes my hands in hers. 'You're a good dad, and a good husband. Stop working yourself up about all this stuff.' She strokes my face. 'We've got a lot coming our way in the next few weeks. Just try to relax.'

I bury my face in the nape of her neck, inhaling every ounce of her. Basking in the knowledge that my marriage lives to fight another day, and in my state of vulnerability, I decide to push my luck.

'You know what really helps me to relax...'

I feel Abbie laugh. She pulls away but stays close, a knowing look in her eyes.

'What...here?'

'It'll be just like the old days,' I say, trying to tempt her with nostalgia.

'Hah, when we used to sneak around in car

parks after work?' Abbie bites down on her lip as a naughty smile spreads across her face. It's a look I've seen many times before; one that tells me she's certainly not against the idea.

'What if the neighbours see?' she asks, fleetingly looking behind her out of the passenger window.

'They won't see anything,' I say confidently. It's dark and just about late enough.

Abbie pushes a hand through her long blonde hair to move it aside, and without saying a word, she shuffles over to me, aides me in unbuttoning my jeans and buries her head in my lap. Already aroused, within seconds I'm buried inside her warm mouth. I sit back and relax, savouring every delicious second. As ludicrous as a pretend cancer diagnosis might seem, I'm certain I've made the right decision; sure no other scenario could possibly provide this kind of effect.

CHAPTER 9

ABBIE

It's been a really sunny warm day, unseasonably so considering it's still early spring, but I'm not complaining. Happy to finally enjoy our garden, I lean back on the rattan chair, a mug of tea in one hand, my phone in the other. I can't resist scrolling through a page of flat listings on my phone. Old habits die hard.

Eventually, I put my phone down and take in the view before me. The spring flowers are blooming, and pink blossom decorates the trees. The natural world shows signs of vibrancy and health, but unfortunately the same cannot be said for everything in this house.

Jason started his chemo pills today.

Not knowing what to expect from the day, I headed out to work early this morning to open up. Fortunately, Molly had no lectures so very kindly offered to hold the fort and close up tonight so I could head home early, and I'm pleased I did. I found Jason resting in bed. Although it's a mild day, he's feeling cold, wrapped up tightly in the duvet. I've just delivered him a fresh hot water bottle. The bedroom is stifling, but he insists on having the curtains closed and the door shut as he sleeps through the day. He also complained of a bad tummy this morning, but that seems to have eased off since I arrived home.

Sad as I was about having to turn down the flat, after a week of contemplation, I think it was the right decision. Last night in bed, Jason spoke of all the things he wants us to do together during the break in his treatment. Lunches out, a spa day, maybe even a few nights away somewhere. Maybe it's fear talking, or maybe after years of putting work before everyone and everything else, he finally understands what's truly important. It's just a shame it took a cancer diagnosis to do so. However, I know this is where I need to be: right here, looking after my husband and helping him through this.

'Hey,' says a small voice. I look behind me and see Ellie, dressed in her school uniform stepping into the garden. 'Why are you both home?' she asks in her usual snotty tone, after having seen our cars on the drive.

'Sorry, is my being here interfering with your sex life?' My reply is equally snotty, wondering if her boyfriend with the massive willy is lurking somewhere.

'Shush, I don't want Dad to hear.' There's a look of panic in Ellie's eyes as she sits down on the garden chair next to me.

'Don't worry, he's upstairs asleep.'

'Why?' There's a look of confusion on her face, well aware it's out of character for her father to be home at this time and even more unlike him to be unwell.

'Tummy bug.' This is the explanation Jason wants me to give if anyone asked.

'Maybe it was that Chinese we had last night. I've felt really sick all day, thought I was going to puke during science,' says Ellie, rubbing her stomach.

'Yeah, maybe. So, no sign of your boyfriend today?' I enquire, keen to change the subject.

'No. We broke up.' Ellie's expression is unreadable and I can't tell if she's disgruntled or heartbroken as she stares blankly at the patio.

'Oh, you never said. Why?'

'We just did,' she says flatly.

'Are you OK?' I'm a little concerned not to have been met by Ellie's usual stroppiness.

'Urgh! I'm fine!' she yells, springing up from her seat, the unpleasant teenager I recognise finally returning. She storms back into the house. Alone once again, I decide to finish up my tea before I check in on Jason once more.

JASON

I'm fucking boiling, lying here sweating like a pig on a spit roast.

Day one of 'chemo pills' started off easily enough. Abbie departed for work as usual. Fighting against all my natural urges, I stayed home and, left to my own devices, all was going swimmingly. Although it pains me to be away from the showroom, I had my phone and my laptop by my side and was able to reply to messages and sort through some work. In fact, without the distractions from other people at the showroom, I was able to speed through some of my tasks much faster than usual. However, all that changed when Abbie so lovingly returned home early.

Whilst I've been holed up in the bedroom, Abbie has been bringing me coffee to keep me warm, fresh glasses of water to keep me hydrated and hot water bottles to keep me cosy. As great as it's been to be fussed over, with her here I've had no choice but to stay in 'chemo mode' all day.

In the spirit of believability, I've opted to display full-on flu-like symptoms. Initially, I thought it would be easy enough to convey, what with having mastered the role as a youngster in order to skip school. I'm not sure if I'm simply out of practice, but the role seems more challenging than I remember. Snuggling into a big duvet and cosying up to a hot water bottle is no big ask on a cold winter's day, but with today's temperature peaking at 20 degrees, being shut away in this room has left me teetering on the edge of heat exhaustion.

With the curtains shut and the door closed, I pull my phone out from under the covers and decide to find something to watch. Usually, I would have the TV on, but I've decided against it. I'm going for an 'I'm too poorly to even watch the telly' kind of approach, which I believe could be a simple but effective move, but I am starting to get bored.

As I swipe my phone, I hear a gentle knock on the bedroom door. I whisk my phone under the duvet and lie down, swiftly getting back into character.

'Come in,' I say, and cough, then I light up inside when I see Ellie poking her head around the doorway.

'Ellie belly! Well, aren't you a sight for sore eyes! To what do I owe this pleasure?' I say, surprised and happy to see my baby girl.

'Don't get excited. I left a revision book here I need. What's wrong with you?' she asks, dumping herself down on the bed beside me with said book in her hand.

'Nothing, just a tummy bug,' I lie, trying not to give off too strong a vibe of 'I'm dying' to my innocent daughter.

'Do you think it was something we ate last night, because I feel really sick too,' she says, looking strained.

'Oh no, I'm sorry. You can rest up in here with me if you like. Keep me company,' I suggest, willing to take any opportunity to spend time with Ellie.

'No thanks, it stinks in here,' she says with a grimace. 'What is that smell?'

Sweat, decay, the foul stench of deceit?

'It is warm in here. I think I need to crack open a window.' I sit up and loosen the covers a little.

'Yeah, you look proper sweaty, Dad.' Ellie regards me with disgust. She looks at my bedside table, reaches over and picks up my empty coffee mug from earlier.

'Ugh - that's it, that's what I can smell. Stale coffee.' She brings the mug to her face and takes a sniff from it. Starts to dry heave and within less than a second, she urgently hops off the bed and runs into the ensuite bathroom. I hear retching quickly followed by the gross sound of puke landing in the toilet.

Come to think of it, that chicken we had last night didn't taste too great. And if the smell in this room isn't bad enough already, the stench of Ellie's vomit is certainly an unwelcome addition. I really should get out of bed and check she's OK, but I've always been rather sensitive to other people's bodily fluids. So, I decide to take advantage of my own situation and do what any other cancer-stricken patient in my position might do.

'Abbie!' I shout downstairs. 'Ellie's being sick!'

Then I tuck myself back into the duvet before Abbie makes it into the bedroom. It is imperative I don't break character.

ABBIE

Standing at the front door I watch as a worse-for-wear Ellie climbs into the front seat of her mum's car. After emptying the contents of her stomach into my ensuite toilet as well as onto the floor tiles, I thought it best to call Kelly to come and pick her up. I have enough on my plate with Jason. A teenager with food poisoning really is an unwanted addition to my day.

I can see Kelly at the wheel. She doesn't get out of the car, nor does she so much as glance in my general direction. I can see she looks disgruntled. Maybe because of the interruption to her evening, or maybe it's due to the reminder of my very existence. I wave anyway, a gesture that's ignored by both her and Ellie. With that I turn around and step back into the house, closing the door behind me. Back in the living room, I plonk myself down on the sofa. I really should think about making some dinner but I don't know if Jason can stomach anything and the sight of Ellie's vomit has made me lose my own appetite somewhat.

On the large coffee table in front of me sits Jason's laptop. It's closed, with his black dogeared notebook resting on top of it. He said he wouldn't, but I'm sure he logged on this morning. I know he finds it hard to switch off, but right now I really want him to concentrate on his health although I also realise how important work is to him. It'd be unrealistic of me to think he could ever turn himself off completely.

Keen for the living room to be a non-work environment, I stand up and slide Jason's laptop towards me. As I pick it up from the coffee table, his notebook falls at my feet. I tuck the laptop under my arm and bend down to pick up the notebook. It's fallen open on a page of numbers and workings out, possibly prices; their purpose something I can't quite interpret. I casually flick through the pages. His whole life is here: lists of jobs to do, prices and figures, contact names, phone numbers and email addresses, and I smile to myself at how 'old school' Jason is. Making handwritten notes on everything rather than storing such information electronically like most other people.

Just as I'm about to close the notebook I spot a list that stands out from the others, titled *Testicular Cancer*. It's an extensive list, taking up over two pages. He's recorded types of treatment, side-effects, timescales. He's researched charities and fundraising ideas. Marathons for Cancer Research. He's even written down a coffee-cake recipe under the title 'Macmillan Coffee

Mornings'. All this from the man who can barely run a bath, let alone a marathon, and I'm pretty sure he doesn't even know how to turn the oven on, far from bake a cake from scratch.

Over on the second page, in the top corner he's drawn a little heart, the initial A inside it. I close the book and feel a rush of guilt so strong I have to sit down.

Imagine if I'd left him.

Imagine if I'd delivered my news before he'd delivered his. He'd be all alone, ill and scared in this big house. I feel tears prick at my eyes which quickly run down my face. I wipe them away and stand, keen to go and check on him. That's when Jason walks in. His navy-blue bathrobe is loosely tied around his waist and his chest is visible.

'Hey, what are you doing up?' I ask as he approaches. He looks well, I note. A little tired and drained, but otherwise good.

'I'm feeling a little better now and needed to get out of that stuffy room. Are you all right?' he asks, searching my face. It's pretty obvious I've been crying.

'Yeah, I'm fine, it's just been a busy day,' I say, sweeping my hand through my hair.

'Do you want me to take that?' Asks Jason, nodding at the laptop and notebook tucked under my arm.

'It's ok, I was just gona pop it upstairs out of the way.' I say, making to leave the room.

'Oh, don't go. I came down to see you,' Jason tells me. 'I wanted to say thank you for looking after me today, and Ellie. God knows what I did to deserve you.' He wraps his arms around me. His body is warm and comforting against mine, and I realise just how much I love being held between his arms. I well up again and start to cry at the very thought of losing him.

'Hey, hey, what's wrong? Is it Kelly - did she upset you again?' he asks.

'No, no. Nothing like that.' I try to hold myself together before bursting out, 'I just can't bear the thought of losing you.'

Unwrapping me from his arms Jason smiles at me with loving eyes, before pulling me into his embrace once more. 'I'm not going anywhere,' he whispers into my ear, his breath against my skin giving me goose bumps.

'Promise?'

'I promise,' he says, holding me tightly in his arms.

CHAPTER 10

JASON

It goes without saying that sitting on the bathroom floor in my underpants is not the most comfortable place to spend the day, but it does possess a certain advantage. Tucked in closely next to the toilet, I'm able to work from my phone whilst staying firmly out of view.

It's day three of 'chemo pills' and after spending the past two days sweating in bed, today I've decided to switch things up a little, opting to display symptoms of nausea. The constant retching has taken its toll on my throat as well as my jaw, but I'm able to fake the sound of vomit easily enough by tipping a glass of water down the toilet at various intervals.

For the second day running Abbie has decided to stay home with me. A sweet gesture, but her constant presence means I've really had to be careful to never break character. Any time I sense she's near, I hide my phone behind the loo, and so far I've done well not to get caught. However, trying to run a business from a tiny screen whilst slumped on the bathroom floor has been no mean feat. Dean needs confirmation on some paperwork for a Ferrari part-exchange, and without being able to make a normal grown-up phone call I'm struggling to convey all the information.

While I'm doing my best to tap out an email on the keypad, a text message comes through from Gerald. It's a photograph of his fiancée Suzie, dressed in a flowery summer dress and large sunglasses, draped over the bonnet of the yellow McLaren I just sold him. The sun is burning high in the bright blue sky, and I sense this picture may have been taken in the South of France where I know Gerald has a place. I can't help but feel a prickle of envy at the glamorous sight. Clearly Suzie is more than happy to indulge in the rewards of Gerald's hard work without complaining. I bet he has never had to pretend to be half-dead on the bathroom floor to keep her affections.

The love of my life reads the short caption attached to the picture, and I'm genuinely not sure if Gerald means Suzie or the car, but either way I smile, happy in the knowledge of another satisfied customer.

I reply to Gerald. *Brilliant picture. South of France?*

Before I return to my email to Dean, I take a second to 'be sick'. I heave loudly then tip some water from my glass down the loo before throwing in another retch and a loud gagging cough for good measure along with another tipple of water. My throat is really sore.

I flush the clean toilet and decide to finish my reply to Dean before Abbie comes back. Landing on the draft email, I notice a mistake. The email starts with *Hi Jean,* rather than *Dean.* I need to rectify the mistake, but as I try to highlight the name, I accidentally send the message.

'Oh, for fuck's sake,' I groan, having just about had enough of a numb arse and the measly working conditions.

'Everything OK?' Abbie calls sweetly.

Uh oh - she's in the bedroom. I hadn't realised. I tuck my phone behind the toilet and slowly rise off the floor with all the grace of an arthritic octogenarian. I turn and see Abbie standing in the doorway, her blue eyes anxious.

'Yeah, I'm just fed up with feeling rough,' I say, which is no word of a lie. My back and neck are hurting and my irritation levels are increasing by the hour. I rub the back of my aching neck and stumble a little, having lost most of the feeling in my left leg. The instability enough to cause mild panic.

'Oh no, be careful,' fusses Abbie, placing her arms around me, trying to keep me steady. 'You're probably dehydrated, you've been puking for hours.'

'I think I need a lie-down,' I whisper, resting my head on her shoulder and we stand together for a moment while Abbie tenderly strokes my head.

'Come on, let's get you into bed.' And she helps me out of the bathroom and over towards the bed. There, she pulls back the covers and thumps my pillow before I climb in. The moment I lie down and stretch out, my aching body thanks me for the comfort, my back and neck recovering almost instantly. Abbie places the covers over me, but I stop her.

'No, no. I'm so hot,' I cry out, unable to bear another day sweltering under the duvet in this stuffy bedroom.

She nods understandingly and folds the covers down over my feet. Pouting sympathetically, she then places a hand on my head and strokes me, in just the same way she does to Daisy the cat. I close my eyes, enjoying the feel of her touch.

'Have a rest,' she murmurs, and I open my eyes and see her turning to leave.

'Don't go,' I plead, reaching out to her, willing her to return.

'I'll be right back. I'm just going to fetch you a bucket in case you need to be sick again.' She goes trotting out of the room with some urgency, worried about any potential damage to the carpet.

I'm so happy to finally be out of the god-forsaken bathroom – but then I remember the Ferrari part-exchange and my phone concealed behind the toilet. I quickly leap from the bed and hurry to the bathroom, where I grab my phone, sprint back to the bed, hop in and tuck the phone under my pillow, managing to resume my position just in the nick of time as Abbie walks back into the room and places a lime-green bucket on the floor next to me at the side of the bed.

'Is there anything you want me to get you?' she asks.

I've barely eaten a thing all day. In the spirit of authenticity, I've had to be seen to be unable to stomach anything, but now it's way past lunchtime and the two cereal bars I hid in my bedside table are long gone and my stomach is making a noise reminiscent of our once broken tumble dryer.

'Could I have a coffee please, and maybe a slice of toast, oh and maybe a couple of biscuits... Please?'

Abbie frowns, looking a little puzzled by the size of my order. 'Are you sure?' She's no doubt wondering where my appetite has suddenly sprung from.

'I need to try and eat something, to help my energy levels,' I explain, my voice croaky from all the retching, but the desperation is genuine enough. I'm fucking starving.

'OK. Anything else?'

I reach for Abbie's hand and look into her beautiful blue eyes. 'And maybe a cuddle?'

Abbie smiles at me and I smile back, feeling hopeful.

'OK, I'll make you something to eat first, then we'll have a cuddle.'

I kiss her hand before she slips it out of mine, leaving the bedroom and heading downstairs for the kitchen. That's when I seize the opportunity to write the overdue follow-up email to Dean. I pull my phone out from under my pillow, desperate to get the Ferrari paperwork wrapped by the end of the day.

ABBIE

Life is a funny old thing.

It's strange how quickly things can change. How things that seemed so important one minute suddenly don't the next, and how other situations can take on a new level of precedence almost overnight.

Only a couple of weeks ago I was desperate to walk away from my marriage and equally desperate for my business to survive. Now it's as if the two things have swapped places. I'm desperate for my husband to survive a cancer diagnosis, and - although it's tough to admit this - I think it could be time for me to walk away from *Daisy's*.

Sitting in the kitchen in the evening, fretting over the shop's accounts on my laptop is nothing unusual, but tonight I've noticed a difference. Having spent the past couple of days at home looking after Jason, I've discovered that I rather enjoyed not being at work. In fact, I've come to dread the very idea of returning to a daily routine of difficult customers, nagging unpaid suppliers and Molly's political lectures. To give Molly her due, she's being a great help. As she doesn't have any classes tomorrow, she's agreed to open up and hold the fort again. Depending on how things are here I'll try my best to pop by and check on how she's getting on.

The plain fact is, I've known for a while now that *Daisy's* has no long-term future. However, until now I've been unwilling to accept it. Frankly, by now, I've had enough of the whole stressful situation.

'That's a big sigh,' Jason says.

I turn on my bar stool and see him appear, dressed in his navy-blue dressing gown. I hadn't heard him come into the kitchen.

'How are you feeling?' I ask.

'Bit better,' says Jason, pulling from the fridge two mini-cheese sticks and a gherkin, letting the door close behind him as he joins me at the breakfast bar.

'What you doing?'

'Just looking at the shop accounts,' I say despondently.

Jason plonks himself down on the bar stool next to me and hands me a mini-cheese stick. 'Do you need any help?' he enquires, taking a bite from his gherkin.

'No.' I close the laptop. 'I don't want to think about it anymore.'

Jason smiles sympathetically. 'What's on your mind?' he asks.

'Dunno,' I lie. 'What to have for dinner?'

To which he laughs gently. 'Seriously, what's the next step?'

'I know it's probably time to throw in the towel, but . . .'

'But you don't want to?'

'It's not that as such. I've been my own boss for so long, I don't even know what else I would do.' I reluctantly release my worry into the atmosphere.

'You could come and work with me,' says Jason, like a real Mr Fix-it, and I'm a little surprised by his suggestion.

'Haven't we had this conversation once before? I seem to remember you weren't so keen on me working with you then,' I remind him, casting my mind back to the time when Jason was just starting out with *Turner's.* At that time, I was leading a miserable existence working on the service desk at a VW dealership. I hated that job and I resented Jason massively for not letting me work with him instead.

'That was a long time ago,' he says. 'We couldn't both take the risk. One of us needed to hold down a proper job. Things are different now.'

I take a bite from my cheese stick and mull over the idea. I wouldn't mind Jason being my boss, and at least we'd get to see more of each other.

'And what would you have me do?' I want to know, keen to hear what he's got in mind.

'Laura in Accounts is always saying she needs more help, and you understand spreadsheets,' Jason shrugs, eating his cheese stick in one bite.

I pull a face. 'What - that's your big solution to all my problems? Saddling me with Laura, who has only three topics of conversation: the fact she was once a size six, how useless her husband is, and my fertility, which she's always asking intrusive questions about. I think I'll pass, thanks!'

Jason rolls his eyes and climbs off his bar stool to go and help himself to a packet of salt and vinegar crisps. It's unlike him to snack so much at this time. I wonder if his salt levels are low from puking all day, like when a person has a tummy bug.

Daisy jumps on the breakfast bar, bidding for my attention. I stroke her and stand up to give my purry girl a kiss on her head.

'You know what you need.' Jason says, opening his crisps.

'Enlighten me.'

'You need a gimmick. Something that sets you apart from other cafés. The gift shop clearly isn't enough. What if you turned *Daisy's* into a cat café?' Jason nods towards Daisy, the source of all inspiration.

'The premises aren't big enough for that. And even if they were, the place would require a whole remodel.' I know this, having previously had the same idea and thought it through.

'OK - what about a dog-friendly café,

then?'

I gasp and cover Daisy's little ears. 'Don't listen to him, Daisy. He doesn't know what he's talking about.'

'Seriously. You could easily do that. It wouldn't require an expensive remodel, just some re-branding. Molly could help you. She's young and knows how to use socials. You could sell those doggie cakes and biscuits and dog accessories. Hold doggie play-dates. People would buy into that.'

As a self-confessed cat devotee, it does slightly go against my ethos, but I have to admit, it's a really good idea.

Grinning all over, Jason walks back over to me and offers me a crisp from the packet.

'Good to see your appetite's back,' I remark, popping a crisp in my mouth, surprised at how quickly he's bounced back from a day of violent sickness. He chews slowly on the crisp in his mouth before placing the bag down on the counter next to me.

'Yeah. You know what, my tummy's starting to feel a little funny. You finish them, I'm going back upstairs to bed.' And he rushes out of the kitchen.

'Do you want any dinner?' I call to him.

'Erm, not right now. Maybe later,' he calls back, darting up the stairs.

I pick up the crisps and as I munch my way through them, I think I can hear Jason being sick again. My heart breaks for how much he's suffered today.

I contemplate making some dinner for myself, but I don't feel that hungry with all the stress and worry taking away my appetite, and so I decide to take some initiative and do something productive. After licking the salt and vinegar residue from my fingers, I open up my laptop once again and decide to research doggie cafés. Thanks to Jason, I am feeling a sense of renewed hope that *Daisy's* might have some life left in her yet.

CHAPTER 11

JASON

I have approximately one hour and thirty minutes from the moment I enter the showroom to the moment when I need to leave.

Using some gentle persuasion, I managed to convince Abbie I was well enough to be left alone for a few hours. It really was quite the balancing act to display symptoms that were convincing, but not so bad she couldn't leave me. After about an hour of 'vomiting' from the bathroom floor this morning, I decided enough was enough and opted to display severe lethargy, which made perfect sense considering how 'violently sick' I've been.

With my day destined to be spent 'sleeping/resting' in bed, Abbie felt confident enough to go off to *Daisy's*, keen to check in on the shop and Molly. It seems my dog-friendly café idea has been well received and Abbie is eager to get the ball rolling. I watched her leave the house with a notable spring in her step, which was nice to see, then waited guiltily at the bedroom window like a resident stalker as Abbie drove away from the house.

Once I was safe in the knowledge that she was gone, I quickly got dressed and jumped in my car. It's been three whole days since I left the house and it feels *sooo* good to be out and about. It feels even better to cross the threshold of my clean and shiny showroom. Although I have kept in touch with proceedings, my contact has been more limited than usual. Even when abroad on holiday I check in daily with a morning phone call, keep a constant eye on my emails and make sure I'm always available should anyone need me at any time; however, the past few days have seen me take a step back like never before. There have been no morning calls, limited access to my laptop, and any queries coming my way have been dealt with more slowly than usual, all in the name of saving my marriage.

With my laptop tucked under my arm and my black notebook clutched in my hand, I walk into work and feel a sense of great relief. Secretly I was afraid of stepping into a feral pit of disorder, but I'm pleased to see everything looks exactly as it should.

I'm spotted by Dean, who greets me with a welcoming but surprised smile, not expecting me to come in until next week.

'Hiya, boss, nice to see you.'

'Hi, Dean. How's things?' I ask,

immediately getting down to business. I can't afford any frivolous chit-chat. I'm on limited time and I need my update to be brief and to the point.

'Yeah, all good. The—'

But I interrupt him. 'Can you meet me in my office in ten minutes? We need to check in on a few things and I haven't got long,' I add over my shoulder as I stride past the grey Audi R8 on the way to my office. I feel so happy to be back in the place where I belong. Everything looks pretty much how I left it, except for the pile of post at the end of my desk. Some of it has been opened, some not.

First things first. I place my notebook down on the desk, take my seat and open up my laptop. While I wait for it to fire up, I pick up the pile of post and start to rifle through it. When I hear a knock on the glass, I look up expecting to see Dean, but instead it's Laura, my Finance Manager, standing in the doorway. Laura is somewhere in her mid-forties with short thin brown hair. She's not attractive but she makes an effort, always displaying a full face of make-up and always stylishly dressed, even if her figure reminds me of a beer barrel. Short, wide and round.

'Hello, stranger,' she gushes. 'I wasn't expecting to see you until next week.' She has her phone in one hand, a mug of coffee in the other.

'Yeah, I know. I had some spare time today,

SAMANTHA KAY

so thought to stop by while I got the chance.'

'Oh, so you haven't been away?'

'No, not this week,' I say politely, keeping my focus on the post, wishing Laura would leave so I can crack on.

'Oh, have you been unwell?'

'When am I ever ill,' I say smugly.

'Oh. So, is it Abbie, is she unwell?'

I've always believed that one of the privileges of being the boss is not having to explain yourself. While I never told any of my team why I wouldn't be around this week, it has suddenly occurred to me that if I've not been away on holiday, travelling for work, or off sick, then my absence might be causing some suspicion. That's when I decide to go along with Laura's assumption.

'Erm, yeah. Abbie's been struggling with . . . lady problems,' I say, hoping this will shut her up, the very phrase always scaring me enough into changing the subject, but the opposite happens.

'Don't get me started on fertility problems,' Laura replies, her face lighting up at the topic of conversation. 'I know everything there is to know - I've been there. It takes its toll on you. Emotionally, physically, financially. Once, you know, Jason, I was a slim and in love. Now look at the state of me, five rounds of IVF and two kids later. Honestly, that husband of mine used to hang on my every word. Now I

157

have to tell him three times to take the bins out and I'm lucky if I get so much as a grunt of acknowledgement. You'd never believe it, but I was a size six when I met Johnny—'

'Sorry, Laura, got to stop you there,' I say, squirming in my seat, realising why Abbie detested the idea of working with this woman.

'It's all right, boss. I understand. You men aren't always so good at talking about these things. But you tell Abbie that if she ever wants to talk about anything, she can give me a call,' Laura says kindly.

'Will do. Sorry, I just need to . . .' gesturing towards the post in my hands.

'Of course. Good to see you, Jason.' Laura gives me a cheeky wink, pulls the door to and, thank God, walks away.

By now, my laptop is firing on all cylinders. I'm logging in when I hear another tap on the glass. I groan, annoyed to be interrupted again, but it's only Dean, come to see me as requested. Pleased to see him, I beckon him inside.

Dean anxiously opens the door. 'Sorry, boss. Do you want me to come back later?'

'No, it's fine. My bad - I thought you were Laura. Come on in.'

'Was she telling you about her husband's gout?' Dean asks with an air of exasperation.

'Urgh, no, something about IVF and bin day.'

'Sounds like you landed on a lot of areas

there,' Dean laughs.

'I know. Lucky me!' I say with a small chuckle, adding, 'Right, I'm pressed for time, unfortunately, but I wanted to check in on a few things.' I open my notebook on today's list of things to do. 'The Ferrari part-exchange?'

'All done. Handover scheduled for next week.'

'Oh really?' I say with some surprise. I'd been sure this exchange was going to prove difficult.

'Yeah, it's all in hand. Customer's coming in on Tuesday,' Dean says confidently.

'That's great.' I can cross the item off my list. 'And I saw that email about the Lambo. We can't agree anything until we get a price—'

'Already done,' Dean breaks in. 'I called the guy. Got him up to the price we wanted. Driver is on his way to collect it as we speak.' Dean is oozing with pride and I don't know why, because I should be delighted that he's doing such a good job, but something about his competence is annoying me.

'Great,' I say through slightly gritted teeth, crossing another item off my list.

'Anything else?' asks Dean.

I peer at my emails. 'Erm, yeah. I forwarded you an email from someone who might be interested in the yellow 488 Spider.'

'Yep, I phoned them straight away. They're booked in for a test drive at three o'clock today.

Actually, boss, they're really keen - so all being well I'm confident that the deal is as good as done.'

'Is that right? Well, maybe I should just hand you the keys to this place and let you get on with it,' I snap, my words coming out much harsher than I intended. And although I've achieved my goal in wiping the smug smile from Dean's face, I've created an unnecessary awkwardness between us. The fact is, I'm the emperor – me. The empire is supposed to fall without me, not thrive! As glad as I am to hear all is fine and well, it seems Dean's competence is damaging to my ego. I'm resentful!

'Everything OK, boss?' Dean asks, a worried expression replacing his bravado, and I feel bad, aware of how utterly ridiculous I'm being. Dean is *everything* I could ask for in an employee. He shows up, does the work and doesn't ask too many questions. His enthusiasm and work ethic reminds me a lot of myself, and I know how lucky I am to have him on the team.

'Sorry, Dean, I shouldn't have said that. It's just . . . been a difficult few weeks,' I tell him, rubbing my forehead, the strain of the situation at home obvious to anyone.

'I'm sorry to hear that, boss. Is there anything I can do?'

'Yes. Keep doing what you're doing. I'm grateful for everything you've done. Actually, it's likely I'll need the next couple of weeks off also.

But on my return, I think it's time we discussed a pay rise.'

Deans face lights up, reassuring me that the promise of money can quickly repair any damage.

'Need we wait until then?' Dean says bravely - typical salesman that he is.

'Sorry, I have a bit of a timing issue today. I need to be out of here in an hour. Look, I'll schedule a meeting now,' I say, turning to my laptop. I open my calendar and schedule a meeting with him; keen to keep him onside.

'How are you fixed for two Tuesdays from now, say ten a.m.?' I ask, spotting an opening in my schedule.

Dean pulls out his phone and taps through it. 'That works for me,' he confirms.

With the meeting scheduled, Dean and I cover a couple more bases before he leaves my office. Finally alone, I crack on, racing through my tasks. In an hour from now, I need to transform from competent boss to fragile cancer patient, and right now, time is against me.

ABBIE

If only I could split myself in two.

I glance at the time on my watch and gasp at how quickly the hours have passed. I promised Jason, I wouldn't leave him for more than two hours, but it's already been two and a half and I'm still in no position to leave *Daisy's*. The place has been super-busy since I stepped through the door. Ordinarily, this would be great news, but not when I have a cancer-stricken husband waiting for me at home.

Molly keeps telling me to leave, assuring me she's got everything under control, and while I do believe her, there are some odd jobs I need to catch up on and which I haven't had time to get to yet.

As I take payment for a café latte, I feel my mobile vibrate in my back pocket. I hope it will be Jason replying to my message checking in on him. As the customer leaves the counter, I pull my phone from my pocket and read the message.

All fine, take your time. Having cuddles in bed with Daisy. Don't worry. x x

'Everything all right?' asks Molly, setting off from behind the counter to clear a vacated table.

'Yep, all good. He's alive and well. Well, alive at least.'

Molly brings an empty used plate and two glass mugs back to the counter.

'I just worry.' I gabble. 'He's been vomiting so much the last couple of days and hardly eating. I have this vision of him passing out and hitting his head or something awful like that.' Tears fill my eyes.

'Abbie, if you're that worried, then go. I told you - I'm fine here.'

'No, I'm just being over-dramatic. I know he's fine. The nausea has calmed down today, and I really need to sort through those deliveries in the back before I go. And I'm behind on the stocktake - oh, and I need to run down to the bank at some point.' I stand there, listing my to-do tasks on my fingers, horrified at how quickly time is running away.

The bell over the door rings, and I'm surprised to see Mas, a good two hours earlier than he would usually swing by.

'Hey, Abbie. How are you?' he asks with a big smile. He's so sweet and polite.

'I'm doing well, Mas, thank you. How's things with you?'

'Yeah, all good thanks,' he replies, approaching the counter. He looks as if he's just come from uni, dressed in jeans and a T-shirt with a rucksack over his shoulder. I think this is the first time I've seen Mas wearing something that isn't the family kebab-shop uniform. He looks smart and stylish, even a little handsome. He gives Molly a yearning glance but, ignoring him, she walks away, J-cloth and spray in hand to wipe the table she's just cleared.

'Can I get you anything, Mas?' I ask.

'Oh, no thanks, that's fine. Just wanted a word with Molly if that's OK.' Mas moves over to the table where Molly is standing. I stay at the counter, straining to listen to their conversation as a customer wants to learn about our tea options.

'So - are we still on for tonight? Just checking,' I hear Mas say.

'Yeah, I said so, didn't I?' Molly says ungraciously, acting aloof and rather rude.

'Good. I wasn't sure as you didn't reply to my message,' Mas persists, refusing to be discouraged.

'Yeah, well. I've been busy. Just meet me here at five like we agreed.'

'OK. See you later then.' Mas is smiling proudly to himself, and I honestly don't know why he bothers.

'Bye, Abbie.'

'See ya, Mas.' I give him a small wave as he leaves the shop while Molly fails to acknowledge his existence. It's only when the door closes behind him that she finally looks up from the table.

'Two mint teas and one scone. Lovely. Take a seat,' I tell the customer, as Molly makes her way back over to the counter.

'Where are you two off to tonight?' I ask, unable to disguise my curiosity.

'Just some party,' Molly shrugs carelessly, but I can't hide my excitement.

'I knew it! I knew you liked him!' I exclaim.

'No, I don't,' Molly says stubbornly. 'He's a capitalist. I could *never* like a capitalist.'

Personally, I'm not quite sure that Molly herself is the epitome of socialism. Serving coffee from a privately owned business to shoppers who spend their money on knick-knacks that they don't need, doesn't exactly scream Socialist of the Year, but I can't be arsed to get into that now, especially not today.

'Well, they do say opposites attract,' I say archly.

Molly's cheeks flush but before I have a chance to tease her any further, the bell above the shop door dings and a lady customer walks in. She's in her forties, I'd say, with glowing, sun-kissed skin, bleached-blonde hair, and under her arm she carries a tiny, short-haired chihuahua whose coat is the same colour as its owner's hair. The woman glides towards the counter, and I swear an aura of light surrounds her.

In all the busyness of the day, I'd almost forgotten about Jason's doggie café idea, but suddenly here it is, the sign I've been waiting

EIGHT MILLION MINUTES

for: a shining beacon of hope that will save my business, in the form of a human with sun-damaged skin and a little blonde dog. I smile at her and just as she's about to smile back—

'Excuse me! Sorry, no dogs allowed,' bellows Molly, successfully shattering the moment.

The woman stops and scowls, but before she walks away, I jump in.

'Oh no. Don't listen to her.' I spring from behind the counter and guide the woman to a newly vacated table. 'We welcome dogs,' I say gaily. 'All dogs. Big ones, small ones. Even smelly ones,' I trill, smiling and pulling out a chair, feeling only the smallest hint of betrayal towards Daisy. I'm hoping she never finds out about this!

Thankfully the woman takes a seat, placing her tiny dog on her lap. As she makes herself comfy, I head to the counter to grab a menu.

'Since when do we allow dogs?' grumps Molly.

'Yeah, I forgot to mention. We're rebranding as a dog café.'

'But you hate dogs,' sniffs Molly.

'Shush! I *love* dogs, and so do you.' Before Molly has the chance to ask any further questions I head back to my lady and her dog with a menu, keen to make a welcoming impression.

JASON

It's been three and a half hours since I left the house. I know I'm cutting things fine, but when Abbie said she was held up at work, I seized the opportunity to stay a little longer at the showroom. It was a risky move, but as I've no idea when I'll make it in next, it seemed like the obvious decision. I managed to catch up on loads and even had time to stop off for a cheeky McDonald's, which tasted like heaven. After days surviving on nothing other than granola bars and the odd cheese stick, I felt I deserved a treat. However, the impromptu Big Mac meal has delayed my return home even further. I race my car down the road, unsure how on earth I'm going to explain my absence, but as I approach the drive, I breathe a sigh of relief.

Abbie's car is nowhere to be seen.

Thank goodness.

I pull onto the drive, turn off the ignition and hop out of the car as fast as I can. Carrying my laptop and notebook, I run to the front door and hurry to insert my key. The front door flies open, the beeping from the house alarm preventing me from running straight upstairs.

In my haste I tap the code in incorrectly.

'Fucking hell!' I groan, trying again, finally getting it right.

I race through the house, up the stairs and into the office, where I dump my laptop and notebook exactly where I found them this morning. Just as I do, I freeze at the sound of a car pulling up. I look out of the office window. It's Abbie's red Mini, parked on the drive in its usual spot. She's home.

I made it back just in the nick of time.

'Sorry I was gone so long!' Abbie calls from downstairs.

I don't respond. I creep out of the office. Abbie can't see me in here, it'll look suspicious.

'How are you feeling?' Abbie calls, her voice getting closer. She's climbing the stairs and I'm standing on the landing fully dressed in jeans and a sweatshirt when I'm meant to be sick. I lift my sweatshirt up, ready to whisk it off, but I haven't got time to remove my jeans too! So I pull my sweatshirt back down. While conducting a Mexican wave with my sweatshirt, Abbie's footsteps get ever closer. I stand still on the spot. Panicked, motionless.

'Oh God! What are you doing?' gasps Abbie, clearly not expecting to find me stalking the landing.

When she joins me I have no plausible answer to give. I open my mouth to speak, but no words come out. So instead, I enfold her in a hug

SAMANTHA KAY

and hold her close to me, enjoying the feel of her body against mine.

'I'm so happy you're home,' I murmur, and I really mean it, although ten minutes later would have been preferable.

'Are you going somewhere?' Abbie asks, understandably confused. Three and a half hours ago she left behind a patient who could barely make it out of bed. Now, as if by some miracle, that same man is bright-eyed and bushy-tailed, fully dressed and standing upright on the landing, for no obvious reason.

'Not without you.'

Abbie loosens our embrace and looks at me quizzically.

'I'm feeling a lot better,' I explain. 'I thought we could go for a walk - just to get some air.' Proud of my ability to think on my feet, I kiss Abbie on the lips to prove just how happy I am to see her.

'Are you sure you're up to it?' she wants to know, voicing some concern.

'I've been cooped up for days,' I point out. 'I need a change of scenery.'

'Well, all right. You want to go now? Because I was going to run a quick bath.'

'Have a bath when we get back. Come on. I've been waiting for you.' And like an excitable puppy I take Abbie's hand in mine and lead her back down the stairs.

'Where are we going?' she asks.

169

'Wherever the mood takes us!' I say gleefully, such a display of enthusiasm very out of character for me.

Then, realising how incredibly odd everything may seem, as we reach the final stair, I pause for a moment, take firm hold of the banister and wobble - just a little, just enough to indicate all is not as well as it might seem.

Abbie's eyes widen as I catch my breath, as if the very act of walking down the stairs requires me to take a second to gather myself.

'We'll walk slowly,' I say, letting go of the banister and giving my best sad eyes.

Abbie smiles lovingly at me. She loops her arm into mine and at a sedate pace, leads us out of the house.

*

About two roads away from our house is another road. If you turn left, at the end of it you'll find a great big park with a lake, huge, beautiful oak trees, a cricket pitch and a spacious green café that sells coffees and ice lollies.

When we bought our house, we told ourselves we would visit this park regularly. We would bring the kids to feed the ducks and kick a ball and enjoy picnics on sunny summer days beside the water. Well, it's been five years since we moved into our house, the kids are all grown up, and never once have we made use of this park. With work dominating so much of my life,

I now feel regretful for all the memories I never put the time aside to make.

As Abbie and I take a stroll along the tree-lined path under the soft light of the late-afternoon sun, we work our way through ice creams purchased from the café. This is an unexpected treat! While I devour my ice cream, Abbie takes her time with hers as she tells me all about her day.

'I'm just annoyed we didn't think of it sooner. The lady I was chatting to, with the chihuahua, she said that dog cafés are a godsend. Sometimes that can be the difference between going out or staying at home, because she can't leave the dog alone for too long.'

I don't think I've seen Abbie this excited about *Daisy's* since it first opened, and I genuinely hope this idea can be as lucrative as she believes.

'That's why I like cats. Less maintenance,' I mumble, licking the drips around my cone.

'Me too. But if high-maintenance dogs are going to get the till ringing, then I'm all in. I already found a company that makes dog-friendly cupcakes. They're coming by next week for us to check out some of their products. Also, I need to arrange a date next week to meet with the graphic designer to discuss rebranding.'

'Next week? But I have a break in my treatment next week,' I remind her, my tone a little more needy than intended.

'Yeah, I know. That's why I thought it would be a good week to do it.' Abbie's response is perfectly logical.

'But I thought we said we'd do something together next week.'

'Well, we did. But you haven't mentioned anything since. I just assumed you'd be itching to get back to the showroom.'

Her assumption unsettles me, and that's because she's hit the nail on the head. Ordinarily, I'd seize any opportunity to head straight back to *Turner's*, and although the urge is as strong as ever, I now know that putting the showroom before everything else is destroying my marriage. Things need to change, and that change needs to happen now, before it's too late.

'There's more to life than the showroom,' I state, surprised to hear myself say it.

Abbie stops dead in her tracks. She looks at me wide-eyed, her lips parted in shock, unable to believe the words that just left my mouth.

'Sorry, I think I misheard you! Did you just say there's more to life than the showroom?'

I give a tight smile, not quite believing it myself. 'What can I say. Cancer makes you reassess things.'

Talking of cancer, at that point I decide to take a break. We've walked quite a long way. My legs feel tired, and I'm sure I've already pushed myself further than a cancer sufferer should go. I sit myself down on the vacant bench along the footpath and Abbie joins me, sitting closely next to me.

'What if the chemo doesn't work?' I utter quietly.

'But you said they caught it early. That we shouldn't worry.' And although her voice is upbeat, I can sense an undertone of worry, which I'm ashamed to admit makes me happy. It fills me with hope that she does still love me enough to worry.

'What if they haven't?' I press my advantage. 'You hear those stories all the time. "Sorry, Mr Turner, the treatment hasn't worked. It's far more serious than we first thought".'

'Jason, is there something you're not telling me?' Abbie is looking scared, and I know it's my job to reassure her, just like I always have done.

'No, no. I'm sorry.' I take her hand in mine and force myself to relax as I finish off the last of my ice cream. 'I just want us to enjoy all the time we have together. Whether it's one more year or another fifty.'

'Me too,' sighs Abbie, tucking herself in closer to me, resting her head on my shoulder.

For a moment we sit in a comfortable silence before an idea comes to mind.

'What about a cottage in the Cotswold?' I find myself suggesting. 'We'll leave on the Friday, stay a couple of nights, breathe some clean fresh air. We'll get back before my next round of treatment starts. You can still make your meetings, and I'll have time to swing by the showroom if I feel up to it.'

'Sounds perfect,' says Abbie, her voice a bit choked as if she's holding back the urge to cry.

I kiss the top of her head. Abbie doesn't move except to wipe her eyes and I feel confident that everything is moving in the right direction.

CHAPTER 12

ABBIE

Whenever we go away on holiday, a lovely lady named Yvonne stays at our house to look after Daisy. Yvonne loves Daisy, and Daisy loves Yvonne, which is nothing short of a miracle because Daisy doesn't really like anyone expect for me, Jason and the kids.

When Yvonne is here, I can rest easy as I know Daisy is having the best possible care. Yvonne will douse herself in catnip and feed Daisy her weight in cat treats. While Daisy is getting the five-star treatment, Yvonne will also take care of the house. She'll water our plants, bring in our post, she cleans up after herself and one time she even welcomed us home with a batch of freshly baked cookies.

So, when Jason suggested an impromptu trip to the Cotswolds, my initial reaction as always was to call Yvonne. To my dismay, she was unable to book us in at such short notice. Then, just as we prepared to put the trip on the back-burner, a somewhat unlikely volunteer stepped forward to save the day: namely my step-daughter, Ellie.

Unsurprisingly, two nights alone in a large empty house was a rather appealing prospect to sixteen-year-old Ellie. Equally unsurprisingly, my initial reaction was to say no. However, Jason took a different view. He's super-eager for us to get away before his treatment starts again next week, and he also felt it was about time one of his kids was handed some actual responsibility for once in their lives.

After much persuasion from both Jason and Ellie I finally caved in and agreed to leave my precious Daisy in her care. I'm not overly happy about it, but Ellie does adore Daisy so I'm willing to give her a chance to prove herself.

It's early on the Friday morning when we leave, but we're eager to get going as soon as possible, wanting to make the most of our day. I'm standing in the kitchen with Ellie who's still dressed in the oversized yellow T-shirt she sleeps in, running through everything one final time before we head out and she gets herself ready for school.

'Remember, she has biscuit in the morning and meat in the evening. And if you run out of biscuit, there's more in the cupboard under the stairs.'

'I have fed the cat before, Abbie, I'm not dumb!'

Debatable.

I bite my tongue, determined not to leave the house on a sour note. 'The number for the vet, have you saved it in your phone just in case?' I ask.

'*Yesss!*'

I know I've woken her up earlier than usual, but I'm not quite sure why Ellie is in such a bad mood. Her attitude doesn't exactly fill me with reassurance, but it's only for two nights, I tell myself. How much could possibly go wrong in two nights?

'Let me check.' I pull out my phone and cross-check the number against the one on Ellie's.

It's then that Jason breezes into the kitchen, freshly showered and changed, smelling all yummy. For the first time in years, he has agreed not to bring his laptop on our trip. Instead, he left it at the showroom with Dean. It might not sound like the grandest gesture in the world, but the very idea of not having to share Jason with his laptop is quite a turn-on. Something has certainly shifted in him, and it's nice to see.

'Everything in order?' he asks, throwing an arm around Ellie and kissing the top of her head.

'Yep,' Ellie beams happily, saving all her stroppiness especially for me.

'I'm happy for Grace to stay, but no boys and *no* parties. There are cameras outside, so I'll see if people are coming in,' Jason warns her.

'I'll have to try and sneak them in another way then.' Ellie says cheekily, and although I'm confident she's joking, I still feel uneasy. After all, she did manage to smuggle in the boy with the giant willy for God knows how long. She clearly has trusted methods.

'Very funny. I've sent you money for a takeaway. If you have any problems, just call us, or your mum,' Jason tells her.

Oh no! The very idea of Kelly stepping into this house while I'm not here fills me with horror. If she so much as makes it to the doorstep, I'll have to conduct an exorcism.

'Or knock for Demi and Angie across the road. You know them. They're really nice,' I throw in, desperate to offer any other alternative.

'I'll be fine. Grace is coming over later. She's bringing face masks and snacks,' Ellie says, smiling sweetly at her dad.

'Sounds good,' chirps Jason, innocent and unaware of his daughter's antics in this house. He turns to me. 'Ready for the off?'

'Yeah.' I nod.

We say our goodbyes to Ellie and leave the kitchen. As Jason heads towards the front door ready to pile our luggage into the car, I go upstairs to say one final goodbye to Daisy, hoping my doubts about Ellie will pass.

*

After a couple of hours of busy A roads and a succession of motorways, we gradually emerge into a different world. Queues of traffic, clouds of pollution and angry drivers hooting their horns have disappeared into oblivion, replaced by quiet country roads, quaint churches and lush village greens.

Although Jason and I have been to some far-out and exotic places together, we've never explored the UK beyond trips to the coast and a one-time trip to York for a friend's wedding, and I'm starting to think we've been missing out. It's still officially morning on a beautiful spring day, the pleasant conditions bringing the village scenery into high definition. It's not as if I've never seen cherry blossom or a daffodil before, but here, everything seems brighter, healthier. A lack of car fumes will do that to a place. Everything is so vibrant.

After another half an hour or so, Jason finally pulls our red Ferrari up outside Rosewood Cottage.

'Here we are,' he says, turning off the roaring engine.

I look at the scene in front of us. Standing all alone in the middle of nowhere is a white picket fence surrounding a cottage with marshmallow-pink walls and a large thatched roof with two chimneys, one sticking out at either end. What the cottage lacks in size it certainly makes up for in charm. Indeed, it looks as if it's fallen straight out of a fairytale.

'We're staying here,' I say, stating the obvious.

'Yeah, this is us,' nods Jason.

I release my seat belt and climb out of the car. As beautiful as the Ferrari is, it's not the most comfortable on long journeys, and I'm keen to stretch my legs. Jason follows suit, both of us standing outside the cottage. I look at it in complete awe. Colourful spring flowers line a pathway that leads to a white front door. The fragrant air is so sweet I wish I could bottle it up and keep it. I can hear birdsong, in a way I've never really heard it before. Away from the hum of traffic or the bustling of people, their volume is turned all the way up, and the melody provides a perfect musical backdrop.

'But if we're staying here, where are the seven dwarfs going to stay?' I quip.

'Do you like it? I know it's a little different from the kind of places we usually stay at.' Jason is pulling off his sunglasses as he speaks, and I note a hint of hesitancy in his voice.

True, there is a lack of palm trees and sandy white beaches, but something inside me believes a change to the usual routine is exactly what we need. I loop my arm into his.

'I love it. I can't believe places like this really exist,' I say, unable to hide my smile.

'Oh good.' Jason sounds relieved. With that, he pulls our luggage from the front of the

SAMANTHA KAY

Ferrari, and we practically skip our way along the flowery footpath towards the front door.

We step straight into the living room, and I'm pleased to see that the cottage interior is modern. A pink sofa faces an open fireplace that certainly makes for an effective feature and would be very practical during the winter. There's a couple of plush coffee tables and a rather small flat-screen telly filling the space to the left of the fireplace.

We step in a little further and close the front door behind us. I pick up the couple of shopping bags full of the food we've brought with us and head on through to the kitchen on my left, it being the only other room down here. I pass a small bookcase jampacked with paperbacks and boardgames, and raise a smile at what looks like a very old edition of Monopoly.

The kitchen is cute, with its white wooden units - modern and airy while still retaining all its character. I dump the shopping bags in the middle of the table and start to unpack, keen to get our chilled things in the fridge before we do anything else.

'Lights on!' commands Jason. 'Lights on!' he repeats.

'What are you doing?' I call from the kitchen.

'Living-room lights on!' he says, his voice getting louder.

I wish he'd stop. 'Why don't you just use

the switch?' I want to know.

Jason enters the kitchen, phone in hand, looking flustered. 'Because there aren't any.'

'Oh, that's just great. What do you mean, there aren't any?' I grimace, looking around me. Indeed, there aren't, at least not in the kitchen.

Strange.

'It's supposed to be more energy efficient. All the lighting is designed to run off voice command, or motion sensors or something,' frets Jason, waving his hands above his head as if bringing an aeroplane into land, before giving up and tapping frantically through his phone.

'You probably need to connect your phone to the Bluetooth then,' I suggest, placing the bacon and milk into the fridge.

'Yeah, I get that. That's what I'm trying to do, but it's not working. I can't even get WIFI!' grumbles Jason, becoming increasingly frustrated.

This little scenario makes me wonder what else in the cottage might not work if we can't even make the lights turn on! But I choose not to pass on my own concerns and continue to unpack the food.

'The whole reason I booked this place was because they promised that the WIFI signal was good.'

And there was me thinking it was for the birdsong!

I suppose I shouldn't have been quite so

naïve. After all, Jason is having treatment for cancer, not a personality transplant. He might have left his laptop at the showroom, but I know he can still access everything he needs from his phone.

Jason starts marching around the kitchen, peering into the corners of the ceiling for motion sensors, then holding his phone above his head, trying to find a signal.

'We've got hours until it gets dark. I'm sure we'll work it out by then,' I say, secretly quite liking the idea of a WIFI-free weekend.

Jason starts huffing and puffing while I try my hardest not to laugh.

'Anyway, what's the plan?' I ask to distract him, wanting to bring his mind round to more pleasant matters.

'Dunno. Find a pub. Get some lunch,' he says distractedly, finally looking away from his phone, anguish etched across his face. Although I do feel a little peckish and quite like the idea of exploring our surroundings together, what I really want is for my man to relax.

Maybe it's this place. Being in the middle of nowhere with no distractions. Maybe it's the fresh air or maybe it's just that holiday feeling, but I want him . . . right now.

'Could do,' I say, closing the fridge then making my way over towards Jason.

'But you know, I don't think there's anything or anyone around for miles . . .' I gently tug the bottom of his sweatshirt and pull him in closer.

'What could two people, all alone with nothing to do, *possibly* do to pass the time,' I croon into his ear, kissing the skin on his neck in the way I know he loves.

He moans softly, leaning his body into mine, and without uttering a single word, he takes my hand in his and, giggling like two randy teenagers, we run upstairs as fast as we can.

CHAPTER 13

JASON

I wrote a very angry email to the cottage provider about the faulty Bluetooth and WIFI - but it won't send! Out in the middle of nowhere I have very little signal of any kind, which is not only frustrating but impractical. With no connection, I can't check my emails or even make the lights turn on. The sun has set, plunging the cottage into darkness and the only light source available other than the torch on our phones is the single scented candle we found in the bathroom. But I really shouldn't complain.

Despite the lack of lighting, we've had a really good day. We did 'it', not just once, but *twice*! We haven't done 'it' multiple times in one day in at least a decade. After the first time we were going to head out for some lunch, but it started to rain, so we had some bacon and eggs here instead and with nothing else to do, we did 'it' all over again!

Another thing we haven't done in *years* is play Monopoly. When we first moved in together, with very little money at our disposal, Monopoly was a game we'd play together regularly. When Abbie pointed out the very old edition of the game stuffed into the cottage bookcase, we couldn't resist a stab at our old pastime.

Just like old times we've fallen back into our respective roles.

I'm banker while Abbie oversees properties.

As rain pats against the cottage windows, we each enjoy a bottle of beer with the game spread out over the kitchen table. The board is so old the two halves are almost coming apart and we could only find one dice, meaning the game is moving a little slower than we remember - but what's the rush? It's more fun this way.

I roll a five and move my tiny silver car right onto Free Parking. 'Oh, yes!' I exclaim, gathering up a bounty of £150.

Abbie groans loudly. Coming right up behind me, she rolls a four, her tiny boot having just missed out on the sought-after windfall, landing next to me on The Strand.

'That one's mine,' I declare, checking my little card with the red top. 'That'll be eighteen pounds, please.' And I gleefully take Abbie's rent, her pot of money shrinking by the minute.

'Ha, I think this is fast becoming my favourite holiday!' I joke, smugly counting my stash, arranging the notes into neat little piles, having almost forgotten how much I enjoy this

SAMANTHA KAY

game.

'Ha, well, it's no Portugal though, is it.'

'Portugal?' I echo, not quite understanding.

'Yeah, Portugal. That was my favourite holiday,' Abbie says sweetly, taking a swig from her bottle of beer.

'Portugal!' I scoff. 'Are you serious?'

'What? I loved that holiday.'

'We've been to New York, the Caribbean. We went to Monaco last year, for crying out loud, and you're citing Portugal as your favourite!'

'It was our first holiday together.'

'Our room overlooked the bins!'

'I know . . . I know,' says Abbie, smiling dreamily. 'Our room smelled funny and there was that leak in the bathroom that kept us awake at night. But we saved so hard for that holiday. I was so excited the two of us were finally going away together. Honestly, we could have stayed in a tent on the side of the road, and I'd have still been happy.' Abbie has a faraway look in her eyes, while I can't quite believe what I'm hearing.

Stunned, I sit with my mouth open, trying to process what she has just said.

'What?' she asks, sensing my utter bemusement.

'I don't know, I just . . . I think we each remember that time *very* differently.'

'How so?' says Abbie, narrowing her eyes at me, fidgeting with the label on her beer bottle.

'I remember worrying, *a lot*. About how we were going to make it through each month. And I remember that holiday, and honestly, I don't remember it feeling all that romantic. I remember feeling ashamed. That we'd saved so hard and that was the best I could give you.'

Abbie smiles thinly before taking another swig from her beer, and I struggle to read what she's thinking, neither of us looking directly at the other.

'Well, I'm sorry to hear you felt that way,' she says eventually. 'But for what it's worth, I remember it fondly.'

Frustrated as I am by Abbie's Portugal revelation, I know I should feel grateful that my wife loves *me*, rather than all the things I can buy her. However, it grates: I can't help but resent her for being unappreciative. But then, not wanting the evening to be ruined, I pull myself together. I watch the light from the bathroom candle flicker an orange glow across her beautiful face. My heart swells, and I'm feeling so lucky to have her here with me.

'Well, a lot's changed since then,' I conclude.

'Yeah. It's certainly been an eventful sixteen years,' she agrees, pushing back on her chair. She stands, picking up her empty beer bottle 'Another?'

'Sixteen years, two months, one week and three days,' I roll off, as Abbie opens the fridge door. The light from inside brightens up the kitchen and lands on me like a spotlight, making me feel like a superstar mathematician.

'All right, Rain Man! What the hell was that!' Abbie laughs, and I can't quite tell if she's flattered or a little scared. She closes the fridge door, and the light disappears. She places two fresh beer bottles down on the table and takes her seat next to me again.

'That's how long we've been together,' I tell her. 'The day we met was my first day back at work after Ellie was born. She was exactly fifteen days old.'

Abbie rolls her eyes, ever conscious of the controversial circumstances. She reaches for the bottle opener on the table and removes the lid from our bottles.

'The day we met wasn't the day we got together,' she reminds me.

'Granted, but I always count from the day we met. Because that was the day my whole world changed. I've always kept count of it,' I tell her, feeling rather nerdy, but what can I say? I'm a businessman, and numbers are very much my thing.

Abbie looks at me, smiling and doe-eyed, and I think she's touched.

'Aw, you old romantic. I had no idea you had it worked out to the very minute,' she says, leaning in and kissing me on the lips.

'Well, I've never done that, but it's easy

enough to work out,' I say, picking up my phone.

'Oh God,' I hear Abbie utter, but I ignore her and push on, curious now as to the actual figure. I bring up the calculator.

'So, there are twenty-four hours in a day. Times that by sixty, gives us one thousand four hundred and forty. Times that by three hundred and sixty-five . . .' I carry on with my calculations. 'Times that number by sixteen gives us . . . wow, eight point four million. We've known each other for more than *eight million minutes*,' I tell her, placing my phone back down on the table and reaching for my beer.

'Eight million.' Abbie whistles. 'That's a lot of minutes.'

'They've been good, haven't they?' I ask hesitantly.

To my horror, Abbie doesn't answer right away. She looks thoughtfully into the distance, and I feel my stomach knot.

'Mostly . . .' she says eventually. 'Except for that holiday in Cancun.' She grins at me playfully and I feel myself relax again.

'Oh Christ. You're right - that was awful. We all got so ill.' It's all coming back to me now.

'And remember how Harry got bitten so badly by the mosquitos we had to take him to a doctor? Poor thing. He looked like a giant tomato!'

We sit and laugh together at the shared memory in the dim light of our darkened cottage. The very idea of creating new memories without her - it simply can't happen. I take hold of her hand closest to me and look into her pretty eyes.

'I'm really happy we made it here,' I say sincerely.

'Me too,' she says back, and I'm confident she means it.

'Whose go is it?' asks Abbie.

'Mine. And Mayfair is still up for grabs!' I let go of her hand and pick up the dice from the centre of the board, keen to add to my property portfolio. There's no sentiment in business!

ABBIE

It's 5.30 in the morning. I've woken early after little sleep. Last night, I lay awake for ages. A lot of different thoughts and memories swirled around my head, preventing me from switching off. I kept going over our conversation from last night, and annoyingly, I'm starting to think Jason may well have a point.

Maybe I am remembering everything through a rose-tinted haze, because the more I think about it, the more I remember just how hard things used to be. Maybe the trauma of it all caused me to block it out, or maybe time has changed my perspective. But as I lay here in the early morning light, I began to feel so guilty, the emotion gnawing away at me.

I mean, who am I kidding! I don't want us to go back to that time. What - to cramped living conditions and fretting over bills? I remember one time when our bank accounts were empty, and dinner consisted of one slice of toast and two and a half fish fingers each. It wasn't cute or romantic. It was sad.

It's only as a result of Jason's drive and determination to make things better that we no

SAMANTHA KAY

longer live like that.

I love him so much.

I love how much we've overcome together. I love him for how hard he's worked for us and how much he's sacrificed. And instead of being grateful for our life, I've done nothing but obsess over the negatives.

Jason stirs a little in his sleep and rolls over onto his side. I turn to face him. He looks peaceful, still fast asleep.

Although I don't miss making do with toast and fish fingers for dinner, I do miss the amount of time we used to spend together. The loneliness, the distance I've felt from him these last few years has been nothing short of agonising. For a long time, I saw no way of it ever changing.

But then cancer happened, right when it was supposed to.

A week, a day later, I'd already have announced my plans to leave him.

Would I have come back?

Quite possibly, but the damage would have been done, and who knows if we ever could have worked past it. The very thought of leaving him to cope alone wrecks me with guilt, but he'll never know how close I came to walking out of the door.

Never.

Cancer has given us the time we needed to gather some perspective. Maybe we'll finally

193

figure out a work-life balance that suits us both.

I watch as he stirs again. I gently stroke the stubble on his jawline with my thumb. He groans a little and rolls away from me. I move in a little closer, wrapping an arm over his chest and hold him in a spoon cuddle. I rest my face against the back of his neck. I feel myself relax against his warm skin and my eyes start to feel heavy.

CHAPTER 14

JASON

As another day without any pressing engagements begins, we choose the luxury of sleeping in late. Eventually we peel ourselves out of bed and decide to enjoy some breakfast in the cottage garden. The sun is out, accompanied by a warm breeze, perfect for sitting-in-my-pants-and-T-shirt conditions.

The iron table and its matching chairs aren't especially comfortable, but they blend in nicely with the picturesque country garden. The lush green lawn is lined with rose bushes and blooming spring flowers. A small stone wishing well, about waist-height, features in the centre of the lawn. Anywhere else, it might seem a little kitsch, but alongside the birdsong and the bright blue sky, it's all rather perfect.

Abbie looks happy and relaxed. Sitting closely beside me in her PJs, we each devour a plate of avocado and tomato on toast. I lean back on the uncomfortable chair and take a sip from my coffee, unable to remember the last time I felt quite so relaxed. Maybe it's the lack of WIFI, or maybe it's the fresh country air, but either way, I wonder if a life away from the hassle and bustle could well suit us.

'Do you think this could be us one day? A house in the country?' I muse, watching two tiny bluetits
hop around the wishing well.

'You want to move to the country?' queries Abbie, unimpressed.

'Not now, but maybe one day - when we retire. It could be a project, like those *Escape to the Country* people on TV. We could buy an old cottage and fix it up together.'

Abbie licks some tomato off her finger and makes a face. 'Really? Couldn't you just go and play golf or something?'

'I hate golf. And I'm really bad at it. Just imagine, we'd get ourselves some chickens and a couple of goats. Grow our own carrots and potatoes,' I rattle on, going full sales mode as I pitch the idea to a very reluctant customer.

'That sounds like a lot of work in retirement. Can't we just blow all our money on cruises instead?' Abbie suggests.

To be fair, that's not a bad suggestion. Idyllic as the idea may sound, the reality might be more trouble than it's worth.

'Like my mum and dad, you mean?' I ask.

'Yeah. We could be just like them when we're old. Spend the winter cruising and the summers—'

'Going to funerals,' I interject, to which we both laugh.

The past few years have seen my parents attend a laughable number of funerals. Naturally, at first it was all very upsetting, since it all seemed to happen in one big, unstoppable wave. The senior members of our family gradually became depleted, with the passing of grandparents, great-aunts and great-uncles, etcetera, but now it's turned into something of a pastime for my parents. It seems they love nothing more than a good funeral. Funerals of old friends, former colleagues, friends of friends, friends' former colleagues!

It's become a running joke in our family - my parents seeking out funerals for a good social occasion and a decent buffet.

'I spoke to Dad the other day,' I tell Abbie. 'He told me they'd been to another one!'

'No way!' laughs Abbie, and I think how much I love hearing her laugh; it really is the most wonderful sound in the world. 'Who was it this time?'

'Some elderly neighbour. I don't think they knew him that well.'

'When did that ever stop them!'

'Sounded quite sad actually. Dad said there weren't even twenty people there.'

Abbie sighs. 'Hmm, I suppose that's the price you pay for living a long time. All your friends are dead. Everyone you grew up with, long gone.' She picks up her mug of tea and leans back on her own uncomfortable iron chair, tilting her head and admiring the natural beauty of the cottage garden before us.

'I hope I get a good turnout,' I say out of nowhere, hating the idea of no one turning up to celebrate my life.

'Stop it. You know I don't like it when you talk about dying.' Abbie's upset and it's my fault as I'd forgotten all about my 'cancer' during our conversation.

We pause for a moment as the birdsong continues all around us.

'We should talk about it though,' I stupidly persist.

'We have! We have wills and insurances. What more is there to talk about?' Abbie is getting annoyed, her voice rising an octave.

'Well, we've never discussed our funerals. What songs we'd like, flowers, all that stuff.' I understand that Abbie doesn't want to think about such things, especially in light of the current 'circumstances'. However, my recent 'diagnosis' has made me realise one universal truth.

None of us are getting out of this world alive.

Ever the pragmatist, I simply think it might be helpful to be clear with one another about our wishes for when the worst happens.

'What song would you like at your funeral?' I ask.

'I don't know, Jason, what song would *you* like?' Abbie comes back in a mocking tone.

'House of Pain "Jump Around"' I answer without hesitation, to which Abbie lets out a beautiful loud belly laugh.

'Really? That's the song that sums up your life?' she asks, surprised by my choice.

'I love that song. *We* love that song. Remember when the kids were little and we used to have Jabbie's "Nightclub"? It was the one song all four of us used to love. It reminds me of some very happy times.'

Abbie smiles and nods. She's looking slightly more relaxed now, for which I'm pleased.

'OK, well, I'll have the same one,' she says casually.

'No way, you can't have my song. Pick your own,' I say, put out by her lack of thought. These things matter.

Abbie crosses her arms and looks thoughtfully into the distance. The sunlight illuminates her blonde hair, her blue eyes sparkle, and I think how incredibly beautiful she is and how I never tire of gazing at her.

'Taylor Swift, "Wildest Dreams",' she answers eventually, uncrossing her arms.

'Why that song?'

'It's a good song, one of my favourites, and it's the words. She's looking pretty, wearing

EIGHT MILLION MINUTES

a nice dress, looking out over the sunset. That's how I'd like you to remember me,' she says with a cheeky grin.

'OK.' I nod. In a world where most Taylor Swift songs sound the same to me, it's quite remarkable that I think I know it. It's one Abbie and Ellie used to play a lot, and Abbie's right, it's a nice song.

'What about flowers. You want flowers?' I ask, to which Abbie tuts loudly, wanting to be done with the topic of conversation.

'Yes. I want flowers.' She takes a sip from her mug of tea and to my surprise, has more to add on the matter. 'Actually, I really do want flowers. None of this "no flowers, donate the money to charity" nonsense. Help a small business like mine and commission lots of bright and beautiful flowers from a local florist.'

'Noted. Any flowers in particular?'

'The ones from my wedding bouquet,' she tells me.

I look at her blankly. Touched as I am, I have no clue what flowers were used in her wedding bouquet.

'Pink gerberas and white roses,' she says quietly.

I nod. I know full well that I won't remember that, but thankfully there are pictures I can refer to should I ever need to, another many million minutes in the future.

'What about you, You want flowers?' It's

200

SAMANTHA KAY

her turn to ask.

'Yeah, why not. I'll have the same as you.'

'So, I can't copy your song, but you can copy my flowers?' she protests.

'They were my wedding flowers too.' I reach for her hand, bring it to my lips and kiss her soft skin.

'You know what I would like?' I say.

Abbie looks at me wide-eyed, waiting for my revelation.

'Instead of black cars, I'd like a convoy of Supercars,' I announce, impressed by my own idea.

'Which ones?'

'Just whatever's loud and fast.'

'That's certainly very you,' Abbie says sweetly.

'Thank you.' With her hand still in mine, I kiss it once more and give it a reassuring squeeze, hoping that one day, when the inevitable happens, I'm the one to go first, knowing I couldn't possibly live without her.

CHAPTER 15

ABBIE

Our lazy morning was followed by a slow walk into the nearby village. There wasn't a great deal to see, but it was quaint and very pretty. We found a small shop and bought some groceries as well as some candles, which will come in handy later when the sun goes down and the lights in the cottage refuse to turn on. On the way back, we stopped off for a drink at a tiny picturesque pub beside a small stream. The stop-off was really just an excuse for Jason to use the pub's WIFI, but I didn't mind. I understand he can't be off-grid forever.

I think all the walking and fresh air took its toll on him, since once back at the cottage he retired to the bedroom for a nap while I decided to busy myself in the kitchen. Earlier, whilst making breakfast I found a deep cake tin in the back of one of the cupboards. Although I may sell my fair share of cakes at *Daisy's*, I never make

SAMANTHA KAY

them myself, and I'd decided it was time to have a go. Having purchased the right ingredients from the village shop, I set about making us a coffee and walnut cake. After spotting the recipe in Jason's notebook, I've had a real hankering for it and figured it might be a nice treat for us both.

It's been a long while since I made a cake from scratch, and I soon remember why I never bother. The kitchen looks as if a small nuclear bomb has exploded in it, and I'm exhausted. There was no electric mixer, so I had to mix everything by hand. Nor were there any kitchen scales, so I measured all the ingredients by the 'cupful'. Eventually I managed to get the cake into the oven and, according to my timekeeping, it should be ready now.

I open the oven door. Pull the tin out a little and peer inside. The sponge is looking rather flat and shiny with air bubbles all over the surface, reminiscent of an Aero chocolate bar and it hasn't risen in the way it should. I half-wonder if I should leave the mixture in a little longer, but I don't want to risk an oven fire in a thatched cottage, so I make the decision to take the cake out and put the tin down on the wire rack to cool. Maybe it'll taste better than it looks. Also, it still needs to be iced – which should help with the aesthetics, I'm sure of it.

'Is it ready?' I hear Jason say as he walks into the kitchen. I'd not heard him wake.

'Er, I'm not sure.' I give the cake a tentative

poke, as if it's a weird science experiment.

'Should it look like that?' Jason queries, standing next to me wearing a t-shirt and his boxer shorts, his hair a little bed heady.

'I'm pretty confident it *shouldn't* look like that. But I still need to ice it,' I add hopefully.

Jason nods and smiles, aware as I am that no amount of icing is going to make this cake any better.

He dips his fingers into the tin and digs out a small piece of cake and bravely pops it in his mouth.

'Well?' I ask.

He coughs. 'It's . . .different.'

'Is it moist?'

'It's not . . . dry,' he manages, struggling to swallow it.

I copy Jason, digging my fingers into the oily sponge to sample a piece. Ugh! It's definitely not dry. Instead, it's greasy and eggy and I think it's still a little raw. I spit it out into my hand.

'That's bloody horrible!'

Jason laughs as I toss the masticated cake into the sink and turn on the tap, shuddering, washing it away along with any hope of becoming this week's Star Baker.

'I think you did a good job,' Jason says supportively, cuddling me by the kitchen sink, his body all warm and cosy.

'You're so full of shit,' I mumble into his shoulder, and I feel him laugh.

'Are you still going to ice it?' he asks.

'Nah. There's no point. And have a headache. I just want to get tidied up.' I finally admit defeat, more than ready for a bath and a lie-down.

'Shall I make you a tea?' Jason offers.

'Yes, please. That'd be lovely.'

As we buzz about, Jason fills the kettle and fetches down two mugs from the cupboard above the sink.

'Where do you want this stuff?' he asks, pointing towards the bags of flour and caster sugar and a half-used box of eggs.

'Pass it here.'

With two mugs in one hand, Jason passes me the eggs and then picks up the paper bag of flour. I reach out to take it from him, but I'm too late. Without any warning, the bag splits and an avalanche of flour descends onto the kitchen floor.

'What the—' I gasp, peering through a white cloud.

Jason stands open-mouthed, an empty torn bag of flour in his hand. He looks around, trying to piece together what has just happened.

'Oh. The draining boards wet. It must have soaked the bag.' He's trying to suppress a laugh, but I fail to see the funny side.

'Urgh! I just wanted to do a nice thing! The cake's a disaster, and the kitchens a mess, I have a headache and now this!'

I whine, almost on the verge of tears as I drop to the floor beside the pile of flour, my reaction maybe a little overdramatic, but the task of cleaning up the kitchen has just multiplied, and I really do have a horrible headache.

'Please don't get upset. The cake's nice, honestly,' Jason lies.

'Oh, shut up, Jason.' I cry. 'The cake's a pile of shit!'

Jason doesn't say anything. He joins me on the kitchen floor, sitting himself next to me, and starts playing with the flour, sprinkling it back onto the kitchen tiles.

'It's like snow,' he muses, picking up a small handful and throwing it gently into the air between us, creating a little blizzard of flour, most of which has just landed in my hair.

Finally raising a smile, I too pick up a handful of flour, and as if it were a small snowball, I toss it at Jason. He retaliates immediately, with his own flour-ball and joyfully aims it at me. Before we know it, we're fully embroiled in a flour-ball fight right there on the kitchen floor. Laughing and playing like two naughty kids, with no care for all the mess we're making nor how long it will take to clear up. Giggling and covered in flour-dust, Jason kisses me. His lips are dry and unsurprisingly taste like flour. Then, in one final flurry, he chucks a handful of flour down the back of my top and over the both of us, before taking my hand in his

SAMANTHA KAY

and pulling us both to our feet.

My head still hurts, we're covered in flour and the kitchen is in a shocking state, but there's nowhere else in the whole wide world I'd rather be right now, than here in Rosewood Cottage with my lovely husband.

JASON

As far as I am concerned, there is no greater pleasure in life than having my wife lay her naked body across mine in a warm bath full of bubbles. Covered in flour and with no solid plans on how to spend our final night in the cottage, soaking in the bath together seemed like the only logical way to spend our evening after we finally got the kitchen clean again.

As expected, the lights are still failing to come on, which means our only light source is provided courtesy of the candles we purchased from the village shop. They're dotted around the bathroom and create a romantic and relaxing scenario. The bath is large and just the right size for the two of us. Abbie has nestled herself comfortably between my legs, resting her head on my chest, our bodies fitting together perfectly, just like two pieces of a jigsaw.

'How's your head?' I ask, and tenderly kiss her temple, my arms wrapped loosely around her chest, resting under her lovely boobs.

'Hmm, better.' she murmurs. 'The paracetamol's helped.' She says, closing her eyes and relaxing in my arms.

'It's a shame we have to leave tomorrow. Maybe we should have booked for a couple more days,' I say. This is so unlike workaholic me. Tough as it's been to be out of constant contact with the showroom, I've enjoyed the two of us being locked away in our own little world. It's the first time in years we've spent some real time together and it's been wonderful.

'That would have been nice. But you can't put off your treatment,' Abbie reminds me.

'Yeah, you're right,' I sigh, having momentarily forgotten all about my pretend cancer.

'Anyway, I don't really want Ellie alone in the house for more than a couple of days,' Abbie goes on, and I wonder what she means by that exactly.

'No? Why? You don't think she's sleeping with this boyfriend, do you?' I frown, wishing immediately that I hadn't asked, positive I can't handle the answer.

'Oh, she's not seeing him anymore,' Abbie says. 'She told me they broke up.'

'What happened?' I want to seem concerned but am secretly relieved. I was a sixteen-year-old boy once, and the very last thing I want is one anywhere near my daughter.

'No idea. Ellie just said they'd broken up, then she stropped back into the house.'

It's not gone unnoticed by me how difficult Ellie has become, especially towards Abbie. The constant sulky moods and snarky comments are no doubt contributing towards Abbie's unhappiness.

'I'm sorry she gives you such a hard time,' I say, and I mean it. 'I'll have a word with her about her attitude.'

'It's OK. I'm sure I was just as much fun to be around at her age.'

Abbie's voice is downcast, making me wonder just how many layers there are to her unhappiness. I know I need to be around more, and I need to speak to Ellie about her behaviour - but what if it's even deeper than that? Could it be that Abbie is seeking something more meaningful than the life she has now – something that my own selfish behaviour has made impossible? Would everything be as difficult if the adolescent upsets were coming from a child of her own? It's a route I'm reluctant to take, but if it saves my marriage, I could be swayed into changing my mind.

Lying intimately together as we are, it's as good a time as any to approach the subject.

'Do you think we'll ever regret not having kids together?' I ask, keeping my voice casual, trying not to squirm.

Abbie lifts her head from my chest and looks around at me, her expression horrified. 'No, I do not! Why, do you?'

Thank God! What a relief.

'No, not generally,' I say, trying to sound

SAMANTHA KAY

casual. 'It's just, all this cancer stuff. It's starting to dawn on me that that window really is coming to a close now.'

'And I'm perfectly fine with that. And you were always adamant that you didn't want any more kids,' Abbie responds, and I can tell she's worried I've suddenly had some kind of epiphany and changed my mind.

'I just want to be sure I didn't deprive you of babies – our own kids,' I say, as keen as Abbie to move away from the subject.

'Just because I have a womb doesn't mean I'm contractually obliged to use it!' she says angrily, rearing up.

Now I've well and truly poked the bear awake, and I feel bad for ever doubting her feelings on the matter.

'I know, I know. I'm sorry I brought it up,' I soothe her, kissing her remorsefully.

She's still frowning but silently nestles herself back down on my chest, poking her pretty painted toes out of the water. I notice the bubbles are starting to dwindle and the water is cooling, I should add more hot water, but before I make the suggestion, Abbie has something she wants to say.

'Harry and Ellie. They might not be *mine*, but I've always felt they were *ours*. They each have a room in *our* house. I've fed them dinners; we've taken them on holidays. They've given me lip and driven me mad. I've parented those kids.

I've hardly missed out on anything, if that's what you're worried about.'

'I'm sorry. I shouldn't have brought it up. It's just been a weird time. I just need reassurance that you're happy.' I say truthfully, holding her a little closer.

'I'm very happy with our choices, thank you,' Abbie says, matter-of-fact, dipping her toes back under the water.

'Good. Me too.'

'I know people think I'm weird, because I don't want babies.' It's true - Abbie has spent her adult life defending our decision to well-meaning strangers, friends and now me, which makes me feel so guilty.

'I don't think you're weird. I think you're lovely,' I say, kissing her again. 'And these boobs, they're lovely too.'

To my relief, Abbie laughs gently, and I feel her body relax against mine again.

'Honestly. They're perfect,' I say, admiring her breasts, so perfectly round and pert like those of a Roman statue of a goddess, her rose-pink nipples poking out of the water. '*You're* perfect.' No one else in the world could make me as happy as she does.

Abbie smiles at me then arches her back, lifting her breasts out of the water completely. As I admire the view, she takes my hand in hers, dipping it under the water, and seductively places it between her legs and I'm surprised but

SAMANTHA KAY

delighted to feel she's turned on.

She groans softly as I kiss her neck and make her come in the bath by candlelight; this very moment making for the most wonderful end to our day together.

CHAPTER 16

ABBIE

It's early. We're up, dressed and packed, ready to start our journey back home. As nice as it might have been to drag out a couple more hours at Rosewood Cottage, Jason wants to get off. If we leave now, we should make it home by 10 a.m.

If I'm honest, I too am eager to get back. After leaving Ellie home alone for two nights I need to know that she, the house and Daisy are all still in one piece. Also, Jason has expressed his wish to swing by the showroom. He wants to pick up his laptop and check in on things before his chemo pills start again tomorrow. Of course I understand, but I can't help feeling a bit sad. I know we must return to reality at some point, but it would have been great to put it off a little longer.

While Jason is outside loading up the car, I'm still in the cottage, tidying away from breakfast and checking we haven't left anything behind. The Monopoly we played on our first night has been left haphazardly on the small sofa facing the TV. In the interest of leaving things how we found them, I pick up the box and head towards the packed bookcase. The box is so old it's barely holding together, the lid not closing as it should. While I'm trying to make room for it in the bookcase, three tiny green houses and a red hotel tumble out and land on the floor by the wall.

I kneel down, placing the tatty box beside me, pick the pieces up and put them back with the others. As I stand back up, I notice something square, white and plastic on the wall hidden behind the bookcase. I feel around and come up with a small box, and in the middle is what feels like a switch. I press down on it, and by some kind of miracle, the downstairs lights turn on.

I chuckle to myself. Jason said there'd be a master switch somewhere. It never occurred to either of us to look behind the bookcase.

I hear Jason at the front door and impulsively turn the switch back off, all the light disappearing in less than a second, and get back to squashing the Monopoly box into the bookcase as he re-enters the cottage.

'You nearly ready?' he asks.

'Yep, just putting this away,' I tell him, keeping my discovery firmly to myself.

*

Our journey has been a good one. Surprisingly, we hit very little traffic and now here we are,

EIGHT MILLION MINUTES

back home. Quaint villages and tuneful birdsong are now nothing more than a distant memory. I messaged Ellie about an hour ago telling her we were enroute but received no reply. Only moments away from our street, Jason is still ranting about the cottage's faulty lighting.

'Don't let me forget to put in a complaint,' he says. 'Where do they get off renting out a place with no working lights!'

I suppress a smile. 'It wasn't that bad, was it - going back to basics and all that,' I say, having found the experience rather cathartic.

'Easy for you to say,' he grumps. 'You don't have to stand and point to pee. You try doing that in the dark.'

When he pulls the Ferrari onto the drive, I'm pleased to see that the house is still standing with no obvious signs of anarchy having taken place. I unclick my seatbelt, but Jason remains firmly in position, the loud engine still running.

'Aren't you coming in?' I ask.

'No. I need to pick up the laptop and check on a few things.'

Earlier, when we stopped off at the service station, Jason got very stressed. Tapping through his phone, huffing and puffing about all the things he's missed and needs to catch up on, eager to get back to work. The holiday might never have happened. We're straight back in the old routine.

'I just thought you might want to see Ellie,

SAMANTHA KAY

that's all.' I was kind of hoping Jason would be with me to deal with any potential problems. My headache from yesterday is there again, and a row with Ellie really is the last thing I can cope with this morning.

'It's not that I don't want to see her, but it's still early. I want to get as much done as I can before my treatment starts again tomorrow. Next week I'm gona be out of it again all week and I —'

'All right, all right, I get it,' I say, interrupting him as he becomes more agitated. 'I've actually got some work to do too. Adminy bits – you know,' I add, not wanting to part on a sour note.

Jason smiles in relief, happy I won't be nagging him any further. 'I won't be back late. I promise.'

I nod and smile, not quite believing him, but I can't be arsed to challenge it.

I make to climb out of the car, but before I do, Jason reaches for my hand, stalling my exit.

'Hey, Abbie, I...I hope you had a nice time . . . with me.' He looks at me with large puppy-dog eyes. I think he's worried that I'm upset with him, but I'm not. I'll never stop wanting him to be around more, but I understand what he needs to do to keep the very nice roof over both our heads.

'Of course. It was lovely,' I say truthfully.

'There really is no one else I'd rather sit in

the dark with for two days,' he says and I laugh, turning to face him properly.

'Same.'

I lean in and give him a lingering kiss on the lips. 'Go. Get your work done and come home to me.' I tell him. I jump out of the car, take out our luggage from the front boot and wave my husband off to work before heading to the front door.

Stepping into the house, I dump our bags and baggage by the front door, vowing to sort through it before the day is over. I'm greeted by Daisy.

'Hello, lovely girl,' I say, bending down to meet her. She's a happy girl, tail up and trotting towards me. I pick her up and cradle her in my arms, pleased as ever to see my purry girl. Everything is still and silent in the house, eerily so. Although it's about half past ten, I assume Ellie is still in bed, which is fine by me.

I head into the kitchen, wanting to check that she did at the very least get up to feed Daisy, and get a surprise when I see a teenage girl who isn't Ellie eating a bowl of cereal at my breakfast bar. It's Grace, Ellie's best friend.

'Oh hi, Abbie,' she says, just as surprised to see me, as if not expecting me to walk into my own kitchen.

I've known Grace since she was about seven years old. She's a nice girl. A bit stupid, but nice. She's quite short, with massive boobs that make her look top-heavy. She has curly chestnut-brown hair and these days her face is usually caked in make-up, so it makes a nice change to see her fresh-faced and casual, dressed in an oversized Spice Girls T-shirt like she's oh so retro!

'Hi, Grace. You ok?' I say, placing Daisy down on the floor.

'Yeah, all good, thanks. How was your break?' Grace enquires, before slurping a spoonful of cereal into her mouth.

'Lovely, thank you. Really relaxing. Is Ellie about?' There seems to be no obvious sign of her existence. I do, however, spot out of the corner of my eye a full bowl of cat biscuit by the back door, so that's something.

'Yeah,' Grace answers sheepishly.

'Where is she?' My head is beginning to throb so I open the kitchen drawer where we keep the paracetamol and other medical potions, such as Jason's cancer meds. I really should get these headaches checked out; maybe I need an eye test.

'Upstairs.'

'Oh, still in bed, is she?' I assume, snapping two pills and fetching myself a glass of water.

Grace just gawps at me. Anyone would think I had asked her for the square root of sixty-four.

'Erm, I'm not sure,' she finally utters, looking back down into her bowl of cereal, and I'm at a loss to understand why this conversation

EIGHT MILLION MINUTES

is quite so strained. I swallow my pills and hope they'll kick in soon.

'Grace, is everything OK?' I ask, starting to feel a little concerned.

'We didn't think you were coming back until later.' Grace is looking scared.

'What's going on?' I ask, my voice sterner, my stomach starting to knot itself with worry.

Grace nervously licks her lips. Unable to look at me, she looks down at the counter-top and to my frustration, stays silent.

'Grace, where's Ellie?'

'She's upstairs, in the bathroom. She's not feeling very well.' Says Grace, her voice small and worried.

'What's wrong with her?' I'm feeling really worried now.

Grace finally looks up at me but stays painfully silent. Her mouth opens, but no words escape.

Beyond frustrated, I leave her and head straight upstairs to find Ellie. Her bedroom door is open and as I approach, I can hear her sobbing. The light is on even though sunlight is streaming in through the large window. I turn the light off. The bed is unmade and on the messy desk I spot Ellie's mobile phone. This is unusual, as it's usually glued to her hand. A pair of worn leggings lie on the floor by the ensuite door, which is ajar. I can hear Ellie in there, the weeping louder on my approach.

220

I'm not sure she realises I'm home. Not wanting to startle her, I gently tap on the door.

'Come in,' Ellie says between sobs.

I open the door gingerly and find Ellie in a heap on the hard bathroom floor, curled up into a ball in the foetal position. She's facing away from the door wearing nothing but the oversized yellow T-shirt she sleeps in and a pair of black knickers.

'Ellie, it's me. Are you ok?' I ask.

Ellie lifts her head from the floor, and I can see the obvious horror etched on her face on realising I'm not Grace. She is clutching her tummy, her face is ashen, and I can see she's in a lot of pain.

'Is Dad here?' she asks, her eyes wide and panic-stricken.

'No, no, he dropped me home and went straight to the showroom. He's got some work to do.'

She crumples from relief. Lies back down on the floor and continues to weep.

An open pack of sanitary towels sits on the shelf above the bathroom sink and as I edge my way further into the bathroom I notice a couple of spots of blood on the bathroom floor. That's before I see the state of the toilet. The water in the bowl is deep red, full of blood and some large clots. I've experienced a heavy period or two in my time, but this seems extreme.

I kneel beside Ellie and rest a hand on her

shoulder, trying my best to soothe her.

'Are you having a bad period?' I ask, but Ellie is crying too much to answer. I'm worried. There's not much I can do, and the amount of blood she's lost is concerning. There's no way I can leave her in this state. I stand up, deciding to fetch my phone.

'Look, I'm going to call for some help.'

'No, don't, please don't!' she screams.

'I have to, Ellie. It's not normal for a period to be this bad.'

'It's not my period!' cries Ellie, her voice hoarse from weeping. 'It's not my period!' She is struggling to catch her breath between sobs.

I freeze and it takes a moment for me to comprehend what Ellie has just said. I look at the scarlet toilet bowl, then back at Ellie and her tear-stained face, and gradually, all the pieces fall into place.

No wonder Grace was acting so weird.

'Oh please, *please*, tell me this is some kind of a wind up.' I say, my face buried in my hands, not quite believing the bloody great big mess I've unwittingly walked into.

'They said it would be done in a few hours, but it's been ages, and the pain and the bleeding won't stop.'

Poor Ellie. Clutching her abdomen, she looks so young and scared and my heart aches for her. I reach for a towel on the chrome towel rail, fold it over into a square and kneel on the floor

SAMANTHA KAY

beside her.

'How far gone were you?' I ask gently, lifting Ellie's head and placing the towel under her, trying my best to make her comfortable.

'Why does that matter?' huffs Ellie, and I note how, even in a state of utter agony, she's still able to issue her standard stroppiness towards me.

'So I know how to help you,' I say, keeping my voice level. I sit myself down beside her head, leaning my back on the bath panel.

'Five or six weeks,' answers Ellie, which comes as a great relief. Five or six weeks is fine. If she had said five or six months, we'd have a very different problem on our hands.

'I took the pill at six a.m. I thought it would be over before you got home,' she says, her weeping subsiding slightly.

I take a look at my watch. It's 10.45 a.m. If we had stayed at the cottage a while longer, Ellie might well have been back up on her feet or lying in bed with some excuse before our return and no one would have been any the wiser. But as fate would have it, here I am. Sitting on the bathroom floor with a pounding headache, aiding my stepdaughter through an abortion.

I stroke a hand through her tangled hair. She shouldn't be going through this alone with just Grace in the house, who frankly seems more interested in her cereal than helping Ellie.

'It should start to ease up soon,' I comfort

her. 'We'll give it a couple more hours, and if you're no better, we'll call for some help.'

Ellie closes her eyes and nods her head. I sit with her and eventually she calms down. The crying stops and she makes herself as comfortable as a person bleeding out on the bathroom floor can. I cover her with a blanket from her room to keep her warm. Then, confident that she's through the worst, I get up from the hard floor, flush the toilet and throw some bleach down it before opening the bathroom window, the metallic smell of Ellie's blood rather overwhelming.

I head downstairs to fetch Ellie a glass of water. I thank Grace for all she's done and advise her to head home. I think she's glad to escape, having been quite out of her depth.

With Grace out of the way, and Ellie a little calmer, I rummage through the kitchen drawer hoping to find something a little stronger than standard paracetamol to ease Ellie's pain. I locate some ibuprofen. I have a feeling her pain levels are too high for this to do anything, but it's worth a try. I run back upstairs with the pills and the glass of water, and hope to God Jason will break his promise and return home late.

*

It's 5 p.m. and thankfully Ellie is feeling better; delicate, but better.

After she'd taken the ibuprofen, I helped her from the bathroom floor to her bed. She

SAMANTHA KAY

managed to rest and after a few hours perked up a little. Keen for her to have a change of environment, I've managed to prise her out of her bedroom, convincing her to join me and Daisy on the sofa with the offer of a cup of tea and a packet of chocolate digestives. She hasn't touched the biscuits, but I think the tea seems to be doing the trick. Sitting lazily beside one another, Ellie has one hand wrapped around her mug, the other stroking Daisy's head. Ellie's eyes are sad, but I'm confident the worst is over.

I really want to use this opportunity to understand what's going on inside Ellie's head.

'How are you feeling?' I ask, taking a sip from my tea.

Looking into her cup and releasing a jagged breath, it's evident just how sensitive the situation is.

'Crap,' she says.

'Does he know - your boyfriend? About . . .' I don't need to finish my sentence for Ellie to know exactly what I'm referring to.

She shakes her head as a single tear falls from her right eye. She quickly swipes it away.

'No. No one knows. Except you and Grace. And some woman at the abortion place,' Ellie tells me, and I can see it's taking all her inner strength to hold herself together.

'So that's not why you broke up?' I probe, acutely aware that I'm walking through a minefield here, terrified one wrong step could cause Ellie to explode.

Ellie presses the heel of her hand against her forehead, her anguish palpable.

'There was a video, of me and him that everyone saw.'

I wince, an involuntary reaction to the sick feeling hitting my stomach.

'What kind of video?' I ask, not actually wanting to hear the answer.

'One of us. *Together.*'

OK, no doubt in her opinion I'm the dumbest person in the world, but I'm not, I just want to be sure I'm understanding everything.

'So, then it was over?' I ask.

'He stopped talking to me, like I'm the one who's done something wrong,' she says resentfully, 'when that video can only have come from him.' This time she doesn't wipe away the tears, allowing herself to cry it out on the sofa.

I take Ellie's cup of tea from her, put it along with mine down on the coffee table in front of us and wrap my arms around her. As Ellie sobs on my shoulder, it occurs to me that I don't even know the name of the utter scoundrel who knocked up my step-daughter and left her a hysterical mess on the bathroom floor. I feel angry on her behalf, but I can't let it show. My own emotions are not important right now.

After a few moments Ellie pulls away. I reach for the box of tissues that live on the table and hand them to her. She pulls some out, mops her face and blows her nose.

'He gets to look like some fucking king, and I'm just this slut with a missing period, throwing up before maths,' Ellie says furiously, and I feel awful in the knowledge of everything she's been keeping to herself.

'Does your mum know - about the video?' I ask, hoping that someone responsible has been helping Ellie through this mess in some way or another.

'No.' And then she panics. 'Oh God, you're gonna tell mum and dad, aren't you? You're gonna tell them what's happened and the truth about why I wanted to stay here –'

'Ellie, Ellie. I'm not gona tell anyone anything.' I interrupt her rant.

She looks surprised, clearly not expecting such a response.

'You know what, sometimes the whole truth thing...it can be a tad overrated.' I say, taking Ellie's hand in mine.

Ellie frowns, my words surely going against every moral lesson she's ever been taught.

'I don't mean that in a deceitful way,' I hasten to explain. 'It's just, we all have private stuff. All of us. And we don't have to tell everyone everything all the time. We are allowed to keep some things to ourselves. Right?'

In truth, and for all sorts of valid reasons, I probably do have some kind of duty to notify

Ellie's parents about what has been going on with her, but I don't want to betray her secret. Parenting protocol isn't what Ellie needs right now. She needs someone she can trust and confide in, and I'm happy and willing to be that person. Plus, Jason would *absolutely* lose his shit if he knew, and quite frankly, he has enough going on right now. A shock like this on top of cancer could send him over the edge.

'Thank you,' mouths Ellie, 'How was your trip?' she asks politely, needing a change of subject.

'Yeah, it was really good. Different, but good.' It is most unusual for Ellie to take any interest in anyone but herself, but I'm happy to roll with the conversation, equally keen to move on to lighter subjects.

I pick up our mugs up from the coffee table, handing Ellie hers.

'Yeah. What'd you do?' Asks Ellie, dapping her eyes.

'Not a lot actually. We hardly left the cottage,' I say with a coy smile.

'Urgh, you two are so gross,' Ellie responds in her default tone of disgust.

I laugh inwardly, the past few days feeling like a lifetime ago now. It's then we hear the front door open. Ellie looks over at me, her eyes panicked.

'It's fine,' I whisper. 'Your secret's safe with me.'

A few short moments later, Jason enters the living room, his face alight at the sight of Ellie, not expecting her to still be here.

'Ellie belly,' he beams. 'You're still here.' He takes a seat beside her, wrapping an arm around her shoulder and kissing her cheek. Then he takes a closer look at her. 'Everything ok…?'

It's clear Ellie is not her usual picture of health and vigour, and it's obvious that she's been crying, as her eyes are still red and puffy. She's also still wearing her yellow T-shirt from earlier, an obvious sign she hasn't showered or got dressed today, which is very unlike her.

'Ellie's not been feeling too well,' I explain. 'Lady problems,' I throw in, the very mention of 'lady problems' always sending the fear of God into Jason.

'Oh. I'm sorry to hear that,' he says, doing a very good job at not squirming. 'Are you stopping for dinner?' he asks, predictably changing the subject as soon as possible.

'Yeah, if that's all right.' she replies, looking at me before adding, 'Actually, would it be OK if I stayed tonight?'

'Of course. Make sure you let your mum know.' Says Jason, over the moon, delighted to spend some unexpected time with his daughter.

I'm conscious that Jason's treatment starts again tomorrow, but after the day we've had, I know I can't simply shove Ellie out of the door and back to her mum in the state she's in. Kelly would be bound to find out the reason behind it. Hopefully, Jason's chemo side-effects will kick in after Ellie has left.

'I'll message her now.' She picks her phone up from the sofa cushion.

'Lovely. Shall we get a takeaway?' Jason suggests. 'I'm starving.'

'Yeah, sounds like a plan.' I don't have much of an appetite and my headache hasn't budged, which is hardly surprising considering the day I've had. Needing a breather and in search of some more painkillers, I leave the others in the lounge together and set off for the kitchen.

After putting my mug in the dishwasher, I stand alone for a moment, reflecting on the past few hours. I hope that if nothing else, today might mark a positive step forward in my relationship with Ellie and I feel profoundly thankful that we each made it through this terrible day in one piece.

CHAPTER 17

JASON

I feel glum.

It's a beautiful sunny day out there, not a cloud in the sky, zero threat of rain. The perfect day for a drive. Or at least it would be, if I hadn't made myself a voluntary prisoner in my own bedroom. I stand at the window looking up at the clear blue sky and think of Dean. He has a test drive scheduled at 2 p.m. today in the McLaren 765LT. While he whizzes around the track having the time of his life, I'll be huddled over the toilet bowl, conveying sickness by chucking a glass of water down the loo.

But it's only for one more week. One final week and with any luck, that should be it.

Job done.

Marriage saved.

Dull as it is being holed up in the bedroom, it's got to be a damn sight easier than the alternative. Marriage counselling, expensive solicitors, the dividing up of our belongings, sleeping alone - no, it doesn't bear thinking about. And anyway, I've learned my lesson. I know I must be around more. More present. I don't need some smug counsellor to tell me so, I just needed time to make some changes and gain some perspective.

I'm confident that our trip to Rosewood Cottage sealed the deal. Board games, baths by candlelight, plenty of sex. Abbie certainly didn't behave like a wife ready to walk away from her marriage. No, I'm confident all is well. Just one more week of sickness and vulnerability and I'm on the home straight.

Just one more week.

Today is week two, day one of 'chemo pills.' Usually, I would take the pill first thing in the morning, my theory being, the sooner I take it, the sooner the 'side-effects' will kick in and the sooner they will begin to wear off. Unfortunately, today I'm running a little behind schedule.

Ellie stayed over last night. It was lovely having her here, even if she wasn't feeling 100 per cent. Abbie said she was struggling with 'lady problems', but I wonder if she's caught some kind of bug. She hardly touched the pizza we ordered last night and still didn't seem herself this morning. I'm not sure that she will make it to school today, but I'll be leaving that decision in Kelly's hands. One good thing is that Ellie and Abbie seem on much better terms, the atmosphere between the two of them was much lighter than usual. Maybe they bonded over lady problems, or maybe Abbie spoke to Ellie about her attitude, but I dare not ask any questions. They're getting on and that's all that matters.

With Ellie here for breakfast, I didn't want to start my 'treatment' in front of her, nor for my 'side-effects' to kick in while she was here.

After breakfast, Abbie very kindly dropped Ellie back to Kelly's and as soon as they had left, I took my 'medication'. I like to give myself an hour or so before the so-called side-effects show themselves.

I decide to stop hanging around feeling depressed at the bedroom window. Abbie will be home any minute, just in time for the sickness to start. I wonder if I should make better use of my time and fill up on snacks while the house is empty. I've hidden some granola bars in my bedside table again, but in truth they didn't touch the sides on easing my hunger pains last time.

Just as I leave the bedroom, I hear the sound of Abbie entering the house, and I'm annoyed with myself for letting my only opportunity pass me by. I can hear her coming up the stairs, so I nip back into the bedroom and do the only logical thing I can think of, which is to hop into bed and burrow under the covers.

'Hey, how you feeling?' Abbie asks, entering the bedroom and joining me on the bed.

I clear my throat for effect.

'I'm fine. Starting to feel a bit groggy, but otherwise it's not too bad. Was Ellie OK?' With her phone in her hand, Abbie makes herself comfortable next to me, stretching out her legs and resting her back on the headboard.

'Yeah, she seemed a little better actually.'

'Did Kelly say anything?' I'm always worried she might shoot some venom in Abbie's direction.

'I didn't see her. I dropped Ellie off in the car and sped away,' Abbie says, before looking down at her phone and tapping the screen. '*Anyway*, the graphic designer has sent me through some new logos for the shop. Want to see?'

Abbie's taken another day off work to nurse me through my treatment. I told her it wasn't necessary, but she insisted. I feel so guilty. I know only too well how important her business is to her, and how hard she's working on this rebrand. Now really isn't the time for her to be shutting shop for days on end, but I tell myself again that it's only for one more week.

I nod, genuinely keen to see the new branding. I sit up, resting back on the headboard beside her.

'So, there's this one.' Abbie shows me option number one. A picture of a cartoon chihuahua, licking its lips behind a giant cupcake, with *Daisy's Doggie Café* written along the bottom of the cake.

'Or this one.' Abbie swipes the phone to option two. It's a pawprint, surrounded by daisies. *Daisy's Doggie Café* is written inside the pawprint.

'Or this one.' She swipes to option three. The cartoon chihuahua is back, licking his lips, but minus the cupcake. Instead, he's surrounded by the colourful daisies seen in option two. *Daisy's Doggie Café* is written across the top.

'What one do you like best?' Abbie wants to know.

'The last one,' I say without hesitation. 'It sends the clearest message. Dogs are welcome to a café called *Daisy's*. Job done.'

Abbie nods, showing that she's heard, but she carries on swiping back and forth through the images, still looking unsure.

'You don't like that one?' I ask, keen to hear her thoughts.

'I do. I just really want to get this right.' Abbie stops swiping and puts her phone down on her lap. She rubs her head, looking worried. 'The past couple of years have been such a struggle and I ploughed every penny of my inheritance into *Daisy's*. I don't want my parents to have the satisfaction of seeing it fail.'

The amount of hurt and upset that Abbie's parents have caused continues to anger me. To disown your child because of who she fell in love with is bad enough, but to let an inheritance cause such hatred and contempt towards her is downright despicable. I fought so hard to maintain contact with my own children, so how anyone can voluntarily cut themselves off from their own child like this . . . it beggars belief.

I can't imagine my kids ever doing anything that would make me treat them so badly. Abbie is a wonderful person, and her parents are the idiots who have missed out by not wanting her in their lives.

'It's not going to fail. You have a great new idea and it's going to be a success,' I promise, wrapping my arms around her; gently snuggling us down on the bed. I hold her in a lovely spoon cuddle, both resting our heads on the same pillow.

'It was your idea,' Abbie says fairly, not wanting to take the credit that's due to her.

'Maybe, but you're the one putting the work in,' I say, moving her blonde hair out of the way to plant a little kiss on the back of her neck.

'Right, so it's option three,' she says. 'I'll let the guy know. Then I need to sort out the website and the socials and get some flyers made.'

'Flyers? It's not the 90s,' I scoff, not sure why Abbie would waste money on such a thing.

'I know, but I'm only going to get a hundred or so printed. It won't hurt to leave them in the other shops. If I make them into some kind of ten per cent off voucher, it might help get people through the door.'

She's still rattling off her ideas, unable to relax, unlike myself. Enjoying her proximity, I yawn and can feel myself starting to drift off. I force my eyes to open. I can't afford to fall asleep! I'm at a very delicate point in this process. I need to be as convincing as I was in week one. My marriage depends on it. As close as I am, I'm not over the finish line yet and mustn't get complacent.

I groan.

'What's wrong?' Abbie asks immediately.

'I'm going to be sick.' And with great urgency, I spring from the bed and race to the bathroom. I'll be so pleased when all this is over and done with.

Worried in case Abbie might enter the bathroom, I decide it's not wise to chuck water down the loo for vomit-like sound effects, and merely gag and heave as loudly as I can muster.

'Did you take the anti-sickness pill?' Abbie calls from the bedroom.

'Yes, but it doesn't seem to be working,' I call back, heaving once more and groaning, the echo from the toilet bowl working wonders for the acoustics.

'Do you need anything?' Abbie asks kindly.

'No!' I call back, my response a little curt, which is normal for me when I'm under the weather.

'OK, I'll leave you to it. Call me if you need

anything,' Abbie says, and I hear her leave the bedroom, kindly granting me some privacy.

ABBIE

Fortunately, today has gone smoothly enough so far. I managed to drop Ellie back to her mum this morning without arousing too much suspicion. Physically she was certainly much better, but the emotional wounds might take a little longer to heal. She was quiet at breakfast and in the car. Usually, I would have welcomed this, but I worry that her quietness will alert everyone to the fact that something is very wrong. Although having said that, Jason didn't seem all that concerned - but then again, he has a lot on his mind.

His second stage of treatment started today.

He was quite sick after I returned home. After a couple of hours spent puking in the toilet he eventually retired to bed. He wrapped himself tightly in the duvet and was becoming very sweaty, but otherwise, he didn't seem too bad. I made sure to keep him hydrated and sat with him for a little while. As nice as it's been to be together so much lately, I look forward to the time when things go back to normal. He seemed so vulnerable and sad in bed, which is so not like him. I want my husband back - just not the one who works an eighty-hour week. I suppose we'll just have to wait and see how that pans out.

Earlier today I received a message from Denise – the lady who owns the hairdressers next to *Daisy's.* She's kindly taken in my delivery of some doggie bandanas and shiny bright collars. *Daisy's* has remained shut today while I've stayed home to look after Jason. I could have asked Molly to open for a few hours, but I worry that I've been putting a little too much on her of late. Also, all the extra responsibility would surely warrant a pay rise, and I literally can't afford for Molly to be getting any such ideas right now.

With Jason safely wrapped up in bed, I felt confident enough to leave him alone for a couple of hours, just long enough for me to nip out, pick up my delivery from Denise and pop inside *Daisy's* to check all is fine. Driving there, I finally reach the High Street and am lucky enough to spot a parking space right outside the shop. As I pull up, my heart jumps into my throat when I see that the shop's shutters are up. They were definitely down, the last time I closed up, and no one has been in since.

I hastily turn off the ignition and hop out of the car. Standing on the pavement, I can see the shutter isn't up all the way, just enough to clear the door. The lights inside are off, and peering through the window everything looks as it should do. I can see no sign of a forced entry but all the same I wonder if I should call the

SAMANTHA KAY

police.

I try my keys and am pleased to discover that the door is locked. I tut to myself. I'm so sure I closed the shutter, but I've got so much on my mind right now, with Jason and the rebrand, not to mention this bloody migraine thing I seem to have developed. I really must make an appointment with the GP. There must be pills you can be prescribed for migraines. I need to sort myself out pronto. The very last thing I need right now is a burglary claim on my insurance that would have been all my own fault.

Once I've opened the door and stepped inside the shop, everything looks fine, although I can hear something that sounds like two giant hamsters scurrying around. My heart begins to beat furiously in my chest. Someone is here.

Picking up a large jam jar containing some half-dead short-stemmed white roses which I'd placed there last week to decorate the shelf near the door, I creep deeper into the shop. Past the tables and towards the counter . . . and then I get the fright of my life when I see two half-dressed bodies huddled together on the floor behind it, like corpses that have been dumped there.

I scream in absolute terror.

The sound scares them, so much so they jump in shock, thus revealing that they are alive. It's then I realise who they are.

'What the fuck are you doing!' I shout.

'Sorry, Abbie. I'm so sorry.' It's Mas,

EIGHT MILLION MINUTES

cowering, fearing that I'm about to strike him with the jam jar. His hair is messy and his jeans are just about on and undone so I can see his red underpants.

Molly has her modesty covered, just about, using her chunky cardigan as a blanket on her top half. However, her legs are exposed and bare, apart from a pair of grubby white socks.

'What the fuck!' I explode again. How is it that I've suddenly acquired a habit of walking in on fornicating couples?

'I'm so sorry, Abbie,' repeats a red-faced Mas, scurrying to his feet.

'This is my livelihood - not a bloody knocking shop!' I bawl.

'I know. I'm sorry. So sorry.'

While Mas continues to apologise profusely, Molly remains silent and fused to the floor, fear etched across her face. I turn away, too angry to even look at her.

With his trainers held in his hand, Mas struggles to button up his jeans one-handed.

'Is there anything I can do?' Asks Mas, still displaying impeccable manners.

'Yes. You can leave,' I tell him fiercely.

He makes his way out from behind the counter, and I notice him hovering, no doubt waiting for Molly. While his chivalry is endearing, it's not necessary.

'Don't wait for her,' I say curtly. 'We need a word.'

242

Mas bites down on his lip. He doesn't argue, simply nods his head and heads towards the door.

'OK. Bye, Abbie, again so sorry.'

'Goodbye, Mas.'

Once he's gone, I lock the door behind him and turn on the lights. That's when Molly reluctantly comes out from behind the counter. She's decent now. Her floral mini-dress is on the right way round, the top two buttons left undone, her chunky cardigan draped over her arm. Her cheeks are flushed, and she looks as if she's about to burst into tears.

'What the hell is going on?' I demand. 'I gave you those keys because I thought I could trust you.' I'm trying my level best to contain my anger and not intimidate her.

'I'm sorry,' Molly whispers.

'I thought we'd been burgled. I thought there was an intruder in here.'

When she says nothing, I carry on: 'What if you had an accident? What if there was a fire? Are you going to pay for the damages? I need staff I can trust, Molly, not staff who think it's OK to fuck on my floor!' I hear the coarseness in my words and wince, realising I may have gone too far.

'I'm so sorry, Abbie. I'm really, really sorry. But you don't know what it's like, trying to find somewhere private to go, and I really didn't think you would find out.'

EIGHT MILLION MINUTES

I shake my head in disbelief, really wishing she'd stopped at 'sorry'.

'You're going to sack me, aren't you?' Molly says, inhaling a deep breath. Tears begin to flow down her flushed cheeks.

As furious as I am, her sadness and embarrassment pull at my heart-strings.
Despite the political lectures and having sex on my shop floor, I genuinely like Molly. She's really stepped up over the last couple of weeks and I greatly appreciate her being a safe and reliable sounding-board for all my problems. I look at her, all weepy and pathetic and force myself to calm down.

'Fortunately for you, I don't have the time or inclination to hire anyone new right now.' And I thump my jam jar of white roses down on the counter, not wanting her to think my decision comes from a place of sympathy or kindness.

'So, I'm not sacked?' she asks, sounding rather surprised.

'No, you're not. But I swear to God, Molly, if you pull a stunt like that again—'

'It will never happen again. I promise.'

We stand silently for a moment. Molly looks awkward, not quite knowing if she's free to leave or not, so I take the opportunity to prod her a little.

'I *knew* you liked him. Why did you deny it for long?' I say with a smile, the atmosphere lifting.

244

Molly bows her head. 'He's a capitalist,' she mutters, shame oozing from her at such a level I can't help but laugh. She looks up at me, not appreciating my reaction. Her principles are so rigid I often worry that she deprives herself of worthy life experiences and general happiness.

'You know, it is possible to like people who hold different views to you,' I say kindly. 'After all, I'm a capitalist. Admittedly, not a very good one, but we get on, don't we?'

'Yeah, I suppose so,' she replies reluctantly, wiping her nose with the back of her hand.

My head is still pounding, recent events surely not helping my stress levels. I often find caffeine eases a headache, but I'm not in the mood to start up any machines or commit to tidying up. So, I head over to the fridge where we store the cold drinks and pull out two ice-cold Cokes and hand one to Molly. It's a peace offering. Still standing, we both open our cans by the counter. As angry as I am, I worry I was a little too harsh on Molly. Although we're poles apart in many ways, I wasn't always the angry old woman who stands before her today. Her mishap has in fact ignited some memories of my own.

'I do know what it's like, you know,' I tell her, taking a sip from my can, leaning on the counter. 'To have nowhere private to go. Jason and I used to have sex in the stock cupboard at work all the time.'

Molly laughs in surprise and nearly spits

out her drink. She wasn't expecting such a revelation from her boss.

'Did you know you liked him - straight away?' Molly asks, her question making me wonder how long she's forced herself to deny her feelings for Mas, and whether she feels bad for giving him the cold shoulder all this time. I, on the other hand, never suffered from the same dilemma. The attraction between me and Jason was as instant as a packet of Super Noodles.

'Yeah. I really did. He had this confidence, this self-assurance that boys my own age just didn't have. That was really sexy to me.'

'Did you know he was married?' Molly asks curiously.

Maybe unbeknown to Molly, that's a question I've been asked a lot over the years. I think it's people's way of gauging what kind of person I am.

A naïve girl with no idea what she was getting herself into. Or:

A home-wrecking slut.

Often people are surprised to hear it's the latter, and although I can't undo any of the hurt and pain I caused, I can at the very least, be honest.

'Yes,' I say, without hesitation. 'I knew.'

Molly's eyes widen. I can tell she's shocked. 'Didn't you feel bad?' It's a fair question, asked politely enough, but I can hear the judgment in her voice just like I've heard it from so many people over the years.

'I just pushed it down, kind of ignored the fact that his wife and children existed, until I couldn't ignore it anymore.'

'Until she found out?'

I nod. 'It was a horrible time,' I say, casting my mind back to a dark period of my life, one I don't often care to remember. But now that I've seen Molly half-naked on my shop floor, I guess there's no topic off-limits, so I continue.

'We broke up. He was going to do the right thing by his wife and kids. I was absolutely heartbroken. And we were still working together so it was beyond awkward, still seeing each other every day. But after a while, normal order was resumed. And a few weeks later we were back at it in the stock cupboard.'

'God, that's wild.' And I can tell that Molly is enjoying hearing the more sordid details of my life.

'Eventually he left her. Got a place of his own and we moved in together. That's when my parents finally found out that I was with an older guy who was married with kids - and well, they hit the roof.'

'But even after all these years, they've not accepted things?'

Another question I'm asked a lot, people finding my complex family dynamic a subject of deep fascination.

'There was a short ceasefire once, but

then came the fall-out over the money my grandad left me. We haven't spoken since then,' I conclude, not caring to elaborate on the upsetting details.

'You must have really loved Jason, to have gone through all of that.' Molly takes a thoughtful sip from her can of Coke.

'I still do,' I say defensively.

Molly furrows her eyebrows. No wonder. Just a few weeks ago I was on the cusp of walking away from Jason, ready to start a new life without him, and now I'm standing in front of her practically declaring my undying love for him. Molly must think I'm crazy!

'True, the past few years have been challenging,' I add hastily, 'but I'm confident we're in a better place now.'

Molly looks at me thoughtfully. 'A married man . . . I could never do that,' she says. Virtue signalling is the very thing Molly does best, but I try not to take offence. She's young and doesn't understand that not every great love story starts under a Disney-style rainbow of butterflies and purity. Some love stories contain a little more controversy, and while I'm not proud of all the details, I am proud of the life Jason and I have built together.

'Well, you're doing a capitalist. Some might say that's worse.' And with that, I enjoy reminding Molly that I'm not the only person in the room who's chosen a path they never imagined themselves taking.

CHAPTER 18

JASON

'Why didn't you sack her!' I exclaim, absolutely outraged by what a pushover my wife is.

'I dunno. I thought it a little hypocritical. You and I used to have sex at work all the time,' Abbie reminds me. She's lying back on the sofa as I rub her feet that are nestled in my lap. She came home from *Daisy's* a short while ago, complaining of a sore neck and feeling sick, which isn't surprising, considering the day she's had.

Personally, I'm feeling much 'better' than I was this morning. Wearing my boxers and dressing gown I decided to join Abbie on the sofa. Her eyes are closed, a hand resting on her aching head.

'Oh come on, that was a bit different,' I scoff.

'How so?' she asks, and yawns, exhausted.

'We never broke into the premises and went at it on the showroom floor. *And* we never got caught.'

Abbie opens her eyes. 'That's not true. We

once got caught in that car park behind the leisure centre.' A soft laugh falls from her lips.

'But that wasn't at work.' I say, pointing out the vital difference.

'No, we were responsible employees. We always locked that store cupboard from the inside.' And we both laugh.

'You seem better,' says Abbie. 'How are you feeling?'

Abbie's simple question suddenly makes me self-conscious. Am I too well? Too jolly? My 'side-effects' certainly haven't been as extreme today as they were during the previous round of treatment. This whole cancer act is exhausting, but it's important I don't become complacent.

I'm not out of the woods yet.

'I'm OK,' I say, gently rubbing her legs. 'The doctor said the second week should be less harsh than the first - you know, as the body gets used to it.' I'm winging it, trying to explain why cancer-stricken me looks and feels much brighter than Abbie right now.

'Talking of which, when is your next doctor's appointment?' Abbie asks, forcing herself to sit up, resting her weight on her elbows. She looks so strained and I feel so guilty, since I am the cause of it.

'Don't you worry about me. You need to rest.' I try my level best to avoid the question. But Abbie's having none of it.

'Do you need to call the hospital? Or will

they call you?' She's like a dog with a bone.

I clear my throat, needing a second to navigate my answer. 'Erm . . . I need to finish this round of pills. Then they'll book me in.'

'For what, exactly? A scan, blood tests, a chat?'

'Yeah, all of that.' Outwardly I remain cool, calm and collected, while inwardly I'm beginning to panic. I thought once this week was over, that would be it. Cured. Back to normal. No more 'medication', no more bouts of 'sickness'. No more straining my throat on the hard bathroom floor. But oh no, she wants follow-up appointments! How did I not prepare myself for follow-up appointments!

'I'd like to come with you this time, to your next appointment. I hate that you've gone through so much on your own. I really want to be there with you, and I've also got a few questions I'd like to ask.'

'OK.' I nod weakly, and by some divine miracle, my phone rings unexpectedly - and not a second too soon. I pick it up to see it's Gerald calling. Desperate to remove myself from the conversation, I lift Abbie's feet from my lap and get up from the sofa.

'Who is it?' she asks, sinking back onto the cushions and closing her eyes.

'Gerald. I should take it. You rest - I'll take this elsewhere,' I say, walking out of the living room.

SAMANTHA KAY

'Hi Gerald, how's things?' I say cheerily, gravitating towards the kitchen.

'Jase, that you? Where are you?' Gerald asks. It sounds as if he's speaking to me from the car.

'Oh, nowhere exciting. Just at home.'

'I swung by *Turner's* for a bit of window shopping, expecting to see you and they told me you've not been around for a couple of weeks. No one seemed to know why. Everything OK with you?'

'Yes, all's well, thanks. I just decided to take a break, step out for a couple of weeks. I've had a few personal matters to deal with.' I'm careful with what I say, conscious that Abbie could well be listening.

'Ah, I thought as much. How are things? You still married?' asks Gerald, slight concern in his voice.

'Yes. Actually; things are going really well.'

'Good. I'm pleased to hear it. I'm sorry to have missed you today. I was hoping to discuss something with you. Suzie's birthday is coming up and I wanted to get her something nice.'

'I'm assuming you mean something nicer than a box of Milk Tray?'

'Ha, absolutely! I spotted that little white Porsche you had. The 718.'

'Yep, I know the one you mean.'

As I chat with Gerald I spot my box of medication on the counter opposite me,

253

EIGHT MILLION MINUTES

the statins the GP prescribed for my high cholesterol, the very same pills that I pretend are my chemo medication. It was very careless of me, to leave them lying around. I really am becoming complacent. Last week, I organised all my pills into my handy day-of-the-week pill organiser, and now look at them! A box of my so-called 'lifesaving medicine' is sitting haphazardly beside the kettle and an empty pill organiser, receiving the same level of importance as a packet of paracetamol!

Holding my phone in place with my shoulder, I begin the process of sorting a pill into each compartment. I open the drawer under the breakfast bar counter where my small bottle of vitamin D pills - my so-called 'anti-sickness pills' - live. I forgot to take one of those this morning. I remove the cap from the small bottle and add one alongside each 'chemo' pill.

'I'll be back at work next week,' I tell Gerald. 'Why don't you come by and—'

'No, next week's no good. I'm travelling to Italy.'

I can't afford to miss this opportunity. Gerald is my most loyal and lucrative customer. I'm also keen to get rid of that Porsche. Nice as it is, it's not had a single bite. I think quickly. If I want to keep up appearances, I really can't swan off to the showroom right now, but surely a mate popping over can't hurt. If anything, it'll be good for me, for my recovery, to see a friendly face.

Especially if that person is going to make me money.

'Well, if you want a chat why don't you pop over here now? We can discuss some numbers and have a catch-up,' I offer, placing my final pill into the organiser and snapping it shut inside.

'You have coffee?' asks Gerald.

'Of course. Coffee, tea, running water. The full works!'

'All right. As it happens, I'm not all that far from you, so I'll be with you shortly,' Gerald decides, sounding rather chipper.

'OK. See you soon,' I say. I swipe my phone to close the call and put it down on the countertop next to the box of statins, the small bottle of vitamins and the pill organiser.

Abbie comes into the kitchen at that point, and I notice that she's rubbing the back of her neck. I wonder if maybe she's caught whatever it was Ellie had. With any luck, I might catch it too, since it could greatly enhance the conviction of my performance.

'You don't mind if Gerald pops over for a little while, do you?' I ask, unsure whether Abbie will appreciate me bringing work into the house, especially if she's feeling under the weather.

'Shouldn't you be resting, rather than working?' she says, fetching herself a glass and filling it with water from the fridge.

'Oh, it's not really work. It's Gerald. He's a friend. We're going to have a coffee and *if* he brings up buying a car, then so be it.'

Abbie rolls her eyes at me. 'Whatever. I'm off to have a bath,' and she leaves the kitchen holding her glass of water. I don't think she's got the strength to argue today.

Satisfied with my small victory, I pick up my pill organiser and follow Abbie upstairs to change out of my dressing gown and into something presentable.

ABBIE

Like most people, I get headaches from time to time, often if I'm tired or really hungry, but just lately I've had more than my share. What's more, this headache feels different. It's worse, somehow. Even the back of my neck feels stiff today and a pain above my right eye has developed since I got home. As ever, I blame it on the stress of the last few weeks. I just wish the bloody thing would shift.

Despite the discomfort, I enjoyed my soak in the bath. It's still rather early and the sun hasn't even set yet, but I'm ready to call it a night. Before I do that, I need to pop downstairs and take a couple more painkillers. Annoyingly, Gerald is still here, which means I feel obliged to partake in the customary 'hello, how are you?' small-talk ceremony. I feel like utter crap and I'm hardly looking my best, make-up free and dressed in a tracksuit with my hair caught up messily on top of my head.

As I approach the kitchen where the painkillers live, I overhear Jason say, 'Surely Suzie will want to have a test drive?' I knew full well this was never just a social visit.

EIGHT MILLION MINUTES

'No need. If she doesn't like it, we'll exchange it for something else,' I hear Gerald reply casually, and I laugh inwardly at how he can blow thousands of pounds on a car with the same ease as buying a pint of milk. The ridiculousness of it all is never lost on me.

'Hello, Abbie, so lovely to see you.' Gerald rises from his stool at the breakfast bar and takes my hand in his in the way he always does as we kiss the air at the side of each other's cheeks.

'How've you been, Gerald?' I enquire politely although I feel pretty awful.

'Tremendous. Honestly, never better. And yourself?'

'Very well, thanks,' I lie, the pain in my head starting to make me feel even more nauseous than it did earlier.

Gerald takes his seat back on the stool at the breakfast bar, the space now doubling up as Jason's office, with his laptop, notebook and phone all laid out across the work surface along with mugs of coffee and biscuit wrappers. Dressed casually in jeans and a sweatshirt, Jason looks happy and focused. He's in his element. Doing what he loves most, talking cars and making money.

'And Suzie, how's she doing?' I ask, it being only polite to always ask after Gerald's latest flame. Before he has a chance to answer, Jason's mobile rings, the vibration making it buzz on the counter. I can see it's Harry calling. But Jason

SAMANTHA KAY

seems unwilling to talk to his son now he's in the middle of a sale. He flips the phone over, ignoring the incoming call.

'Isn't that Harry?' I ask. 'Don't you think you should take it?'

Jason looks at me, his mouth a hard straight line. I don't care, I won't be put off. He knows as well as I do that no conversation with Harry will ever last more than two, maybe three painful minutes. I widen my stare at him, silently berating him with unspoken words: *It's after work hours, we're at home. Speak to your son!* Surely, he can spare a few minutes for his own flesh and blood.

He finally caves in. Letting out a not-so-subtle huff, he picks up his phone and answers it.

'Hiya Harry, what's up?' he says, badly hiding his impatience. While Harry speaks on the other end, Jason looks up towards the ceiling, his mouth now back in that hard straight line.

'I'm so sorry about this, Gerald. I won't be a second,' and he excuses himself, hopping of the bar stool. 'You know, you can also ask your mum for money. God knows I've given her enough!' Moans Jason as he leaves the kitchen.

'Teenagers,' I say, to which Gerald nods understandingly. He's a nice man. Anyone else might be put out by the interruption.

'Is Jason looking after you? Would you like another drink?' I ask, conscious I'll now need to hold the fort until Jason returns.

'Oh no, I'm fine, thank you. Will you join us for a drink?' Gerald asks in a manner that is so charming, I feel bad that I'm going to decline.

'Usually I'd love to,' I explain, opening the drawer next to Gerald, relieved to see we still have the box of ibuprofen. 'But I've got this horrible headache. I think I'm going to take these and head on up to bed.' And I rattle the little packet of painkillers at Gerald to show him.

It's then I notice Jason's box of chemo pills alongside his bottle of anti-sickness pills sitting amongst the mess on the breakfast bar countertop. Positive they should really be put away somewhere safe and, dare I say it, out of sight, I pick up the box and the bottle and place them in the drawer next to where Gerald is sitting, leaving it open while I fetch myself a glass of water to help me swallow the ibuprofen.

'Dearie me, it's all those biscuits he scoffs, I suspect. That'll do it,' Gerald comments with a playful tut.

'Sorry?' I say, not quite understanding his comment.

'The cholesterol pills. I gather they're Jason's,' Gerald replies, nodding towards the drawer.

'What cholesterol pills?' I ask, bemused as to why exactly Gerald is talking to me about cholesterol.

'The Statin's. I take them too. Cheese; that's my weakness.'

'What are statins?' I ask, snapping my painkillers from the foil and gulping them down with my glass of water. I have no idea what Gerald is banging on about, and frankly, I don't care. I just want Jason to come back so I can go to bed.

'Those pills,' Gerald says patiently, gesturing towards the packet of medication lying in the drawer next to a small bottle containing Jason's anti-sickness pills, 'I take them too, every day. For my cholesterol.' he repeats.

'Oh no, that's not what those pills are for,' I correct him, finally making sense of what Gerald is talking about.

'Yes, they are. Statin's - I've got that exact same box at home. Doctors prescribe them to old men like me with high cholesterol no willpower.' As he speaks, Gerald cheekily reaches for another biscuit.

This man is getting on my nerves. I get the sense he's someone like me, who wants to be right about everything, but in this instance he couldn't be more wrong. Jason doesn't have high cholesterol from too many biscuits. *He has cancer.* I want to scream it, to put Gerald right, but I know I can't. Jason is adamant he doesn't want anyone knowing about his diagnosis, at least not at the moment, and as his wife, I have to respect that decision.

'That's not what those pills are for,' I snap,

creating a distinct awkwardness between us.

'What do I know,' Gerald says and smiles, holding up his hands in surrender, admitting defeat. 'I'm not a pharmacist. I'm sure people take those things for all manner of reasons.'

Having taken my painkillers, I shove the packet of Ibuprofen back in the drawer alongside Jason's pills. I can't say I've paid any attention as to what those pills are called – until now. I look at the box curiously. *Atorvastatin*, that's what's written on the box, in bold black writing. *40mg film-coated tablets. Statin* for short, I guess.

I'm confused but my mind is racing. Gerald certainly seems confident in his knowledge of this medication. He may be old, but he's far from senile. In fact, he's sharp as a tack, smart and eloquent, and I can't get my head around this. How can someone of Gerald's advanced years take one of these pills every day, and experience no visible side-effects? Yet, when Jason takes them, he's sick as a dog. So sick that he has to take a week off work.

I pick up the pills, taking a closer look at the box, and ask: 'When you take these pills, do they make you sick, like physically sick?'

'No, I can't say they do,' Gerald shrugs.

'And how long have you been taking them?'

'Maybe...ten years.'

'Every day?'

'Yes. My high cholesterol is somewhat of

an ongoing problem.' Gerald explains, looking at me with a hint of concern due to the weird atmosphere between us. The poor man's no doubt wondering what on earth he's walked into exactly, and he's not the only one.

Confused and with my curiosity now in overdrive, I open the box and pull out the information leaflet.

'Sorry about that, Gerald. Now, where were we?' I hear Jason say, his voice hearty as he comes back into the kitchen and hops back up on his bar stool looking happier than he did a moment ago. Quickly, I slip the leaflet in the pocket of my tracksuit bottoms, out of sight.

'I'll leave you guys to it,' I say. 'Lovely seeing you, Gerald.'

'Take care, Abbie,' Gerald says kindly.

'I'll be up shortly.' Jason assures me, wrapping an arm loosely around my waist before gently kissing me on the cheek.

I leave them both to talk business while I drag myself up to bed, happy for Jason to take his time, giving me a chance to read over the information in my pocket.

CHAPTER 19

JASON

Well, that was certainly time well spent. It looks like I'll finally be rid of that Porche, Gerald left a happy man, I was able to catch up on some work emails, all while lining my belly with chocolate biscuits. All in all, it's been a very good evening indeed.

I lock up the front and back doors, check the windows are all closed, and before I go up to bed, I pop back into the kitchen to tidy up. I shut my laptop and my notebook. I take the used mugs to the dishwasher, placing them on the top rack and throw the biscuit wrappers in the bin, wincing at quite how many I've eaten. I really need to cut back; a dose of diabetes really is the last thing I want to add to my list of ailments.

With everything looking neat again, I turn off the kitchen light and head upstairs.

Only six more days, I tell myself. Only six more days until everything can return to normal.

Upstairs, I ease the bedroom door open, and I'm surprised to see that Abbie is sitting up and still dressed in her comfy tracksuit.

'Hey, how's your head?' I ask, going and plumping myself down on the bed next to her. She doesn't respond, her head resting against the padded headboard, her gaze fixed on her phone, Daisy curled up lovingly beside her.

'Hey, you OK?' I ask again, playfully poking her in the ribs, bidding for her attention much like a needy toddler.

'Yeah, I'm fine,' she mutters, keeping her eyes on the screen.

I know full well that when my wife says she is *fine,* she is anything but. Maybe she's cross about Gerald coming over. I know she hates it when I bring work home at the best of times, let alone when I'm supposed to be battling cancer and putting my health first. In no mood for a lecture, I head into the ensuite to brush my teeth. Standing in front of the sink, I squeeze some toothpaste onto my electric toothbrush, pop it in my mouth and switch it on. In the mirror I see Abbie enter the bathroom.

Initially I assume she needs to use the loo or the sink, but she simply remains standing in the doorway with her arms crossed. I turn off the toothbrush, muting the loud buzzing.

'What?' I ask, looking at her in the mirror, my mouth full of foam.

'How comes you never mentioned your

cholesterol?'

My heart stops dead in my chest. How does she know about my cholesterol and why is she asking about it? Catching sight of my shocked face in the mirror, I quickly change my expression, afraid of giving anything away.

'What?' I ask, playing dumb, quickly switching the toothbrush back on.

'Do you have high cholesterol?' Abbie asks, moving away from the door and standing next to me at the sink.

I don't answer straight away. Instead, I continue to brush my teeth, hoping if I can drag the activity out long enough, Abbie might tire of waiting and return to the bedroom, but no such luck. She's still standing here, waiting for an answer.

I spit into the sink, rinse and wipe my mouth using the towel next to me.

'I might do. So what? Is it a crime?' I ask, trying to keep things light-hearted.

'No. I just don't understand why you've never mentioned it.'

That's when I notice she's holding a small, folded piece of paper in her hands, the type found in a box of pills - *my* box of pills - telling her all the information I don't want her to know.

'In the grand scheme of things, it's really not important right now,' I say, leaving the bathroom, hoping this will be the end of the matter.

'So, you do have high cholesterol?' Abbie asks again, following closely behind me.

Standing by my chest of drawers I remove my watch and place it down next to a silver framed picture of us taken at the top of the Empire State Building.

'And that's what you take those pills for,' she persists, 'the ones downstairs, in the drawer, under the breakfast bar?'

In reply I half-shrug, half-nod, my mouth releasing a non-word that implies yes but without giving any solid confirmation, the panic inside me rising rapidly.

'So, if those are your cholesterol pills, where are your chemo pills?'

In a flash of inspiration I say, 'There,' pointing to the pill organiser on my bedside table, as I open my top drawer and take out a clean T-shirt. Praying that the sight of the pill organiser will draw a line under this and get me out of a sticky situation. I go back into the bathroom, pull my sweatshirt off over my head, and in the second of darkness, I hear the sound of Abbie's voice once more.

'Those pills. The ones in that box, downstairs in the drawer . . . we sat, in the kitchen *together*, snapping them and placing them in that organiser.'

I can picture her working out the timeline in her head, piecing the short series of events together, making unwelcome sense of it all.

'That was a different box,' I call out, putting on my fresh T-shirt.

'No, no it wasn't. There was only one box, and it was definitely that one.'

I step out of my jeans and pull off my socks, trying desperately not to lose my cool. It's no use. I scrape my small pile of clothes up from the bathroom floor and throw them with some force into the washing basket behind the door. I inhale a deep breath.

Abbie is at the bathroom door, her eyes piercing through me. She's worked it out. I don't know how or why this has suddenly happened, but while I've been downstairs talking cars and eating biscuits, she's been up here, crime-solving. But I can't admit to anything. In just a few short weeks, we've come so far, I can't let it all unravel, not now, not like this. Please God, I can still save us; I can still pull this back.

I wrap my arms around her, and gently stroke the back of her head.

'I think you're tired, and you're getting confused. You need to rest,' I murmur lovingly, but Abbie's having none of it. She pulls away, placing her hands either side of her head, pressing her fingers into her temples in pure frustration.

'Yeah, I am confused, Jason. I'm confused as to why you've been palming off cholesterol pills as chemo bloody therapy!' She looks and sounds as if she's about to burst into tears.

'Honestly, Abbie,' I huff. I lose patience and storm from the bathroom, not wanting to hear another word.

As predicted, she follows me back into the bedroom.

'I'm on loads of pills!' I yell. 'Chemo, anti-sickness, cholesterol. Look!' Yanking open my bedside table, I pull out the surplus vitamin D pills hidden at the back. 'I've even got these ones for vitamin D! What do you want? An inventory!' I cry out, flashing the green box of pills at her before throwing them down on the bed.

'Jason, I swear to God, if you don't tell me what's going on right now—'

'What, Abbie? What are you gonna do? Give Hamza a call? Tell him you want to move out of here and rent a flat!' I roar, my words taking us both by surprise.

Abbie's mouth falls open and her eyes widen in shock. We stare at one another in a stunned silence, as both our secrets finally lay themselves bare in all their twisted truth.

'You fucking sicko,' she utters quietly as everything sinks in, making perfect disturbing sense.

Fucking sicko.

I can't argue with that. Feeling so ashamed, I look down at the floor. I've hit a dead end. There really is nowhere else to go from here.

'How'd you find out about the flat?' asks Abbie, and I can hear the anger in her voice,

EIGHT MILLION MINUTES

making it shake.

Still unable to look at her, I choose to stay silent.

'*Jason!*'

'I used your laptop. One time - when mine was broken. I saw an email.' I'm finally telling the truth.

'You sick bastard.' Abbie's voice is muffled because her hands are covering her mouth, as if in prayer, and I watch as she shuts her eyes tightly and screams all her anger and frustration into her hands.

'I'm sorry!' I shout over her scream, to which Daisy jumps from the bed and runs under it, scared by the argument.

'But – wait a minute,' Abbie says suddenly, dropping her hands from her face, 'you were actually throwing up. You were in the bathroom, being sick. I heard you! You were in bed, shaking with a fever. And the lump, there *was* a lump! I felt it,' she rants, maniacally recounting everything.

'It's just a cyst,' I say dully. 'I had it checked. It's nothing to worry about.' Part of me hopes that the news that I'm not dying after all might, if nothing else, will come as a great relief. Unfortunately, judging by her expression, it doesn't. In fact, her face reddens and I worry she might actually explode.

'So that's what you did. *You pretended it was cancer!*' Abbie screams.

'You were going to leave me!' I cry out, trying to make her understand my predicament.

'And you thought that was the answer! That cancer would make me stay!"

'At least I put in the effort to save our marriage,' I say passionately. 'I didn't sneak around behind your back looking for somewhere else to live!'

'EFFORT!' she screams, then, seething with anger, picks up a pillow from the bed and hurls it in my direction. It doesn't hit me, landing about a foot away from me on the floor.

'That was you putting in an effort!' she bellows, picking up another pillow and charging towards me with it, whacking it hard across my torso and shoulders. 'You could have just turned up to the theatre on time, Jason! Or made it home for dinner once in a while. It would have been a lot less fucking *effort*!'

Concerned about what Abbie might throw at me next, I step out of the line of fire and head towards the door, but not before saying my piece.

'Oh well, sorry I might have missed dinner once in a while!' I shout from the bedroom doorway. '*I have to work*. People need me, people are relying on me!' And I thump down the stairs, wanting to put some distance between us, in the hope it will calm things down.

'You sell expensive cars to rich old men. You're hardly curing cancer!' She's right behind me.

EIGHT MILLION MINUTES

'No, but it keeps the roof over our heads!' I shout. When I charge into the living room. I look at the sofa with some angst, concerned by the number of cushions on it, worried Abbie might use them as further target practise. She's still hot on my heels, neither of us ready to wrap this up yet.

'And you know what?' I go on. 'I don't hear you complaining about any of this.' My arms outstretched, I gesture to the luxury and opulence that lie before us. 'The house, the holidays, the cars!'

'I never wanted any of this,' Abbie argues.

I snort in derision. '*Everybody* wants this! The comfort, the security, the options.' I don't believe a word that just came out of her mouth, furious about how bloody ungrateful she is being.

'All I've ever wanted was you. But you're never here. And even when you are, your head is elsewhere.'

'What do you want from me!' I shout, dramatically shaking my hands in front of my face, at an absolute loss as to how to please this woman.

Abbie stands before me. She anxiously licks her lips. Her cheeks redden and I notice he pretty blue eyes pool with tears.

'I just…'. She says, inhaling a jagged breath, 'I want it like it used to be. Before all this.' Fleetingly looking around the room, tears fall from her eyes.

'Fuck me, Abbie.' Exhausted, I drop down onto the sofa. Sick of competing with this distorted past version of us she holds onto so dearly. 'You look back at it as if it was a big romantic adventure. And it wasn't. We had nothing. It was awful. It was so hard.'

'But I was happy then,' she tells me, her voice high and strained. Her words hit me like a bulldozer, as she stands there blissfully unaware of just how hurtful and insulting she's being.

I place my elbows on my knees and bury my head in my hands. 'Well, I'm sorry,' I say in a choked voice. I'm so, so tired. I look at Abbie, and she's crying properly now - tears streaming, nose running, using the sleeve of her top to wipe her eyes.

'I'm so sorry I've worked so hard to give us so much and it made you so fucking miserable!'

Feeling agitated I climb to my feet, my nervous energy needing somewhere to go, I start to pace the room.

'Maybe you should give your mate Hamza a call!' I sneer, my ego having taken an almighty pounding.

'Maybe I will. Maybe I'll call him first thing,' Abbie says through her tears, confidently calling my bluff.

'Good, you do that!'

'I will,' Abbie fires back.

'Why were you looking at such dingy flats

anyway?' I want to know. 'You would have got half of everything.' I'm genuinely baffled. Why is Abbie suddenly so keen to be a martyr?

'I'm not Kelly. I'm not out to destroy you.'

'How very noble of you.'

A heavy silence falls between us, the only sound that of Abbie sniffing. There's really not much else to say, and feeling utterly exhausted, I decide to step out. I think we both need some space from each other, and I for one need a stiff drink. I walk past Abbie, and as I reach the living-room doorway on my way to the kitchen, she speaks.

'I want a divorce,' she says, her words clear and assertive, stopping me dead.

I know we've just thrown a lot around, both of us, but surely none of it was serious, not really. We've rowed before. In sixteen years, we've both said horrible things we didn't mean, but never, *never* has the word 'divorce' been uttered.

I turn to look at her. Standing straight and confident in the centre of the room, her tear-stained face stern, her eyes looking at me with such conviction, I know she's deadly serious.

'You don't mean that.' And I can't recall a moment in my life where I ever felt as frightened as I do right now.

'Yes, I do. I'm not happy. I haven't been for ages.'

'I know that, Abbie, I know that now. And

I've been trying, I really have.'

Despite everything that's just happened, I really did believe we were finally in a better place. That our love was strong enough to keep us on track. I go over and take her hands in mine, her perfect soft hands, and hold onto them tightly, kissing each one.

'That's why I did what I did,' I say, desperately trying to make her understand.

But Abbie shakes her hands free from mine and takes a step back as if she can't bear to be near me, to be touched by me.

'What, you thought a good dose of emotional blackmail would save our marriage? Really? Do you even realise how messed up that is - pretending to have cancer!'

'I know I shouldn't have done it.' My own eyes are starting to pool with tears, brought on by the fear of losing her. It can't end, not like this.

I embrace her, holding her in my arms, burying my face in her hair, her lovely clean smelling hair.

'I can't lose you, Abbie. I can't,' I sob, clasping her to me, but she fails to hug me back, keeping her arms firmly by her side, making her stance clear.

'I love you. I can change. I have changed,' I plead.

She says nothing. Gives me nothing. I can feel her crying into my shoulder, my t-shirt quickly becoming damp from her tears, her body gently shaking as she sobs.

I let her go, and in an act of pure desperation, I drop to my knees in front of her, taking her hands in mine again.

'Abbie, all I have ever done is put you first. All of this, *everything*, it's for you, it's all for you. Our home, the showroom. You are the reason for all of it.' I am pleading with her to understand.

She shakes her head. 'You still don't get it. I don't care about the house and I don't give a shit about the showroom. It's not important.'

And as much as I love her, and as desperate as I am for her to change her mind, her words make me furious.

'What - you don't give a shit about the showroom? My livelihood, *our* survival, isn't important to you?' I demand, frustrated, unable to understand her way of thinking. I climb to my feet, tired of going round and round in circles with her.

'No, you're twisting my words,' she says immediately, back-pedalling, but I'm too angry to let it go.

I know I've made mistakes; I know I've done wrong. I know I need to be at home more and be more present. But I can't quite fathom a world where she believes our livelihood isn't important. The very thing I've poured my heart and soul into, the very thing that keeps us from starving, isn't important.

'Then what *do* you mean exactly? What *do*

SAMANTHA KAY

you want, Abbie? Do you want me to be more like you, is that it? Should I let my business fail too - would that make you happy? Then we could both be failures together!' I jeer at her, trying to make her see how ridiculous and also how bloody rude she's being.

'Oh, fuck you!' she shouts in my face. Then she charges past me, knocking into me with her shoulder as she marches out of the living room and runs up the stairs. 'You're going to die rich and alone, and I hope you'll be very happy with yourself!'

'Oh, don't you worry, I'll be ecstatic!' I bellow back as the sound of our bedroom door slamming shut echoes through the house, followed by a loud thud, no doubt the sound of something being thrown on the floor.

Then silence.

I stand alone in the living room, quivering with shock, knowing I went too far. I shouldn't have mocked her like that. I shouldn't have let my ego and temper get the better of me. I should apologise. For the sake of my marriage I *need* to grovel at her feet.

I charge out of the living room and up the stairs. Standing outside the bedroom door, I can feel my heart beating furiously in my chest. I feel nervous and in truth, I still feel really fucking angry. I need a moment to calm down. We both do. If I go in there now, it could make everything worse - if that's even possible. I stand and listen at the door for a moment. I can't hear anything. No crying, no banging around or any more objects being thrown, which I take as a positive.

Then, feeling utterly drained, I let my tired feet guide me back down the stairs towards the kitchen in search of a stiff drink.

CHAPTER 20

JASON

I can't sleep. It's 2.30 a.m. and I've been lying wide awake in the spare room for hours, dwelling over every sorry shot fired between us and every terrible decision I've made. After pouring myself a whisky to take the edge off, I sat in the kitchen for quite some time and had the good sense to draft a sincere and heartfelt apology in my head which I plan to deliver in the morning.

Eventually I decided to call it a night. I came in here hoping to get some much-needed rest, but it seems my brain isn't ready to switch off. We've had some rows over the years, but never anything like the one we had tonight. The more I think about things, the less I believe we can work this out, but I can't give up hope, not yet.

In the morning, we'll both have calmed down. The worst of the storm will have passed and maybe, just maybe, we'll be able to sit down and talk like grown-ups.

EIGHT MILLION MINUTES

I turn onto my side and close my eyes, replaying our recent trip to Rosewood Cottage in my mind. We had so much fun. It can't be denied how much love we still share. We're good together. *It can't be over,* I tell myself, clinging to bleak hope.

Just as I feel my body begin to relax, a loud meow startles me.

Daisy!

She does this from time to time. Meows in the dead of night for no apparent reason. Keen to get some rest, I ignore her. I snuggle down into the duvet, begin to settle, and that's when she meows again. My eyes flash open. That one was really loud. I bet she's been out night-hunting and has caught something - a mouse, most likely. Usually, she's far too lazy and spoilt to bother with hunting, but every now and then she gets the urge, and is always keen to show off her prizes.

She meows again, that one unusually deep, nothing like her usual call for attention. Worried she might be hurt, I climb out of bed. Her meowing has now become constant, every call getting louder than the last. I patter down the landing, following her calls to our bedroom.

I huff, unsure as to why Abbie won't open the door to let her out. Probably just to annoy me!

I turn the handle on the bedroom door and gently push it open, but I can't.

Somethings blocking the door. Daisy is

still meowing, pawing at the door to get out, but I can't get it open.

Has Abbie barricaded herself in?

I knock gently.

'Abbie, I can't get the door open,' I say in a hushed tone, although I'm unsure as to why I'm keeping my voice down. Abbie can't possibly be asleep with all the racket Daisy's making.

Putting some weight behind my shoulder, I push on the door, but it hardly moves.

'It's OK, it's OK,' I say calmly, trying to pacify Daisy who's becoming stressed, her clawing against the door becoming frantic.

'Abbie, can you open the door!' I say, my voice louder.

I wait a second, hoping she will respond, but there's no sound of Abbie moving around inside, just Daisy's meowing.

Something's definitely not right.

I start to panic. Using the side of my body, I shove all my weight onto the door and feel whatever's blocking it move enough for Daisy to escape through the gap, almost flying across the landing and racing down the stairs. I manage to push the door open a little more, just enough to allow my own body to slide into the dark bedroom, and instantly notice the empty bed. Abbies not in it.

Finally, on the other side of the door, I look down to see what's blocking it.

I freeze in horror.

It's Abbie. She's lying on her side on the floor, her head resting by the corner of the door. I drop to my knees beside her.

'Abbie, Abbie, are you ok?'

Her eyes are closed, her lips parted. She's still wearing her tracksuit from earlier.

I take her shoulders in my hands and gently shake her, but her head lolls back and her body is stiff.

'Abbie? Abbie, wake up. Wake up, Abbie.' I plead, 'It's me. It's Jason.' I try to rest her head on my lap, wanting to make her comfortable, but her body is heavy like a piece of furniture refusing to budge.

'Abbie, wake up. Please wake up Abbie.' I beg.

I shake her shoulders again, more vigorously, desperately trying to wake her, willing her to respond in some way.

'Abbie,' I sob, tears of panic streaming down my face. 'Abbie, wake up. Please wake up, Abbie, please.'

With the back of my hand, I stroke her face, trying to comfort her, to rouse her, to reassure her of my presence.

Her skin is cold.

Well, no wonder, I tell myself. She's been lying on this cold hard floor for God knows how long. I clasp one of her hands in mine. It's cold, her hand is stiff, the fingers curved slightly downwards in a claw. I sandwich her hand between mine and rub it vigorously between my palms, trying to warm her up, to wake her up, but it's not working. Nothing is working.

I need to get help. My phone, it's in the spare room.

I don't want to, but I let go of her hand and climb to my feet. I rush over to the bed and grab the duvet, pull it off the bed and bring it to her on the floor. I cover her, tucking it round her to keep out the draughts.

She's so cold, I need to keep her warm.

'It's OK, you're going to be OK.' I say, struggling to get my words out, my voice shaking and my teeth chattering in fear. 'I'm going to get you some help. I won't be long, I promise. I promise I won't be long.' I wipe my tears away. She can't see me panic, it'll make her panic too. We both need to stay calm.

'I love you,' I say, kissing her hair, tucking the duvet under her chin, making sure she's comfy.

With a surge of adrenaline rushing through my body, I slide myself back out of the room through the partially opened door, careful it doesn't hit her head, and hurry down the landing to the spare room in search of my phone. I tap the emergency button and almost immediately I'm asked what service I require.

'Ambulance. It's my wife, she's cold and unresponsive. We need some help,' I beg them, racing back to the bedroom with the phone, desperate to be by Abbie's side, not wanting her to be alone.

CHAPTER 21

JASON

'It's a big day tomorrow. Your big day. Funny things really, funerals. You get this great big party thrown in your honour, and you're the only person who doesn't get to see it. All seems a bit daft really.

'The kids have helped a lot. They've been amazing . . . they've really stepped up; surprisingly. It seems maybe we were doing something right, after all. Although I'm not sure I should take too much of the credit, considering how much I was never around.

'Harry took charge of the music. I told him about the Taylor Swift song, the one about the nice dress and the sunset. The funeral people said you could have two songs, so I suggested House of Pain "Jump Around". I'm not sure your parents will approve, but sod them. We loved that song. It's going to play along to a slideshow of pictures. Harry sorted that too. We sat in the kitchen for ages, the three of us, looking over old

EIGHT MILLION MINUTES

photos. You would have loved that. There were so many.

'Ellie helped me with the flowers. She was adamant to get you exactly what you wanted: the white roses and the pink daisy things. I know you weren't so bothered about charity donations, but I've encouraged it anyway. I came across this brain charity. It's a good one. They help people who've suffered brain aneurysms and their families. It seemed like the right thing to do . . . after everything that's happened.

'If I hadn't been so wrapped up in myself maybe I would have spotted the signs. Your headaches. The stress I put you under. I read how a burst of anger can cause an aneurysm to rupture. Ever since I read that . . . I can't get it out of my mind. Because I know it's all my fault. For how angry I made you that night.

'I stood outside the door. I stood outside, ready to go in and apologise. And I think about that all the time. The doctors told me it wouldn't have made any difference. That you were already gone. That so few people survive those kinds of ruptures in the brain. But it haunts me. That whole day haunts me.

'I worry that you were scared or in pain.

'I hate that you were alone. The doctors told me that you wouldn't have known anything, that it would have just been like a light going out, but that doesn't make me feel any better. There's so much I would have done differently. I can't believe those were the last words we said to each other. If I'd known, I would have told you how much I love you. How wonderful you are, how important you are.

'It all feels so surreal. As if it's some kind of bad dream.

'There's this moment in the mornings, when I wake up, and just for a second, I forget what's happened. I roll over in bed and when I see your side is empty, I realise you're gone, and it breaks me so bad every single time I have to get out of the house. It's too early to work and I'm struggling to focus, so I go for a run, just so I don't have to be in the house alone without you. I don't enjoy it. It gives me this pain in my side, and it hurts my ankles, but I welcome the distraction.

'I'm dreading tomorrow. It all feels too final. After tomorrow, once it's over, there's no more. As if the very last piece of you will be gone.

'I'm so sorry. For everything. But please know, I did what I did because I love you so much. I did everything I could to try and make us right. The irony is that whatever I did, whatever lengths I went to, you were never destined to stay.

'I hope we do you proud tomorrow in a way I couldn't when you were here. I got you something, some photographs - just a little something to keep with you. Ellie chose them. One of you and Daisy, she misses you very much.

She keeps meowing at the front door, waiting for you to come home. And one of the four of us, on the beach in Cancun at sunset. It's a lovely photo. We all look surprisingly happy, considering it wasn't our best holiday. But it's not about the best memories, is it, it's about *all* the memories. Every shared minute that wrote our story, all eight million of them.'

I lift the thin lace covering over the open coffin and place the pictures between her hands, her perfect and lifeless hands. Abbie looks beautiful, peaceful, exactly how she wished. She's wearing a nice dress - the light blue one with the flowers on it - her hair and make-up are perfect, with red lips and rosy cheeks, just like in the song.

Through flooded eyes, I absorb her, unable to comprehend it will be for the very last time.

'We'll always be with you. And you'll always be with us. I love you,' I choke, replacing the lace cover and finally breaking down. Then I back away, knowing if I don't leave now, I never will.

Outside in the corridor of the funeral home, the daylight hurts my burning eyes after the lamplit quiet. Wiping my soaking face with my hand, I take a deep breath, trying and failing to pull myself together, and stand alone in the corridor, crying my heart out. Just when I'm about ready to fall to my knees, I feel two sets of arms wrap themselves around me, keeping me safe.

'It's OK, Dad. We're here,' Harry says.

I rest my weeping head on his shoulder, as each of my children hold me tightly.

'Come on, Dad. Let's go home,' Ellie says through her own tears, her simple words filling me with dread. The idea of returning home without Abbie crushing me further.

In what feels like an absolute blur, the three of us walk out of the funeral home. Standing on the busy street outside, we weep together, each of us holding the others up, my heart shattered beyond repair.

CHAPTER 22

JASON

I feel numb. I stand alone at the open garden door with a bottle of beer held loosely in my hand, looking over our lush green lawn. A warm soft breeze blows through.

It really is a beautiful day. The sky is blue, not a cloud in sight. The sun is shining, the birds are singing, the world oblivious to the ungodly sadness my day has endured.

By some miracle I made it through the service. It was by far the most difficult thing I've ever had to do. Being eleven years older than Abbie, I always assumed I'd be the first to go, and I was pretty comfortable with that. In fact, I'd never prepared myself for it being the other way around. I never imagined that *I* would be the one saying goodbye. That I would be the one left alone in this great big house, with a great big hole in my heart.

Our home is currently full of people. At the time it seemed like the easier option, holding

SAMANTHA KAY

the wake here rather than scouring around for the perfect venue, but now I'm starting to regret it. As much as I hate being in the house alone, I just want everyone to leave. I cannot endure all these people with their sympathetic eyes and pained smiles trolling around our home, least of all Abbie's parents.

I spot them – there they are at the end of the garden, standing beside Gerald and Suzie, making polite conversation. Abbie's dad nods intermittently between subtle glances at Suzie's inflated chest, while her mum picks at her plate of food.

Right now, the very sight of them makes me so angry I must stop myself from saying or doing something I'll regret. The kids told me I'm unfairly projecting my own anger and grief onto them, and they may well be right, but I think it's more than that. I witnessed it, the years of radio silence, the unnecessary sadness and pain they gave Abbie, the unfair shame they poured on our relationship. If I had it my way, I wouldn't have invited them at all, but I'm going through this phase whereby I try to do the right thing and be a better person. So, here they are, in my house, drinking my tea and eating my food, as if they're the ones whose world has fallen apart.

When Abbie's mum looks over at me and smiles I look straight through her, pretending not to notice. I see her tap Abbie's dad on the arm and nod towards me, implying she wants to

EIGHT MILLION MINUTES

come over. I snarl and turn around in search of a quiet corner. As I move further into the kitchen, which is bustling with people, I bump into Molly and Mas.

'We're going to head off,' Molly announces, issuing me with a sympathetic smile.

Music to my ears. With any luck this should mark the start of a mass exodus.

'Sorry to be leaving so early. I have to be at work in an hour,' Mas says apologetically.

'Not at all, thank you both for coming. It means a lot,' I say, and it's true, even if I am struggling to speak.

'It was a lovely day, really beautiful. She would have loved it,' Molly says, her voice tight, getting choked up, at which Mas wraps an arm around her waist and smiles at her tenderly.

I clear my own throat. 'Thank you. Listen, I'm sorry I don't have more news at the moment regarding the shop, Molly.' *Daisy's* has remained closed since Abbie's death. Right now, I'm not sure what to do with it - another decision in a long list of things I've yet to tackle.

'It's fine, I understand,' she nods.

'I promise to keep you updated, whatever the outcome,' I say, unable to offer her anything right now other than my word.

'Thanks. Anyway, we've decided to go travelling this summer, so . . .'

'Ah.' That makes me feel a little better. It takes the pressure off, knowing that Molly won't

SAMANTHA KAY

be waiting around for answers. 'Lovely. Where to?' I ask.

'Cuba.' And she smiles.

'It's literally the only semi-appealing communist country. What does that tell you?' Mas says to me, seeking agreement.

'That's not true. What about China?' protests Molly.

'Here we go again.' Mas rolls his eyes and grins.

I laugh. 'I'm sure you'll both have a great time,' I say, feeling envious. They're young and in love. They have it all ahead of them. They have no idea how lucky they are.

'Thanks again, Jason.' Molly steps forward to give me a hug. 'Abbie was a really good person. I'm really going to miss her.'

'Yeah. Me too.' I start to well up.

Molly lets go and I see behind her thick-lensed glasses that her eyes are bloodshot and full of tears.

'Thanks for coming.' I shake Mas's hand, trying to hold myself together a bit longer. 'I'll be in touch, Molly.'

'OK, take care.' And they turn to leave.

At that moment, I notice Abbie's mother from the corner of my eye. She is speaking to one of the caterers, handing over a plate. As she starts to turn in my direction, I place my empty beer bottle down on the counter and hurry out of the kitchen and into the hallway, where I'm instantly jumped on by my parents. Standing with Harry, they're each holding a plate stacked high with food from the buffet. *Of course,* I silently remind Abbie, *they do love a funeral.*

'Jason, poppet. How you doing?' asks my mum, releasing a hand from her plate to grip my hand in hers. I can't escape. Mum is wearing her black pantsuit, the good one she said she saves for funerals. Her blonde hair is freshly blow-dried and her nails are manicured. Mum is always very well turned out, but today she looks a little weary, as if the shock and sadness of the past few weeks has taken its toll, aging her overnight.

'Never better,' I reply dryly, to which Mum squeezes my hand even tighter. I worry she's about to drop her plate, so I take it from her.

'Harry told us you've been going running in the mornings,' she says with such seriousness I'm worried she's about to tell me off.

'Yes, that's right,' I answer sheepishly.

'Good. It's about time you did some exercises,' she says, finally letting go of me.

I pick up a finger sandwich from Mum's plate, debating whether or not to take a bite. I haven't eaten for hours, grief zapping my appetite.

'And you, young man, you're looking after your dad, aren't you?' she asks Harry briskly.

'Course,' he grunts, with a small nod.

For years I've worried about Harry. About

SAMANTHA KAY

his lack of personality and conversation skills, but over the last few weeks, I think it might have become the thing I love most about him. Looking terribly grown up in his black suit and tie, he's been a great help to me of late. He came with me to the undertakers, organised the slideshow of pictures for Abbie's service, and every morning he swings by, even going out of his way before college to make me a breakfast of toast and jam and a black coffee when I get back from my run. He'll sit with me, making sure I've eaten, and through it all, at no point does he burden me with inane conversation.

My boy is smart, caring, strong - and silent. With all the noise going on in my head right now, he's exactly the type of presence I need. He's perfect; my boy is perfect. I just can't believe I didn't realise it sooner.

'Remember Auntie Connie's friend Maggie?' Mum says, taking her plate back from me and handing me another sandwich so I have one in each hand.

'No,' I say, finally eating the cheese one.

'Yes, you do. Eddie, tell him.'

Dad also looks very smart today, if a little hot. It's a warm day and he hasn't taken off his suit jacket or loosened his tie. His face is red, his balding head shiny from sweat, but he seems happy enough.

'Maggie. She's friends with auntie Connie.' Says dad, his mouth full.

'Still, no.' I say, deciding to eat the second sandwich. Egg and cress. It's ok, two tiny finger sandwiches about all the food I can handle for now.

'Well, her mum is on the way out. We'll certainly be at her funeral before the year's done. So do give me the details of your caterers, so I can recommend them. Because these quiches are the best we've had, aren't they, Eddie.' Mum pops a mini-quiche into her mouth, closing her eyes and savouring the moment.

'The best. By. A. Country. Mile,' Dad agrees, his mouth still full, splattering quiche over us in his declaration whilst issuing a very exaggerated hand gesture to show his approval.

I look at Harry. Trying to stifle a laugh he takes a sip from his drink.

'Coming from you both . . . and with your *vast* experience . . . that really means a lot,' I chuckle, wishing with all my heart that Abbie was here to witness and enjoy this ridiculous conversation.

Mum swallows the mini-quiche and sighs in pleasure. 'You want us to stay behind, help you tidy up?' she asks.

'No thanks, it's fine, it's all taken care of,' I assure her.

'Me and Ellie are staying tonight. We'll get it done,' Harry states, and I wish I could just pick him up and squeeze him, like I could when he was little.

'You're a good boy,' Mum says, lovingly looping her arm through her grandson's.

'Jason.'

I turn and feel my heart sink to my toes when I see Abbie's parents standing behind me. I've done well to avoid them all day, but no doubt it was naïve of me to think they wouldn't corner me at some stage, and corner me they have. In the hallway with nowhere to go, I'm well and truly trapped.

'Could we have a word?' her father asks, conveying an air of authority.

'Come on, poppet. Let's give your dad some privacy,' says Mum, ushering Harry and Dad away.

I look at Abbie's parents, standing before me like two steel bollards blocking my way. Abbie certainly had a strong resemblance to her mother, Maxine. They share the same round-shaped face, delicate nose and blue eyes, but unlike Abbie's, Maxine's eyes lack any warmth. They're ice-cold.

Her father, Tony, isn't any better. He's taller and broader than I am, which might be intimating to some, but he doesn't scare me. There's an uneasiness to him, as if he hasn't quite worked out how to assert himself. He still has a fair amount of hair for a man of his age, all of it grey. Tony pushes his glasses back onto his nose and slips his hands in his trouser pockets. He then gives a quick glance behind himself, as if worried the wrong person is about to overhear a dark secret.

He clears his throat before saying: 'I know it's been a long time, and I'm sorry it's taken an event as sad as this to bring us together. We're grateful to you for getting in touch and inviting us into your home.'

For a moment or two, I feel sorry for them. Today, my home is full of the people who loved Abbie, and the people she loved in return. She shared her life with these people, made all kinds of memories with them, and yet the very couple who created her don't know a single person here. They've spent the entire day awkwardly hovering on the periphery, and although it's entirely their own doing, a part of me does indeed feel a tiny amount of pity towards them, for all the memories they missed out on and all the ones that will never be.

'There are some things we need to talk to you about,' Maxine says, taking over.

What more is there to discuss? I've already shared all the information I have regarding Abbie's postmortem. However, standing before me are two people who have just lost their daughter. I expect it makes sense for them to have questions, and it would be wrong for me to deny them the answers.

'OK,' I nod.

Tony sighs. He pulls his hands out from his trouser pockets and, shifting his weight from

SAMANTHA KAY

one foot to the other, he looks over his shoulder again.

'Tony, just do it. Ask him!' barks Maxine and I'm taken aback by how abrupt she is.

'I want to retire. We have debts. Some large debts.'

'Just get to the point,' my horrible mother-in-law presses him.

'Yeah, Tony, why don't you just get straight to the point,' I say, staring him dead in the eye, my hackles well and truly up as the true nature of this conversation starts to reveal itself.

'The money left to Abigail by Maxine's father, it was a large amount,' Tony says.

'It was sizable,' I agree, my voice quiet. It's taking all my strength not to push this sorry excuse of a man to the floor. But I can't have a brawl here, not at my beloved wife's funeral.

'Look, I'm a realist,' he goes on, trying to seem reasonable, 'and I'm sure you've spent some of it on that café thing she had. But that money, it was never Abigail's in the first place.' He looks nervously at his wife, who glowers at us both.

'That's right. It was her grandfather's money and he wanted *Abbie* to have it,' I say, doing well to keep my cool.

'That money, that was mine - *my* inheritance,' Maxine hisses, all her rage and anguish rising to the surface. I watch as her cheeks flush and her eyes fill with unshed tears, showing more raw emotion in my hallway than

299

she did at her daughter's service.

'We're reasonable people, Jason. We're not asking for the full amount, just whatever's left. I mean, it's not as if you need it.' Tony looks around and throws a hand flippantly into the air, clearly believing the 'offer' on the table to be perfectly straightforward, unable to see how inappropriate this conversation is, at his child's funeral, for God's sake!

During my career, I've dealt with many people with many different temperaments. Even when dealing with the most difficult of customers, I take great pride in the fact that I've never lost my cool with anyone, not once. But today, these two sorry specimens are testing my patience like never before.

'What I need right now is for you to get out of my house,' I say quietly and with the utmost seriousness.

'Oh, come on, Jason, we're not asking for anything other than what we're owed,' Tony blusters, his voice raised, his own temper starting to show.

'Owed!' I exclaim, seeing red, unable to hold back a moment longer. 'Owed! What do you want - compensation? Abbie was my wife! Her life wasn't some kind of accident you can make a claim against!' I shout.

'She was our daughter before she was ever your wife,' Maxine shouts back.

'Oh, so today she's your daughter, is that

300

SAMANTHA KAY

right? What about all the other days? All the years spent ignoring her, branding her a slut and a whore? You shut the door in her face and broke her heart!' I scream, finally letting rip all the things I've wanted to say for the past sixteen years. For all that time I stayed quiet, for Abbie's sake, worried that speaking up would make matters worse, but now, well . . . Abbie's gone, my life is in pieces, and there really is nothing in the world I can say or do that will make things any worse than they are right now.

'She broke our hearts too,' her mother bursts out. 'What do you think it was like for us, having to explain how our daughter wrecked a marriage. Was shacked up with some older man with two kids he'd deserted. We couldn't hold our heads up! You can't imagine the shame and embarrassment she brought us,' Maxine explodes, contempt oozing from her.

Shuddering, I feel nothing but disgust for these two people, who after *everything*, still can't look past their own outdated and pathetic hang-ups.

'Abbie wasn't an embarrassment,' I say steadily. 'She was wonderful, she was everything, and all you're obsessed by is some old argument about a sum of money that was never yours to begin with. Do you even care that she's dead!' I start to feel out of control, unsure what will happen next. I can't breathe.

'Dad. Are you ok?' It's Ellie, and the sound

of her voice brings me back to myself. It seems my outburst has generated quite the audience. Packed into my hallway, a dozen or so worried faces gaze on at the spectacle I've created. Standing front and centre are Ellie and Harry, looking sad and worried.

Furious that Abbie's parents should cause any further anguish to my children, I assert myself and take charge.

'Everything's fine. Abbie's parents were just leaving,' I say.

But Maxine and Tony have no intention of leaving. With their business unfinished, they hold their ground, silently refusing to budge.

Ready to take matters into my own hands, I employ a strength I didn't know I had. Throwing a hand on each of their backs, I manage to turn them around, march them past Ellie and Harry and towards the front door.

'Get your hands off me! I'll call the police,' shouts Tony as I clumsily man-handle him and Maxine.

In what feels like an absolute blur, I somehow manage to keep hold of them both, open the door, shove them out and slam the door shut again. I stand for a second, feeling rather proud - that is, until I look down the hallway and see my shocked and silent audience.

Ashamed of the scene I've created I decide to remove myself from the situation. I march towards the kitchen, manoeuvring my way past the caterers and the hovering guests. I open the drawer where I keep my keys, take those belonging to the Lamborghini along with my work keys and leave, charging back through the hallway.

'Dad! Where are you going?' calls Ellie as I head towards the front door.

Unsure of the answer, I don't reply. I open the door and rush out, needing to get out of this house. Keeping my head down, I stumble towards the garage and press down on my key fob to open the door, ducking under as it slowly opens. I unlock the Lamborghini and jump inside, the roaring sound of the engine igniting a feeling of comfort and familiarity. For a few short seconds I feel a little better.

Driving carefully, I edge the car out of the garage and onto the drive. But once off the driveway and on to the street, I put my foot down, racing away from the house like a getaway driver fleeing the scene of a crime. At the same time, I turn up the volume on the radio, and under the afternoon's warm sunshine, I speed down the street in a desperate attempt to escape my devastation.

CHAPTER 23

JASON

Back at the house at last, with the car and myself in one piece, I suppose I should feel guilty about leaving in the way I did, but I don't. If anything, I hate the fact I've had to return. The only thing pulling me back was the thought of Harry and Ellie left here alone, worrying about where I'd gone, what I planned to do - or if I had had an accident.

As it happened, I simply drove, not knowing where I was headed, until the car took me to the showroom. Naturally, the place stood empty and closed today, making it the perfect place to be. With not a soul around, I let myself in, made a coffee, had a cry at my desk and unashamedly caught up on some work. Eventually I left, taking the longer route home, willingly sitting in busy traffic; anything to delay my return.

It's now early evening and as I insert my key into the front door, it swings open, almost causing me to fall through the doorway. On the other side of the door stands Harry, holding a black bin bag.

'Where have you been?' he snaps.

'I went for a drive.'

'You've been gone hours!'

'I know. I'm sorry, I needed to clear my head.' I feel like a naughty child, having not expected to be pounced on and chastised before making it through the door.

Harry sighs and skulks back into the house, finally allowing me to cross the threshold. The house is quiet, and I am relieved to see that every guest has left.

'Where's your sister?' I call to Harry.

'In the bath,' he replies curtly. I think I've upset him.

Satisfied that everything is as well as it can be, and keen to avoid a further telling-off, I opt for the solace of the living room. I walk in, and immediately any sense of relief is evaporated by the sight of Kelly. Standing with a cloth in her hand, looking thoughtfully at the framed pictures on the windowsill.

'Oh, for God's sake. What are *you* doing here?' I blurt out. She's not dressed as if she came by to help with the cleaning. Not when she's done up to the nines in high heels, tight jeans and a white blazer.

'So nice to see you too,' she replies sarcastically, at which point Harry enters the living room, still clutching his black bin bag.

'Why didn't you tell me your mum was

EIGHT MILLION MINUTES

here?' I ask, unable to hide my annoyance.

Harry shrugs, picks up some used napkins from the coffee table and throws them into his bin bag, offering nothing in the way of an explanation.

'Phone you, did they? Fill you in on all the drama?' I say, slumping myself down on the sofa.

'No, actually. I was passing and I thought to pop in. I wanted to check you were OK.' Kelly has picked up a framed photograph of Abbie, taken on holiday about three years ago, looking tipsy and just a little sunburnt. Proudly holding a Pina Colada up to the camera, she has one of those tiny cocktail umbrellas tucked behind her ear.

'Since when do you care if I'm OK,' I scoff. It's hard to believe her visit is a selfless act of kindness.

'I'll tell you what, Jason, why don't we try and be nice to each other. Just this once?' suggests Kelly.

I lift my head and look at her. She has put the photo down and is no longer looking at the pictures, but over at me. There's a softness in her eyes that seems genuine, if most unusual. Unable to cope with more conflict today, I decide to accept the olive branch being handed to me.

'Harry, have you offered your mother a drink?'

'I'll have a coffee, darling,' Kelly says. 'Make one for your dad too.'

306

SAMANTHA KAY

Harry nods dutifully. He picks up a couple of empty glasses, then he and his bin bag leave the living room.

'The kids didn't phone me, but they did tell me what happened with Abbie's parents,' Kelly explains. She takes a seat next to me on the sofa, keeping a notable distance, reflecting the ever-present unease between us.

'It wasn't one of my finest hours,' I try to joke. 'Manhandling two pensioners.'

'I'm sorry I missed it,' says Kelly, at which we both laugh. 'How are you?' she asks.

The truth is, I feel like shit. However, the dark complexity surrounding my grief isn't something I care to get into right now, especially not with my ex-wife, so I choose to stay silent on the matter.

'I still can't believe it. She was so young. She seemed so . . . healthy.' Kelly gestures at the happy smiling picture of Abbie. 'You really had no idea anything was wrong?' Her penetrating gaze makes me feel uncomfortable.

'She'd complained of headaches for a few days before,' I manage, but need to take a moment before carrying on.

'Apparently a brain aneurysm can sit there for a while, undetected. It's like a ticking time bomb. It's not until there's a problem, a rupture, that you'd even know it's there. And by then it's often too late,' I tell Kelly, surprised I was able to say all that without breaking down.

'So, there's really nothing they could have done?'

'They said even if she'd survived the rupture, she wouldn't have been OK. She'd have been left with serious brain damage.' I pause and bite down on my bottom lip. 'I felt as if they were implying that death was the better option. But I would have taken any option over this.'

Unable to hold it together any longer, I crack right there on the sofa, all my pain pouring out of me like a burst pipe.

'I would have got her help. The best help, the best care. I would have looked after her,' I say through each painful sob before burying my head in my hands, wishing I could disappear.

I feel Kelly shuffle herself a little closer. She places her hand on the top of my arm and rubs it gently.

'I know. I'm so sorry, Jase. I really am.'

Kelly and I aren't friends. The truth is, we can't stand one another. Since we broke up, we've never been able to move past the most basic level of civility for the sake of the kids. Is she really here as an act of sympathy, or simply to gloat? Either way, the cynic in me is not quite buying Kelly's condolences. I lift my head from my hands and shuffle away, creating a more comfortable distance between us once more.

'Are you really sorry? You hated her. Isn't this all your Christmases come at once?' I say, my tone aggressive.

SAMANTHA KAY

Visibly offended, Kelly's mouth contorts in the way it always does before she's about to sling an insult in my direction. It's when she pulls that face that I see the strongest resemblance to Ellie in her, which I've always thought a shame.

'Of course not. Is that really what you think of me? I wouldn't wish this on anyone. Not on Abbie or you, and especially not on my kids.' It's seemingly impossible for us to be near one another and not argue.

She stands up, and just as I think she's about to leave, Harry enters the living room and places down two mugs of coffee on the coffee table. Oblivious, or simply choosing to ignore the usual frostiness between his parents, he silently exits as quickly as he entered, leaving us both alone once again.

I start to feel bad. None of this is Kelly's fault, and I know it's wrong of me to take my frustrations out on her.

'I'm sorry,' I utter, picking up one of the mugs and handing it to Kelly, gesturing for her to sit down again and stay.

She doesn't accept it straight away but stands where she is, glaring at me. No doubt there's plenty more she'd like to say, but she's holding back, probably out of pity, or respect for the fact that today was Abbie's funeral. Eventually she sits back down on the sofa and accepts the mug from me. We have created something in the way of a truce.

309

'I shouldn't have said that,' I admit, picking up my own mug. 'I have a lot of anger at the moment. I don't think I'm handling it very well.'

I take a sip from my drink and lean back on the sofa again, trying to make myself comfortable.

Kelly doesn't take a sip from her mug. Instead, she wraps her hands around it.

'You know, the kids . . . they've never known life without Abbie. This is a huge loss for them, for all of you. I really did just want to check you were all OK.' Kelly is perched on the edge of the sofa, staring into her mug, and her words are spoken from the heart. I sometimes forget there is a human being under that cast-iron exterior of hers.

After a moment, she adds, 'It was never personal, you know. I would have hated whoever broke up my marriage. Although the fact she was young and blonde and beautiful didn't help much.' To which we both smile, the atmosphere between us easing.

There was once a time when Kelly and I loved and trusted one another, and I think it's sad, that after all these years we've never been able to move past feelings of hostility. For years, every word between us has been scrutinised, every gesture taken the wrong way. It pains me that I've never been allowed to simply be honest about my feelings, to bare my soul and really be heard.

'It rested heavy on me for years, what I did, breaking up the family like that,' I begin. I see Kelly make a face, but I carry on regardless. I need to say my piece.

'Abbie, she just burst into my life. Unexpectedly, out of nowhere. But from the moment I saw her, I was enchanted by her, by everything about her. I'd never had those kinds of feelings before, not for anyone. It was so powerful that Abbie and I were both willing to risk everything for each other. And I won't apologise for that, because to do so would mean I'm sorry, and I'm not. I'll never be sorry for loving her and for the life we shared together, but it was never my intention to hurt you or the kids, please believe me when I say that.'

Feeling a little nervous, I watch as Kelly takes all this in. I understand that it was probably not the easiest thing for her to hear, but I'm glad that I've got it off my chest.

Kelly is silent for a moment, still absorbing what I've said, I think, until she asks me: 'Do you remember my parents' thirtieth wedding anniversary? They had that do round their house.'

'Vaguely.' I cast my mind back, struggling to remember any significant details about that day.

'It was the weekend before I caught you and Abbie at that hotel. And I remember knowing that something was going on, but I couldn't be sure, I couldn't prove anything. At my parents', you spent the whole day with an absolute face on you. You didn't want to be there; you wouldn't make an effort with anybody. You just sat in the corner cradling Ellie all day. You were so bloody miserable.' There's a strong undertone of annoyance in her voice, and it's good to know she doesn't hold a grudge!

'A week later, at the hotel, I saw you both before you saw me. You and Abbie were snuggled together and you looked so happy and so in love. And I knew that I'd lost you. I hadn't seen you look that happy for a long time, even before we had Ellie. Long before you ever met Abbie.'

I can see a level of vulnerability in Kelly that I've not witnessed in a while. It's nice to both be able to speak honestly in a safe space and not shout at each other for once.

'For a long time,' she goes on, 'I just couldn't get my head around it. I'd given you the greatest gift of all - these two beautiful, healthy babies. But it wasn't enough. It never made you happy. I couldn't make you happy in the way that she could. And I hated her for that.' Kelly's voice is quiet, a little shaky at the risk she is taking, sharing such candour.

The description of her feelings towards Abbie truly makes my heart ache. I find it hard to fathom how we can both harbour such contrasting feelings for the same person.

'God knows,' Kelly confesses, 'I tried

everything to break you, to make you feel as awful as I felt. But it never worked. Years later, I was dropping the kids off to you in a car park somewhere, and I remember that as I approached, you two were sitting in the front of the car listening to some music. I think you were both "rapping" along to that awful House of Pain song you used to love. You were both dancing in your seats like two absolute morons.' Kelly air-quotes the word 'rapping', her mockery reminding me why I dislike her so much.

'I'd put you both through absolute hell, but there you were. Still together, still happy. I know how much you loved her, Jase. People search their whole lives for that kind of love. And you're right, you shouldn't have to apologise for that.'

Kelly smiles thinly. I smile back, appreciative of her words and their honesty. Then I look over at the picture of a beaming Abbie posing with a cocktail in her hand and feel like a fraud.

The last words we spoke to one another were in this room. They weren't kind, loving words, but harsh ugly screams, followed by the sound of Abbie running upstairs to her death, to her collapse on the bedroom floor . . . These are sounds that will haunt me forever, echoing over and over again in my mind. I'm not so sure our final years of marriage were as blissfully happy as Kelly might believe, but I won't be the one to shatter the illusion.

'Thank you, for swinging by,' I say, placing my coffee down on the table. It is the first act of kindness I've received from Kelly in over a decade.

'Oh, I'll go then, shall I?' She looks offended, taking everything I say the wrong way as usual.

'No, that's not what I meant.'

'Relax. I know, I'm only joking.'

We've always struggled to understand each other. This is precisely the reason we were never good together.

'But don't worry, I can't stay for much longer.' She takes a quick glance at her watch. 'I have a date.' She speaks in a hushed voice – presumably so the kids don't hear.

'Oh? Who with?' That explains why she's so dressed up.

'No one you know. He's a friend of a friend. It's early days, but it's going well.' And she issues a coy smile.

'Good. I'm pleased for you.' For years Abbie and I always believed a new love interest would have helped ease Kelly's bitterness towards us. I'm just sorry it's only happening now; the irony is not lost on me.

'Thank you,' mouths Kelly just as Harry enters the room.

'Did you want biscuits?' he mumbles, holding up an unopened pack of ginger nuts he's found somewhere in the kitchen cupboards.

I nod, never one to turn away a biscuit.

Harry plonks himself down on the sofa between Kelly and me. He unwraps the packet and, rather than offering it to anyone else first, he takes out a biscuit and dips it in my coffee before popping it in his mouth. Displeased by his lack of manners, I take the pack from him and offer it to Kelly. She accepts one, just as Ellie appears in the doorway of the living room.

'Hey, I thought I heard you come back. Where did you go?' I can hear the concern in her voice. She's freshly washed and dressed in her yellow bed T-shirt and leggings, cradling Daisy between her arms.

'I just went for a drive.'

'Are you OK now?' I can sense her apprehension as she struggles to read the room. The sight of her mother and me together is an unfamiliar one on what has been a long and difficult day.

'I'll be fine,' I say reassuringly, really sorry to have worried her and Harry.

'This must be the famous Daisy,' Kelly puts in, doing well to lighten the mood.

That's when I realise Daisy and Kelly have never met. I can count on one hand the amount of times Kelly has been in this house, and never has Daisy come near her or by her. Daisy has always feared strangers.

Ellie smiles, sitting herself down next to her mum on the sofa and Daisy settles herself

EIGHT MILLION MINUTES

down on Ellie's lap. Kelly lifts her hand to stroke Daisy, but as she does our cat hisses at her and swipes a paw at Kelly's hand, making her feelings abundantly clear.

'Ah, I see your mummy must have told you all about me,' says Kelly, to which we all laugh.

I pull a ginger nut from the packet, dip it in my tepid coffee and put the biscuit in my mouth. For the first time in as long as I can remember, there's a gentle harmony between the four of us. It's nice, the kind of unity I've always hoped for. I'm not sure why it had to take us so long to get here, nor if we'll ever achieve it again, but I'm happy to enjoy it while it lasts.

*

The house is finally clean, Kelly has gone, the kids have retired to their rooms and I'm ready to call it a night. But before I do, I need to take a shower. Standing in the bathroom, I undress as Prince's 'I Wana Be Your Lover' plays over the speakers. I place my dirty clothes in the wash basket and turn on the shower, letting the water run for a moment before I step in.

Reflecting on the day, I'm grateful it's over, but feel as if I've been hit by an unexpected secondary loss. Organising the funeral and all the necessary paperwork that comes with a person's passing, it was almost as if Abbie was still here. Her presence just within touching distance. But now, it's all over. As if the final part of her I could still cling onto has slipped away

SAMANTHA KAY

too.

However, maybe I shouldn't speak too soon. I still need to make a decision regarding *Daisy's*, and whatever the outcome, it'll take some time to sort out, so there is that, I suppose...

I hop into the shower and welcome the sensation of the warm water cascading over me and stand for a moment, enjoying the fleeting sense of relaxation. I reach for my bottle of body wash, squirt a generous amount into my hands and begin the process of getting clean. Washing my face, underarms and chest, I move ever more south, reaching my nether regions, when I feel something unfamiliar.

Something is missing.

Taking my scrotum in my hand, I have a feel around, paying great attention to my left testicle.

It's gone.

The lump, the cyst. *It's gone.*

I lift my penis, and in the steamy shower cubicle, I peer down at myself. There's nothing there. It's vanished. All on its own - just like the doctor said it would.

I suppose I should be pleased, and I am, but I also feel a wave of sorrow. This unwanted intruder on my body created so much angst and drama, but it also gave me the chance to save my marriage and bring Abbie and me back together – until she discovered my treachery. The lump brought with it a shared experience that was solely ours. And now, it's just another thing that's disappeared without warning.

I lift my face to the water as tears cascade from my eyes and are washed away down the drain.

CHAPTER 24

JASON

Three months later . . .

Sitting with my chin in my hand, I stare blankly at a framed photograph of me and Abbie, taken in my parents' back garden at my dad's birthday barbecue. Blue sky, green grass, two happy smiling faces. It's actually quite an old photo, taken about seven years ago, but it's a new addition to my desk, a recent gift from the kids.

As I sit idly, struggling to muster any motivation, I look away from the photograph and out at the showroom. Expensive shiny cars are paraded on the floor. Everyone is milling around nicely, everything is ticking along as it should, and I think what a strange phenomenon it is, the way in which life has this terrible habit of carrying on. These days, I feel like an unwilling spectator, unsure where I fit into it all. As ever, work has brought with it a reason to get up in the morning, to get dressed and function in the way an adult human should, but without Abbie, it's hard to see the purpose.

I turn back to the photo on my desk. Pick it up, hold it between my hands and stare at us. We certainly look happy, but were we? I know I was, but these days I question everything. Abbie was miserable, I know that now. *I* made her miserable, and it pains me, knowing there's no way I'll ever be able to rectify that.

'Dad!'

I jump out of my skin, dropping the frame on my desk with a loud clank. I look up and see Ellie standing at my open office door. I agreed to let Ellie work here for a few days a week over the summer. So far, she's done little more than make herself endless mugs of hot chocolate and take selfies with the cars, but it has been nice having her around. I think she worries about me, especially now Harry's routine morning visits have come to an end, not that I mind too much. Pleasant as it was having him around, he starts uni soon, and a depressed grief-stricken father shouldn't be his main priority.

'Ellie, what have I told you about knocking?' I say, standing the picture-frame back up on my desk.

'The walls are made of glass. I can literally see you're not doing anything,' she answers me back with a healthy dose of attitude.

'What do you want?' I ask calmly.

'You have a visitor.'

'Who?' I don't have any meetings scheduled for today, but then out of the corner of my eye I spot a familiar figure in the distance, standing next to the yellow Lamborghini and chatting with Dean.

'Gerald,' says Ellie, pointing behind her shoulder.

As my old friend and best customer heads towards my office I push back on my wheelie chair and stand up.

'Make me a coffee, please, and ask Gerald if he would like a drink,' I say, handing my empty mug to Ellie just as Gerald appears at my door.

'Gerald, would you like a drink? The hot chocolate is really good,' Ellie greets him.

'Hot chocolate sounds delightful. Thank you,' and Gerald gives her a grateful smile. With that, Ellie disappears, closing the door behind her.

'I thought you were in Switzerland,' I say, offering my hand, ready to shake his.

Gerald bats my hand away, enfolding me in a tight hug instead, such fondness almost bringing a tear to my eye. I swallow hard, not wanting to look foolish.

'I came back early,' Gerald explains, releasing me. 'There was some business here I needed to catch up on. But I had some free time today, so I thought to stop by and see how you're doing.' He makes himself comfortable in the chair opposite my desk as I walk back around to

EIGHT MILLION MINUTES

my own chair, slumping myself down upon it.

The unexpected act of kindness touches me deeply. For a moment, I can't speak.

'So, how *are* you doing?' Gerald asks.

I'm unsure how to respond. While everyone else seems to have slipped back into a routine, I feel stuck in a rut of my own misery. I find it hard to sleep, I'm surviving on a diet of coffee and biscuits, and I can't stand being at home. The crushing grief and guilt I feel is nothing short of torture, which I'm convinced is punishment for the disturbing act of deception of which I can never speak.

I shrug.

'That good, eh?'

'Yep,' I say, followed by a small sigh.

'There's still a lot to process, no doubt,' Gerald says sympathetically.

'Yeah, I suppose. I was going to sell *Daisy's*, Abbie's café, but something's stopping me. There are some other options on the table, but I can't seem to bring myself to make a decision.' I nervously start tapping my fingers on the desk in the annoying way I do when stressed.

'I meant there's still a lot to process in here,' Gerald corrects me gently, pointing to the side of his head.

'Well, yeah, that goes without saying. To be honest, I don't even know where to begin.' My head feels like an unmade jigsaw puzzle, all the pieces scattered in a jumbled, shaken-up mess.

'Have you thought about getting some counselling?'

'God no!' I exclaim, simply horrified by such an idea, scared of where 'opening up' could lead.

'You know who you need,' says Gerald with a knowing smile, pointing a finger in my direction.

I stare at him uncomprehendingly.

'Reggie.'

'Who?'

'Reggie. He's Suzie's personal trainer-type thing, but he's so much more, like a life coach. He helps with healthy meal plans for her, and they mediate together.'

I think Gerald means meditate, but I don't correct him, keen not to interrupt.

'They sit cross-legged and barefoot on the grass in the garden doing all this breathing and calming yoga stuff. To be honest it's all a load of hippy-dippy nonsense to an old man like me, but Suzie swears by it.'

'Yeah, I don't know, Gerald. Between work and one thing and another, I'm not really sure the whole fitness, lifestyle thing is for me.'

'Nonsense. I thought you'd started running.'

'Yeah, but not because I enjoy it. It just gets me out of the house.'

'Trust me, Jase. You need Reggie. Look, it'll be my gift to you. I'll pay for him. For one month.

EIGHT MILLION MINUTES

And if you hate it, I promise you'll never have to see him again.'

Although not loving the idea, maybe I should try and embrace something that might just lift me out of the funk I find myself in.

'He's not going to make me talk about my feelings, is he?' I ask, making my terms clear.

'I shouldn't think so. Not unless you want him to.'

'Fine,' I agree reluctantly. 'Thank you, Gerald.' After all, who am I to turn down a freebie?

'Great, I promise you won't regret it,' he says, just as Ellie bursts into my office (without knocking), holding a small black tray with two mugs on it.

'Right, so that's one hot chocolate, and one black coffee for you, Dad,' she announces, dutifully handing Gerald and me our drinks.

CHAPTER 25

JASON

It's 5.30 a.m. and I'm stumbling down the stairs trying to navigate my way to the front door.

Having not slept terribly well, my eyes feel sticky and sensitive and it pains me to open them as I search for my door keys in a state of near-blindness.

'One sec!' I call out, as I feel around the table in the hallway, eventually locating my keys. I'm already starting to regret taking Gerald up on his offer. I've recklessly agreed to a morning session with Reggie without any real understanding of what I've signed up to.

I skulk towards the front door, already thinking up my excuses. *Maybe I could have a cold? Or maybe I could have sprained something?*

I've always taken pride in being a morning person, but I cannot be bothered with this. The very last thing I want to do at this precise moment is burn calories, or bloody incense, with some barefoot, tree-hugging vegan. Why can't Gerald just accept that I am quite happy festering

EIGHT MILLION MINUTES

in my own misery!

I unlock the front door, tugging my T-shirt down, checking my boxers are covering everything in the way they should, and am taken aback by the person standing before me. I imagined some sort of hippy – a long-haired, willowy type lacking in iron or possession of a hairbrush. However, this guy resembles a heavyweight boxer.

He's black, I'm guessing somewhere in his mid- to late-thirties, is at least six feet tall and is built like the proverbial brick shithouse. He has a closely shaven haircut, the edges sharp and perfectly shaped around his forehead, and an equally sharp, closely-shaven goatee lines his mouth. He's wearing an Adidas tracksuit, and when I spot a Mercedes car key in his hand, the sight of it instantly makes me feel a little more comfortable.

'Hi, Reggie?' I say, trying and failing to disguise my surprise.

'Jason?' he replies, looking me up and down, seemingly just as surprised by my appearance. It can't be often his clients open the door to him wholly unprepared for his arrival.

I reach out my hand and he shakes it, his grip firm.

'Yes, come in,' I say, letting go and stepping aside, welcoming him into the house.

'Did you forget I was coming?' he asks, a puzzled expression on his face as he looks back at me in my underwear.

I pretend not to have heard. Feeling more vulnerable than I care to admit, I lead a nigh-on stranger through to the kitchen in my underpants.

'I did try to call you the other day, just to get a general feel about things, but you didn't pick up, or reply to my email,' Reggie adds as I head over to the coffee machine, hoping he can't sense my guilt.

I did see his phone call, and I did read the email, but ignored both in the vain hope that by doing so he would assume I was no longer interested - but no such luck.

'Yeah, I'm sorry. It's been a difficult few months. I'm a bit all over the place at the moment.'

'Gerald filled me in. I'm sorry to hear about your wife. Things must be rough right now,' the big man says, his voice kind and understanding, hopefully forgiving the sorry state he's found me in this morning.

'Coffee?' I ask, not particularly wanting to engage in an emotional breakdown right this minute.

'Please. Black, no sugar.'

I turn to fetch down a mug from the kitchen cupboard and start up the coffee machine.

'You have a lovely home,' Reggie tells me, casually pacing the kitchen, stopping at the smart fridge where a copy of the family photo taken in Cancun is attached with an angel-wing magnet Ellie bought me. 'These your kids?'

'Yeah, but that's quite an old photo. Harry's eighteen now and Ellie's sixteen going on twenty-six. They live with their mum,' I explain as the sound of the coffee machine burbles away.

Reggie nods, peering back at the photo, and I can tell he's silently working out the family dynamic in his head.

'So, it's just you, alone in this big house.'

Thanks for the reminder.

'So it seems,' I say curtly.

Reggie visibly cringes, embarrassed by his insensitivity. 'I'm sorry, I—'

I relent. 'It's fine, honestly. It is a big house for just one person. I've been contemplating selling it,' I admit, wanting to make him feel better. I don't wish us to get off on the wrong foot so early on.

'Really? Are you not happy here?' This guy apparently finds it hard to imagine that anyone could be unhappy living in a house as nice as mine. What he doesn't realise is that my beautiful and perfect house serves as nothing more than a cruel reminder of my many failings as a husband and a human being.

'There's a lot I need to work through,' I shrug. 'I've wondered if moving might be the answer.'

'Well, hopefully that's where I can help.'

'Yeah, you wanna buy a house?' I say, handing Reggie a mug of black coffee.

'Ha, no. But I believe if a person can get to grips with their physical fitness and well-being, it helps straighten out everything up here.' And Reggie points to his head in the same annoying way Gerald did the other day. It takes all my willpower not to roll my eyes, and I wonder if he realises how incredibly daft he sounds.

'What?' he asks, sensing my resistance.

'I'm sorry. You seem like a nice guy, and I don't mean any disrespect, but I'm not convinced a jog around the park is going to make my problems go away.'

'Oh, it won't,' Reggie says bluntly, banishing any pie in the sky ideas around what these sessions will achieve. He pauses, taking a sip from his coffee.

'Look, Jason, you're on a very long and painful journey right now, but working on your well-being and fitness could really help you . . . or it might not. But either way, Gerald's already paid me and I'm here now, so you and me might as well give this a try.' He says this, then gives a small laugh and a reassuring smile.

Annoyingly, I think I like might like this guy, and I wonder if many of his other clients need as much persuading as me. Wanting the torture over as quickly as possible, I decide to cave in, hoping the sooner we get started, the sooner he'll leave.

EIGHT MILLION MINUTES

'OK. Let me go and get some clothes on,' I say, finally deciding to stop wasting everyone's time.

'Hey, *that's* the kind of energy we want right there!' Reggie says loudly, his positivity sickening.

I return to the kitchen appropriately dressed in a pair of workout shorts and a hoodie, to find Reggie with his head buried deep in my fridge.

'When did you last do a food shop?' he asks from behind the door, and I note a hint of concern in his voice.

'Erm, yesterday, or maybe the day before.' Why is that relevant?

'Yeah? And what did you buy?'

Reggie steps away from the fridge, letting the door close behind him and moves on to inspecting my kitchen cupboards. I'm nervous. It's been a while since I carried out a significant restock of groceries. The big man stands back and peers inside, shaking his head gently as if having witnessed a terrible accident.

'Couple of ready meals,' I state. 'A loaf of bread.' I omit telling him about the Crunchie bar and packet of bourbon biscuits.

'Yeah, and where did you shop?'

'I popped into the petrol station on the way home from work.'

Reggie turns to look at me, his eyes wide in

horror and disbelief. 'You do your food shopping *at the petrol station*?'

What terrible crime am I being accused of exactly?

'It's a Marks and Spencer petrol station,' I reply defensively.

Reggie nods, then tells me, 'OK, Jason. Me and you are going for a drive. Bring your wallet.' And he strides out of the kitchen with an alarming degree of purpose.

*

It's now 6.15 a.m. Reggie has been in my life for less than an hour, and already he has as good as kidnapped me and held me against my will at my local 24-hour Tesco. The store is pretty empty at this time in the morning, with just us and one other early bird strolling through the fruit and veg aisle.

I slump my body weight on the trolley's handlebar and skulk behind Reggie while he lectures me on the importance of good nutrition.

'Eating well doesn't have to be difficult,' he says, as he places some kind of green foliage into the trolley. 'You'd be surprised by how many things you can make that are super-healthy and quick,' he adds, placing a couple of sweet potatoes into the trolley.

'I thought we were just going to go for a jog,' I mumble resentfully.

'We can't exercise knowing you have no appropriate fuel in the house. It's irresponsible.

EIGHT MILLION MINUTES

Like you taking a car with nothing in the tank on a trip to Scotland via a route with no petrol stations. It's not going to make it.'

I'd like to tell him how wrong he is. I've run many times on an empty stomach and survived just fine on nothing more than a slice of toast and a cup of coffee, but I keep my mouth shut, wanting to avoid a further lecture.

Instead, keen to change the subject, I ask him: 'So, how long have you been doing this fitness, well-being stuff?'

'Over ten years now. Prior to this I was a professional footballer.'

'No way. Who'd you play for?' Should I recognise him?

'Watford, but sadly not for very long. You like football?'

'I used to go to West Ham, but I haven't been for years. For a long time I couldn't afford it and once I could, I struggled to find the time. How come you stopped playing?' I ask with interest.

'I got injured, then I got dropped, then I effectively found myself unemployed. Sport and fitness were all I'd ever known, so to cut a long story short, I started doing this,' Reggie tells me, stopping to ponder over the apples.

I nod my approval. Reggie is obviously a hardworking and talented induvial who hasn't let his setbacks grind him down. He might just be my kind of person.

SAMANTHA KAY

'Do you enjoy it?' I ask.

'What - walking around the supermarket helping a grown man buy apples? What's not to enjoy?' he grins, placing a bag of Granny Smiths into the trolley.

Although I should be slightly offended by his sarcasm, I quite like the fact he's clearly comfortable in my company. We continue to stroll down the aisle, turning left into the next one.

'Gerald tells me you own a car showroom. You're the one who sells him all those fancy fast cars.'

'Yeah, that'll be me,' I confirm.

'And do you enjoy that?'

'I love it - much to the detriment of other things,' I say, my words spoken more mournfully than I'd intended.

Reggie looks at me quizzically, picking up on the many uncomfortable layers in my short sentence. Regretting what I've said, I try to move the conversation on.

'Gerald told me you do yoga and meditation. You don't seem the type,' I say casually, at which Reggie stops immediately in front of me next to the lemons, so suddenly I almost run the trolley into him.

'Why, because I'm a huge black man?' he demands, his face stern.

I decide to opt for an honest approach. 'You know, I really wish I could say that wasn't what I meant, but yes, I think that's exactly what I was implying,' I say truthfully, and nervously.

Reggie's granite exterior suddenly folds, his face breaking into a large, amused smile. 'I have a very varied client base. You like lemons?'

'Who doesn't?' I say, glad to see I haven't caused irreparable offence.

'I cater to everyone,' Reggie states, placing a small bag of lemons into the trolley. 'And you know, fitness isn't all about running and weights. Yoga is great for your core strength and meditation is great for your mental fitness.'

Uh oh. I fear another lecture coming on. While Reggie rambles on, I glance into the trolley and have no idea what the hell I'm supposed to do with sweet potatoes, lemons and foliage.

'You know, Reg,' I pipe up, 'I think we may be running before we can walk. I really don't have any idea what I'm supposed to do with any of these things.'

'I know, but don't worry. I'm going to help you with some meal plans. Then we'll compile a list of groceries, so going forward, you can order them yourself online.'

I nod and smile, trying to hide my resentment. *There was me thinking this couldn't get any worse.*

'What do you usually have for breakfast?'
'Black coffee.'
'And . . .?'
'Just a coffee, sometimes toast,' I throw

in, omitting that toast only really happens if someone else makes it for me, which is never.

'That's not breakfast,' Reggie informs me, his words causing a pang in my heart, and I wonder what Abbie would say if she could see me right now.

'That's what my wife used to say.'

'And she was right.' Reggie leads us away from the fruit and veg and onto another aisle of wondrous nutrition, while I follow behind him like a stroppy toddler.

CHAPTER 26

JASON

After an early start and feeling more tired than usual, I decided to finish work a little earlier today. Back home, sitting in the kitchen at the breakfast bar, I've just polished off a meal of grilled chicken breast and baked sweet potato. It wasn't quite the delight to my taste buds that Reggie had promised, but it's a start. An improvement on a ready meal or a whole packet of biscuits.

With my empty plate pushed to the side, in front of me my laptop is open and alight. It was my intention to finish off some work, but instead I find myself casually searching commercial property agents online. After months of delaying the inevitable, I think the time has come for me to sell *Daisy's*. Naturally, making such a decision has been like pulling teeth. My heart so desperately wants to cling on to any part of Abbie that I still can, but my business head knows it's for the best. I haven't got the time to run two

SAMANTHA KAY

businesses, let alone one that's running at a loss.

I turn to look at the fridge, of the happy picture of us all taken on the beach in Cancun. 'Unhappy for ages'. Those were the words Abbie used, in the last conversation we ever had. Since then, I have tortured myself, wondering how long 'ages' was supposed to mean. A year, two years, or maybe longer? And all the while, I believed everything was fine and dandy, that we had it all, including each other.

How did I not realise she was so unhappy?

In what world did I believe working a fourteen-hour day was going to equate to a happy marriage? And why did I think lying to her about cancer was the solution to our problems?

Am I really that self-involved?

With my trusty notebook next to me, I pick up a pen and open it at the page bearing my recipe notes for a coffee and walnut cake. I smile to myself, recalling Abbie's efforts to bake a cake at Rosewood Cottage, then wonder if there will ever come a day when I don't feel as fucking awful as I do right now.

Doubtful.

I flick through my notepad until I reach a blank page and make a note of the agency and their contact details, vowing to get in touch with them tomorrow morning.

Still feeling too distracted to work, I open up another webpage, this time in search of residential properties. This home is no longer my pride and joy, a sanctuary or a place bearing fond and loving memories. It's a place where the most awful night of my life happened. A place that saw everything I hold dear snatched away. In a short while, Harry will be off at uni and no doubt Ellie will soon follow, making their visits even less frequent and the size of this home unnecessary.

On the property website, I am filling in the boxes with details of homes just like mine, curious about the price this place could fetch, when I hear the sound of the front door open.

'Hello?' I call.

'It's me, Dad!' Ellie calls back. A few moments later, Ellie enters the kitchen, cradling Daisy in the way she only lets Ellie do these days.

'Ellie belly. What are you doing here?' I ask, surprised but pleased to see her. I shut down the property site, keen to avoid any unwanted questions. Ellie places Daisy on the floor and I watch as the purring cat weaves between her legs, happy as ever to see her.

'I'm coming to work with you tomorrow, I thought it made more sense if I stayed here tonight,' she says, wandering towards the fridge.

Usually when Ellie comes to work with me, she's dropped off at the showroom by her mother at the more 'Ellie friendly' time of 9 a.m. It is considered a little harsh to expect her to come in with me at 7 a.m.

'You know, if you want to come in with me, you're going to have to get up considerably

SAMANTHA KAY

earlier than usual,' I remind her.

'I know.' Ellie is tapping the screen on the smart fridge to reveal its contents. 'Oh wow, you actually have food in here for a change!' she says, opening the door and taking out an apple.

'Does your mum know you're here?' I ask.

'Course, she dropped me off.' Ellie takes a bite from her apple while exploring the other shelves in the fridge, impressed by my loot. 'George is staying tonight,' she mentions with her mouth full. George being Kelly's boyfriend. It's now making sense of why Ellie's here. I squirm in my seat, the thought of Kelly having sex somehow making me feel squeamish.

'Oh, so it's going well then. Have you met him?'

Ellie nods, letting the fridge door close behind her, walking over towards me with a can of Diet 7up in her other hand.

'What's he like?' I ask, curiosity getting the better of me.

Ellie puts down her can and loosely wraps her arm over my shoulders then kisses me on the cheek.

'Alright. Bit nerdy,' she shrugs, leaving me satisfied that my kids haven't had to endure the company of an absolute creep. 'What are you looking at?' she asks nosily, letting go of me and peering at my laptop.

'I was researching some commercial property agencies. I think it's time I put *Daisy's*

EIGHT MILLION MINUTES

up for sale.'

'Why would you do that?' Ellie says disapprovingly, taking another bite from her apple.

'Well, it's probably about time now. I've been holding onto it for too long, and I haven't got time to—'

'No, I meant, why would you do that without discussing it with me first?' Ellie says, taking me by surprise.

'What, you think I should be discussing this with *you*?'

'Of course. I'm your daughter and heir. *Daisy's* is a part of our empire. An empire I plan on running one day. Why do you think I've started coming to work with you?'

I shrug. 'I dunno. I thought you wanted to spend some time with me over the summer,' I say naively to which Ellie tuts loudly.

'No way! I want to work with you so I can learn about the business. Honestly, Dad, for a businessman you're not very intuitive.'

Don't I know it.

I watch as she opens her can of 7Up one-handed while holding her apple and takes a large loud slurp.

'So, is that your plan - to study business at uni?' I ask, intrigued as to what Ellie's plans are after she completes her A-Levels.

'No, I don't think I want to go to uni. I just said, I want to learn from *you*,' she says with emphasis, as if unable to understand where I'm getting the notion of uni from.

'Really?' Flattered as I am, this is all coming as brand-new information to me. After all, this is the first time Ellie has ever displayed any real interest in what I do.

Ellie opens her mouth wide, places her apple between her teeth and holds it in place while she pulls out the bar stool closest to me, sitting herself down upon it.

Taking the apple out of her mouth, she faces me 'I'm only doing A-Levels because mums making me.' she says despondently, 'I've been thinking about things. Once I'm done with them...I don't want years of more studying and exams. I want to work and make money. I mean, you never went to uni, Taylor Swift never went to uni. Didn't do either of you any harm.'

I smile. I'm not quite sure my success is on par with that of Taylor Swift, but I am touched to hear my daughter recognises my accomplishments.

'So that's what you see yourself doing - working for the family business?' I ask quite seriously.

'Yeah, of course. Once I'm done with my exams, I figured I can come on board and run Daisy's fulltime,' Ellie says airily, as if the owning and running of any business is really that straightforward.

'But that's still two years away, and I

EIGHT MILLION MINUTES

haven't got the time to run two businesses for that long,' I explain as tactfully as I can, not wishing to crush her dreams.

'But you wouldn't need to. We just get someone else in to run it. And I can help on weekends—'

'It's not quite as simple as that, Ellie. *Daisy's* hasn't been making any money for a while now,' I tell her.

'But what about the rebrand? The doggie café was a great idea! Also, Dad, think about Abbie's parents. If they find out we've sold it, they might come knocking, thinking they can have a share of the money.'

Spoken like a true saleswoman. I laugh inwardly as Ellie tries to introduce a degree of fear into her pitch, leaving me rather impressed.

'Well, that's unlikely and I wouldn't let that happen,' I assure her.

'Even so, do we want them to think it failed? Do we want to give them the satisfaction?' she presses, pitching as if her life depends on it, her raw determination and drive filling me with pride, leaving me in no doubt as to where she gets it from.

'I'm not sure. It'll be a lot of work.' I'm worried that Ellie is romanticising the idea.

'Come *on*, Dad. Abbie put too much effort into the place for us to throw in the towel now. She wasn't going to, and neither should we.'

Ellie sure does put up a strong fight. In

truth, I don't want to see *Daisy's* go either. Ellie makes a valid point. I might not have known how unhappy Abbie was in our marriage, but one thing I do know is how much she loved *Daisy's,* and how much she craved for it to be a success.

If the events of recent months have taught me anything, it's that I don't need to spend every waking minute at *Turner's*. What with my 'cancer battle' and Abbie's passing, the last few months have seen me take a step back like never before, and despite that, everything has been running smoothly. That's because I employ an excellent team of incredibly capable people. So, if I decide to concentrate some of my energy elsewhere for a while, I don't see it being a problem.

Ellie looks at me, wide-eyed and expectant.

'OK,' I say, a smile pulling at the corners of my mouth, the idea of a fresh challenge igniting an unexpected simmer of excitement in me.

'Is that "OK, we're gonna do this"?' she asks with a huge smile.

I hold up my hand, not wanting either of us to get carried away.

'It's an "OK, leave it with me".' I'm keen not to give her false hope. There's a lot to think about before I make that commitment.

'And you promise to keep me in the loop?' Ellie requests, pointing her finger at me.

'I promise.' And I mean it.

Ellie takes a final bite of her apple. She

places the core on my empty plate and fidgets with the ring pull on her drink can. She suddenly deflates: all her enthusiasm evaporates and she looks sad.

'What's wrong?' I ask.

'I just really miss her,' whispers Ellie, wiping away a tear.

'I know. I do too.' Swallowing down my own sudden rush of emotion, I jump off my bar stool and wrap Ellie in my arms as we both grieve, wishing Abbie were still with us.

CHAPTER 27

JASON

It's Sunday morning, and although God was allowed to rest on this day, it seems the same doesn't apply to me.

It's not even 9 a.m. and Reggie has already had me complete fifty press-ups, fifty sit-ups and we're just about coming to the end of our second full lap of the park. Strictly speaking, I'm no longer jogging; merely walking with a less than convincing spring in my step. My knees hurt and I'm beyond exhausted. Usually when I jog alone, I would only do one full lap, allowing myself as many stops as I please along the way, but not when I'm with Reggie.

This is my fourth session with him. He turns up at my house two mornings a week, and although I sometimes resent how hard he pushes me, I enjoy his easy-going company. While we jog, we chat - about the weather or the news or whatever is going on in each other's lives. Surprisingly, I find it quite cathartic, casual chat with Reggie distracting my mind from the everyday guilt and shame that continue to plague me.

Today I'm filling him in on the latest developments regarding my plans for *Daisy's.* I'll be heading over there later today with Ellie to take a look at everything, which she's really excited about.

'What about Harry?' asks Reggie. 'Will he be getting involved too?'

'I'd love him to, but he really couldn't be less interested,' I pant, delighted that a vacant bench is within sight. I power through, using the very last of my energy reserves to make it there, and slump my sorry backside down, seeking respite and shade under the huge oak tree. I take a large gulp from my water bottle, while Reggie remains standing, stretching out his calf muscles.

'Maybe one day he'll change his mind?' he says.

'Maybe. It'd be great if he did, but I don't want to push him into anything he doesn't want to do. And right now, he's really focused on starting uni, which I'm pleased about.' I'm resting my elbows on my knees, catching my breath.

'Well, I think it's a beautiful thing you're doing. Preserving Abbie's memory like that, using it to provide a legacy for your kids,' muses Reggie, finally succumbing to a sit-down on the bench next to me.

I smile thinly, wishing my motivation behind *Daisy's* really was as altruistic as Reggie seems to think, rather than a sop to my conscience.

'What is it? What's wrong?' Reggie senses I'm holding something back.

'It's just . . . I worry I'm in it for all the wrong reasons,' I say.

'How so?'

I look ahead out over the park. My eyes follow a couple walking a chocolate labrador in the distance. I feel Reggie's eyes on me, patiently waiting for me to articulate my thoughts.

'I think it's less about preserving Abbie's memory, and more about *me*. My way of making up for being such a shitty husband.' I say finally.

'Nah - no way were you a shitty husband,' Reggie argues, rooting for me in a way I certainly don't deserve.

'The last words Abbie ever said to me was that she wanted a divorce,' I tell Reggie, my confession releasing itself unprompted, as if the dire state of my marriage refuses to stay secret a single second longer.

'Oh wow,' utters Reggie.

'Actually, that's not strictly true. The last words she said to me were that I was going to die rich and alone. I think about that a lot,' I confide, and place a hand over my closed eyes, trying to hold back my tears. It still hurts so much I can

EIGHT MILLION MINUTES

barely contain the pain.

'Why did she want a divorce?' Reggie asks quietly. He can tell I need to get all this off my chest because this is the centre of everything that is holding me back.

'Because I lied to her,' I mumble.

'About what?' And I hear the note of worry in Reggie's voice, in case I'm about to admit to something heinous.

I look down at my hands that are gripping onto my water bottle, and I force myself to pause, to think about what I'm going to say, what I'm finally going to confess. I like Reggie. We share a good rapport. I certainly feel I can be honest and frank in his company, but the lie I told, it was so big, so manipulative. I'm not sure there's any way I can confess to it without sounding like an absolute psychopath.

In the end, I decide that's a risk I should take, because I can't keep this secret contained a moment longer. The grief, guilt and shame are killing me from the inside.

'I told Abbie that... the house, the cars, were what we needed to be happy, to feel safe. But I was lying - to her and myself. Because they aren't and they never were, but I convinced myself otherwise, and it destroyed my marriage.' And then I stop, relieved I had the good sense to come to a halt right there.

Understandably, Reggie looks a little baffled, not expecting quite such a lacklustre

348

SAMANTHA KAY

confession.

'You know,' I go on, 'I watched this docufilm the other night, which is unlike me, I don't usually watch a lot of telly. It was about soldiers fighting in Ukraine, and at the end of it, the film-makers asked the soldiers what they were most looking forward to when the war was over and they could go home. And they all said things like: "I can't wait to kiss my wife again", "watch my kids grow up" or "take my dog for a walk on the beach". Needless to say, not one person said, "I can't wait to get back into the office for a full fourteen-hour day so I can earn enough money to buy a Ferrari." Because Abbie was right. None of that stuff matters . . . and yet I centred my whole life around it.'

I glance at Reggie and note the pity in his eyes.

'Sorry,' I mutter, feeling embarrassed about my needless outpouring. 'I've never told anyone that, about Abbie asking for a divorce the night she died. I suppose a part of me believes that if I can make *Daisy's* work, it'll right all the wrongs somehow.' Then I hang my head, feeling the full weight of the emotional baggage I'm lugging around these days.

'I slept with my best friend's wife,' Reggie blurts out.

'What?' I exclaim, his words springing from nowhere and taking me by complete surprise.

EIGHT MILLION MINUTES

'Sorry, I thought that's what we were doing – owning up to things we've never told anyone. Don't worry, it's not as seedy as it sounds,' Reggie assures me, sensing my shock. 'There was this girl I used to see at the gym. This all happened around fifteen years ago. We hooked up, maybe three or four times. It was just a casual thing, never anything serious. Then, about five years ago, my oldest friend in the world, known him all my life, says, "Hey, I want to introduce you to my new girl." I walk into the house, and there she is —'

'The girl from the gym?' I interject.

Reggie nods. 'I wasn't sure at first if she'd remember me because it'd been a few years since . . . but I could tell by the look on her face that she most definitely did. I never said anything, and nor did she. I guess between us, we've silently agreed never to mention it.'

'Is it that bad? You couldn't predict she'd end up with your mate one day,' I point out.

'True. But even to this day, every now and then, the whole thing will cross my mind and I feel this crushing sense of betrayal, especially when he made me best man at his wedding.'

'Wow, I bet that was some speech!' I say, unable to stifle a laugh.

Reggie smiles and shakes his head.

'Why are you telling me all this?' I ask.

'I don't really know,' Reggie says, as bemused as I am by our spontaneous brotherly

350

outpouring. 'I get the sense that you're feeling really alone in your head right now. You feel as if you're the only person to have wronged another, but you're not. We all carry regret. We've all done things we're ashamed of. It doesn't make you a bad person, it just makes you painfully human.' He leans forward, his elbows resting on his knees as he delivers a heartfelt and beautiful speech on the human condition.

Despite this, I have the distinct feeling Reggie would have a very different opinion of me if he knew the whole truth of what happened the night Abbie died. About the 'cancer' and all the twisted lengths I went to, manipulating my wife so she wouldn't leave me. I know I can never tell another soul what I did. The lie I told will forever remain my most shameful secret and will die with me as it did with Abbie.

'Come on. We can't sit for too long. We still need to get back so I can teach you how to poach an egg.' And Reggie bounces up from the bench like a springer spaniel. I sit and watch on as he jogs away. I'm so tired and I just can't muster the same energy.

'Come on!' he calls, turning round and continuing to jog backwards.

Show-off.

'You have to keep moving, Jason! Your calves won't thank you for all that sitting!'

I groan, getting up from the bench reluctantly, trailing behind Reggie as he jogs

EIGHT MILLION MINUTES

ahead of me through the park.

CHAPTER 28

JASON

With aching calves and a bitter sorrow in my heart, I roll up *Daisy's* metal shutter with Ellie by my side. I'm holding a small bunch of keys in one hand and my notebook in the other, and between us it takes a couple of attempts to pick the right key for each lock. Eventually we gain entry, pushing open the door and stepping into a place where time has effectively stood still.

I have popped in here a couple of times since Abbie's death, but only fleetingly, just to make sure that squatters haven't set up camp and that nothing has flooded or caught fire. I miss Abbie more than ever when I come here – it's as if her ghost lingers here. So far, I've found it incredibly hard to make a concrete decision on what to do with Abbie's business, but I'm hopeful today might be different.

None of my scruples hold Ellie back as she strides through to the back of the shop while I follow at a much slower pace.

EIGHT MILLION MINUTES

Within seconds, she's turned on the lights, allowing our surroundings to burst into splendid technicolour. For me, this place is an untouched shrine to Abbie's last movements and activities, making me reluctant to move or interfere with anything.

'So, where do we start?' Ellie asks briskly, walking out from behind the counter with her hands on her hips, waiting for some type of instruction.

Taking a deep breath, I straighten my shoulders and look around. On the counter in the corner sits a large glass jam jar containing some short-stemmed white roses, just like the ones we used for the funeral. They must have been here all this time, but I never noticed them before. The flower heads are dry and crispy, the petals brown, and the small amount of water left in the jar is an unhealthy greenish-brown colour. Reluctant as I am to rearrange anything, I believe the dead flowers are a sign.

The time has come to inject some life back into this place.

'I think we should grab some bin bags and have a sort through,' I say, picking up the jar. 'Maybe you could start with the fridge? Check the drinks, chuck out any that are no longer in date.' I am winging it, feeling no wiser than Ellie right now.

'OK.' Ellie disappears out the back again. 'Where are the bin bags?' she calls.

354

SAMANTHA KAY

Realising we've arrived unprepared, I head behind the counter, sure there were some miscellaneous objects stored there that might be of use. I place the keys and my notepad along with the jam jar down on the shelf and begin to have a rifle through. Amongst the cleaning sprays, cloths and paper bags, I spot a roll of black bin bags. I pick them up, to reveal a small pile of post that's been left there. I have a quick flick through some old bills, a couple of delivery notes, and that's when I come across the *Congratulations* card I discovered all those months ago.

The sight of it stops me in my tracks. I open it up and read the message inside. *Congratulations on your fresh new start! So happy for you. Love Molly x* I'm not sure if I feel sad, or just plain angry - angry at myself for being an unbearable human being, an excuse for a husband, a man my wife couldn't wait to get away from.

I tear the card in two and toss the pieces inside a bin bag.

'Oh, you found them,' Ellie says, reappearing.

'Yeah, here you go.' I hand her the roll, then pull out the dead roses from the jam jar and chuck them in my bin bag.

'What time is Molly phoning?' asks Ellie, heading towards the fridge, opening the door and starting the process of quality checking the drinks.

It's almost half past two, which means it's almost 9.30 a.m. in Cuba. Molly has very kindly offered to speak to us, to guide us through a couple of things, since most of the equipment in this place is a complete mystery to us both.

'Soon, hopefully.' I look out over the shop floor, not really knowing where to start, fearing the task ahead might be a bigger challenge than I first realised.

'Dad, why do you look so panicked.'

'Do I?'

'Yeah, what's wrong?' Ellie asks.

'Dunno. Uncharted territory, I suppose,' I reply

'What does that mean?'

'It's when you're in an unfamiliar area with not a lot of guidance.'

'Hmm. I feel like that's partly my fault,' Ellie says, as she inspects the date on a box of apple juice before chucking it in the bin bag by her feet.

'Why would you say that?' I ask, surprised.

'Remember, last year, Abbie asked me if I wanted a Saturday job here. And I said no, as if I couldn't think of anything worse than spending my Saturdays with her. But if I'd said yes...well, maybe one of us would know how to work the coffee machine, or where the bin bags were kept.'

'Well, be that as it may, no one knew what the future had in store.' I say, staring at the till and feeling overwhelmed, wondering why the card machine is nowhere in sight.

'I know. But I was always so horrible to her, and I don't even know why, because she was always nice to me.' Ellie says.

I guess I'm not the only person in this family who is harbouring a big old pile of regret.

'You're a teenager, being horrible is part of the job description.' I tell her, unable to deny how unpleasant she often was.

'I just feel bad. Like I stressed her out with all the stuff I put on her. Can I have one of these?' Asks Ellie, showing me a can of 7up.

I nod.

'What kind of stuff?' I ask curiously, unable to recall Abbie ever telling me of any concerns Ellie was having.

'Just . . . stuff,' Ellie mutters, giving nothing away, taking a large loud slurp from her can of drink.

I can't say I know what it's like to be a teenage girl, let alone one who is grieving a significant loss. Nor do I know what's eating away at Ellie, but I do know what it's like to regret your behaviour; to wish so badly that things could have worked out differently. Sadly, that's something she and I have in common, but Ellie's a teenager who didn't know any better, while I'm a grown man with no excuse.

'You know you can always speak to me, about any of your . . . *stuff*,' I offer hesitatingly.

EIGHT MILLION MINUTES

Ellie laughs loudly at my words, but before I have a chance to feel too insulted, my phone begins to ring. It's Molly calling.

'Hey Molly,' I say, as her face appears on my screen.

Ellie abandons her task by the fridge and joins me behind the counter.

'Hey guys, how are you?'

'We're good, thanks. How's Cuba?' Ellie asks, taking hold of my wrist and lowering the screen to her level, getting into view.

'Amazing, but it's so hot!' sighs Molly. True, her cheeks are bright red, her forehead sweaty - and as I look at her, I wonder what exactly Abbie confided in her about the state of our marriage and what Molly must really think of me.

'So,' she adds, 'how are you guys getting on there?'

'Well, we haven't been here long, but Ellie was hoping you could take her through a quick tutorial on how to use the coffee machine,' I say, ready to get down to business.

'OK, have you brought some milk with you?'

Ellie and I gawp at one another. The idea of bringing some milk here hasn't occurred to either of us.

'No? OK, well, have you tried turning the machine on?'

'Er no . . . we were hoping you could help us with that too,' I say, feeling ashamed of my utter

358

incompetence.

'Oh jeez, right, listen up.'

'Hold on, let me grab my notebook.' I fish it out from under the counter and pick up my pen, ready to begin our first lesson. I'm determined to channel our sadness into something positive. I'm determined to make this work.

CHAPTER 29

JASON

Today marks quite a sad day. After five weeks, ten sessions, hundreds of sit-ups and many a path jogged, today is my last scheduled session with Reggie. Afterwards, exhausted from our workout, I lean against the kitchen counter with a cup of black coffee while Reggie stands as he did on our first meeting, with his head buried in my fridge. He's completing one final assessment on my nutrition, our journey together having come full circle.

'Now, you've got your veg, your fruits and your juices, although I'm not too impressed with the number of carbonated drinks—'

'But they're diet ones,' I interrupt in protest, sure I'm allowed one tiny vice in the form of a fizzy drink every now and then.

Reggie closes the fridge door and grimaces. I know he doesn't agree, but he refrains from making his opinion verbal, for I think he realises he's leaving me in a much better state than the one he found me in.

Thanks to Reggie, I'm now capable and also willing to take better care of myself. Admittedly, my cooking skills require some practise, but no longer do I merely survive on ready meals and biscuits. These days I am a man who can grill a chicken breast and boil rice. I am a man who makes porridge for breakfast, even on warm days, and I have recently mastered how to poach an egg and it's all thanks to Reggie.

Like the saying goes, not all superheroes wear capes. Some wear tracksuits and wake you up at 5.30 a.m.

Although it's safe to say I won't miss the physical exertion that comes with Reggie's visits, I will miss him, having greatly appreciated the kindness and patience he's shown me. His sessions have really helped get me out of my own head, and he's taught me how to take responsibility for my own physical health.

It seems our sessions might be coming to a pause at just the right time. Next week, Reggie is flying out to Trinidad for a fortnight's holiday in the sun, while I'm going to be kept busy with interviews, looking to hire a new manager to run *Daisy's*. While no plans have been arranged for any future sessions, Reggie and I have agreed to chat on his return from holiday, a catch-up I shall look forward to.

Right now, Reggie moves from my fridge and on to my kitchen cupboards. Opening a door with each hand, he peers inside and nods

EIGHT MILLION MINUTES

approvingly.

'Oats, pasta, rice – oh, and some seasonings. It's all looking good, Jason. And it's about time you started using this beautiful kitchen, don't you think?'

'You're right. I should probably make the most of it while I can.' Although I haven't spoken about it for a while, Reggie is still the only person who knows that I've been considering a move.

'Have you put it up for sale?' he asks with interest, unaware of any developments.

'Not yet, but I will. Once everything is up and running with *Daisy's*, the next thing I want to do is put this place on the market.' I speak casually, wanting to play down just how much I loathe living here. If I could, I'd give it away, run for the hills and never return.

'You gotta do what you gotta do,' Reggie nods. 'But it seems a shame. You have a lovely home.'

'Maybe I'd feel differently if the kids were here more, but they have their own lives now, and with just me here . . . it's as if this place can't make new memories anymore. Instead, it just reminds me of all the old painful ones,' I say in a low voice, looking mournfully into my mug of coffee.

'Well, hopefully I won't be one of them!' quips Reggie, which makes me laugh and lightens the atmosphere.

'Far from it. I'm very grateful for all you've

done,' I say, wincing at the thought of the state I'd be in right now without him.

'You're welcome.' Reggie says equally sincerely and with a humble smile, before checking his watch. 'Uh oh, I'd better get going.'

Then, remembering something on his way out, he stops to add: 'Before I forget - and do feel free to say no, - an old football friend of mine offered me his two tickets to the West Ham match tomorrow night. He can't go, some prior family commitment or something, but I thought of you. The seats are in Hospitality. I wondered if you'd be interested?'

It's been a long time since I've gone to a football match. I have no pressing engagements outside of work tomorrow night, but I'm not sure a night alone in the stands will make me feel any better than a night alone at home. At least when I'm home the outside world doesn't have to bear witness to how pathetic I am.

'Oh, I'd love to, but I'm not sure I'd have anyone to go with. Neither of the kids are really into footba—'

'No, sorry, let me rephrase that. *I'm* going to the game, and I have a spare ticket. Would you like to come with me?' Reggie explains, trying not to laugh.

'Really?' I'm touched and truly honoured to learn that Reggie likes me enough to want to see me outside his professional setting. 'Yes, that would be great, thank you.' I beam, feeling like a

EIGHT MILLION MINUTES

five year old on their first day of school, simply thrilled when the cool kid wants to be his friend.

'Good! Right, I really do need to go now, but I'll message you later. See you tomorrow!' And Reggie picks up his sports bag, no doubt on his way to his next client.

I open the front door and see him out, feeling oddly positive, hopeful that maybe there is a world outside of my grief, where new experiences and friendships can be created.

CHAPTER 30

JASON

After weeks of planning, a two-hour drive, three hours of unloading, unpacking, a food shop as well as a Kelly tutorial on how to separate darks and whites and the importance of not overloading the washing machine, it really is time for us to leave.

Standing beside Ellie outside Harry's hall of residence I feel very happy and privileged to be here. There was a time in the history of our family when Kelly would have barred my presence at such an event, and even if she had reluctantly let me join in, the atmosphere would have been intolerable. Abbie and I would have been forced to say our goodbyes the day before, or over the phone, but here I am, thankful that after so many years of mudslinging we've finally been able to put our differences aside, come together and drop our firstborn off at university in a civilised way, just like any other family.

The area around us is a hive of activity,

EIGHT MILLION MINUTES

with freshers like Harry being dropped off by their doting parents. Hordes of people are carrying boxes and random objects from their cars to the halls. The weather has been kind to us, allowing us to manoeuvre Harry's belongings from one place to the other without wind or rain making life difficult. However, as I hang around watching Kelly say one final goodbye, I silently will her to hurry up, as the sun beating down on my neck is making me feel sweaty and uncomfortable.

I could just leave, I suppose. Kelly and I drove here in separate cars, mainly because Harry had us bring so much stuff, but mostly because although things between me and Kelly are much better these days, they'll never be that good. I am keen to get home. I need to feed the cat and, unbeknownst to the kids, tomorrow I have a photographer from the estate agents coming by to take pictures of the house. So, I need to get my house in order as it were and make sure everything is clean and camera ready.

Now I've hired a new manager to run *Daisy's*, and with Harry officially at uni, it felt like the right time to finally put the house on the market. Oddly, as the idea of moving starts to become a reality, I feel daunted by the prospect, wondering if another huge change is really what I need right now.

I hear Ellie standing beside me sigh impatiently and mutter something under her

SAMANTHA KAY

breath, her feelings mirroring my own. Kelly has dragged this out long enough, and for all our sakes it's time for me to take charge of the situation and wrap this thing up.

I go and stand next to Kelly, saying firmly, 'Ok, well I guess that's everything. We should really get going now.'

I note the look of relief on Harry's face, but Kelly is reluctant to let proceedings come to an end and continues droning on with her lesson on basic self-care.

'OK, one last thing, remember you can wash most things at thirty degrees, but if your clothes are soiled, you really should crank up the temperature to forty.'

'Touching. I mean, I don't know if I'm able to match your mums parting words.'

Harry's look of frustration breaks into an amused smile, while Kelly issues me her faithful look of disgust and annoyance.

Ignoring Kelly, I look at my boy, drinking him in. He's all grown up. I have no idea where all the time went or why it had to fly past so quickly, but I honestly couldn't be more proud of him, of the person he is and all he's yet to achieve. I look into his eyes that are just like my own and I think of Abbie. I feel a stab of sadness that she isn't here, that she was never able to witness this moment or see the kind of person Harry will evolve into.

'Have fun, son,' I say quietly, meaning it.

EIGHT MILLION MINUTES

'But not too much fun,' interjects Kelly.

'Don't listen to her. The best years of your life are here waiting for you,' I say, hoping it will be true, that my boy will finally break out of his shell and make lifelong friends, and create scandalous memories that will last a lifetime. I pull him in for a hug, holding him tighter than I ever have before.

'Are you going be OK, Dad?' he says so that only I can hear.

Touched as I am by his concern, the very last thing I want is for him to be worried about me.

'Course. Don't you worry about me. Enjoy yourself, work hard and be good...but not too good.' And I kiss his cheek before reluctantly letting him go. Then I step aside, allowing Ellie her moment to say goodbye to her brother.

Kelly and I watch the kids give each other a brief hug. A bit of banter is exchanged, the lightness in their interaction evidence that today doesn't hold the same level of emotional significance as it does for us.

'Do you want me to take one last sweep of your room before we leave?' Kelly fusses.

'No, he doesn't,' I tell her, placing my hands on Kelly's shoulders and guiding her away. 'We've been here long enough. It's time to go.'

'Get off me.' snaps Kelly, shrugging my hands off, confirming that any physical connection once shared between us is well and truly dead in the water.

Walking away with Kelly and Ellie, I turn around and am pleased to see Harry is still there, outside the entry of his building, watching us walk away. I give him a wave. He waves back, before a girl with blue hair stops to speak to him. On seeing that, I turn back around, granting him some privacy, fully assured all is going to be just fine.

As the three of us stroll towards the car park, I walk a couple of steps ahead of the girls, always preferring to put a subtle distance between myself and Kelly. We've shared a good day, putting on a stellar display of unity for the kids, but as ever, I'm happy for any interaction between us to be over as swiftly as possible.

Ready to head on back to my lonely home, I press down on the key fob in my hand and the headlights on my car welcome me with a flash. Wanting to say a proper goodbye to Ellie, I wonder where she's suddenly disappeared to.

'Where's Ellie gone?'

Kelly points a finger over my shoulder. I turn - and there she is, standing by the passenger side of my car, her head buried in her phone, her fingers tapping away at the screen.

'See you soon, Ellie belly,' I say, ready to hug her goodbye.

'I'm coming with you,' she replies, barely looking up from the screen.

'Oh, OK,' I say, stopping in my tracks.

EIGHT MILLION MINUTES

'Actually, Ellie's decided she'd like to come and live with you,' Kelly says. 'It was her own idea.'

I stand open mouthed and dumfounded, looking back towards Ellie as she slips her phone into the pocket of her baggy jeans.

'Well, don't sound too excited about it,' grumbles Ellie.

'I'm just surprised, in a good way. Are you sure you're ok with this?' I look at Kelly, and to my astonishment I see her nod and smile.

'Well, you know,' Ellie says, 'now that I'm strictly your part time employee at *Daisy's,* I thought it made more sense for us to be close. Also, we think you and Daisy might need some looking after.'

I'm not sure if that *we* refers to Ellie and Harry, or Kelly as well, but I don't ask. Personally, I think I've been doing a decent enough job looking after myself, but I know the kids worry about me. About the amount of time I spend alone and how greatly Abbie's death has changed everything.

'I think you'll find it's my job to look after you,' I remind her, deeply touched. I feel a lump form in my throat.

'I respectfully disagree. We're family. We look after each other,' Ellie says.

I swallow hard, refusing to blink, fearful I might start crying right here in the car park.

'We going or what then?' Ellie asks in

her normal stroppy teenager voice, her patience wearing thin.

'Yes, yes. Let's go.'

Ellie opens the car door and jumps inside. Before I do the same, I turn to say goodbye to Kelly, she looks a little choked up, today marking a much bigger change in her life than I could have realised, and I'm surprised but grateful for her selflessness. A hug or even a handshake is out of the question with us, so instead, I simply mouth the words *thank you* to her, knowing this wouldn't be possible without her blessing.

You're welcome, she mouths back, before climbing into her car.

'Can we listen to Taylor Swift?' Ellie asks when I get inside the driver's seat. She is already tapping away at the screen on the dashboard, lining up the playlist.

'Are you sure your mum's OK with this?' I ask, simply astounded by the day's events.

'Yeah. Now she's all loved up with George she's hardly home, and anyway, I'm sixteen, I can do what I want.'

'Ha, not quite yet you can't,' I tell her, starting the engine and pulling out of our space just as Taylor Swift starts to sing that song about being a twenty-two year old over the car speakers.

'So, I was thinking,' Ellie says loudly, 'that now your house is going to be my official residence, it's time we redecorated my room.'

EIGHT MILLION MINUTES

'Mmm?' I say absent-mindedly, trying to concentrate on the road. The satnav's not picking up our location yet and I can't remember the route back to the motorway.

'I'm thinking mint-green walls with pink blankets and cushions. So maybe we could go to the DIY place tomorrow and pick up some colour samples.'

'Tomorrow?' I echo, suddenly remembering my plans with the estate agent and the photographer.

'Yeah, tomorrow. You haven't got any plans, have you?' Ellie has sensed the reservation in my response.

'Tomorrow...No. None at all,' I reply with a smile, feeling happy - not to mention relieved - to have a reason to cancel my plans. 'If you like, we can go to that homeware store tomorrow, the one on the A12, and get some pink things.'

'Yeah, and they have that café there. Maybe we should get breakfast and check out the competition.'

I laugh inwardly. 'I like your thinking,' I say, simply thrilled that my teenage daughter should want to be seen in public with me, let alone stake out local business rivals. The satnav finally picks up our location, and as we head towards the motorway, I feel myself relax. How strange it is, I ponder, how in the blink of an eye, everything can change. Sometimes for worse, sometimes for better. Less than an hour ago, I

SAMANTHA KAY

was dreading my return home, but now, for the first time in a long time, I feel almost excited by the idea.

I take a fleeting glance over at Ellie in the front passenger seat. She's singing along to the music and I suddenly feel certain that everything is going to be all right. True, my life may no longer look as it did before, the way I had dreamed it would, but I'm grateful for today. Safe in the knowledge that I have everything I'll ever need in the people I love.

EPILOGUE

The sky was dull and grey. The clouds were spitting rain and an unseasonal chill travelled through the air. It was springtime in London, and as ever, the weather was unpredictable, often miserable, and perfectly replicated the physical state Jason found himself in.

His feet were in searing pain, his ankles felt as if they were about ready to buckle and he couldn't bear to think about the untold damage done to his toenails. The carnival atmosphere had lost all its sparkle somewhere around mile 21. At that point, the cheering crowds had long since disappeared, the best London landmarks were either behind them or so far ahead it seemed impossible that they would make it to the Houses of Parliament, let alone to The Mall and Buckingham Palace.

But every time Jason felt like giving up, he would see her face, and remember why he was there. He'd see Abbie, her blue eyes, her blonde hair and pretty smile, and hear her laugh. The mere thought of her spurred him on, forcing him to continue, to push through the pain. He wondered what she would think of it all. Would she be proud of his valiant effort, or would she deem it all a big unnecessary gesture?

In the two years that had passed, Abbie was never far from his mind, and nor was the guilt and deep regret he still felt. He often wondered what life might look like if she were still here. Would they have worked things out, or would they be apart, forging new and separate lives?

It was a question he would never know the answer to, and so he kept such wonderings strictly to himself while he carried on playing the role of doting widower, doing what he could to channel his sadness into a positive legacy. What seemed like a good idea at the time, soon became a full-on training commitment, as well as a financial obligation, the fundraising as important as the running.

But Jason was never alone.

Although Reggie might not have experienced the same emotional connection to the cause, he was a good friend, the best in fact. He'd been there every step of the way. Through every frosty morning and soggy evening, every sore knee, the many moments of self-doubt and every fundraising event. When Jason flagged behind the person dressed as a giant

EIGHT MILLION MINUTES

Dalmatian by Cleopatra's Needle, the two friends remained side by side. Through exhaustion and excruciating pain, they held each other up and willed each other on.

Eventually the crowds returned, and the people cheered, and after five hours and twenty-three agonising minutes, with their hands held onto one another's and thrown high above their heads, the two men crossed the finish line like true champions. With tears in their eyes, elation finally overshadowed the physical pain. But even as Jason collected his medal, he couldn't help but think the day was less of an achievement and more of a penance. His feelings of shame were more tolerable these days, but never gone completely.

Through the drizzle, Jason and Reggie dragged their aching feet along to Horse Guards Parade and were soon spotted by Ellie and Harry. Ellie stood next to her friend Grace, each holding one edge of a large blue and white sign they had made, reading *Go Dad and Reggie!*

Over the past year or so, Grace had become something of a subtenant in Jason's house. She was there most weekends, the two girls often taking over the lounge and the kitchen, drinking all his 7ups and eating all his biscuits, but Jason didn't mind. In fact, he rather liked it. They made the house feel alive again.

As was usual these days, Harry stood surgically attached to Izzy, his girlfriend from university. Today her hair was bright pink, but whilst they'd been together it had been an array of colours, most of which could be found in any standard printer. Hair aside, Izzy was a nice girl, and she was good for Harry, helping to bring him out of himself.

As Jason and Reggie approached them, the four cheered and clapped. Ellie rushed towards Jason, hugging first her dad then Reggie, inspecting their medals. By some miracle, Harry let go of Izzy long enough to hug his father, telling him how proud he was.

The group huddled together for a celebratory selfie on Ellie's phone. Three snaps were taken until she was satisfied enough to release everyone from their positions. As they relaxed, Jason noticed a woman approaching them. She was looking at Reggie, as if trying to place him. Her brown hair was pulled back into a high ponytail and she was dressed in running gear, a number attached to her front just like them.

'Reggie? Is that you?' she called.

He turned to look and on seeing her, smiled widely.

'I thought it was you,' said the woman, and Jason noted an accent in her voice, possibly Australian.

'Crystal!' beamed Reggie, and the two of them hugged briefly. 'How are you?'

'Oh, I'm ace! I feel like I've been hit with

EIGHT MILLION MINUTES

a sledgehammer, but otherwise, all good. How about you?'

'Physically, I've had better days,' Reggie said wryly, 'but all is well. This is my friend Jason and his family. Everyone, this is Crystal, an old client of mine.'

'Oh, snap!' Said Jason, to which Crystal gave a puzzled look, confused by Jason's term of phrase.

'I'm an old client of Reggie's too, but now we're just friends,' Jason told her, proud of his upgrade in status.

'Right . . . so who were you guys running for today?' asked Crystal.

Just like himself, Crystal looked wiped out. She was about his age, maybe a year or two younger. Her hair was frizzy from the elements and her cheeks flushed, her skin glistening from the rain on her face. She had the prettiest brown eyes, he thought, large and kind, and the most wonderful smile. Looking into her face, Jason suddenly felt a little coy, but he wasn't sure why.

'Brains,' he answered, stumbling on his response. 'A brain charity. My wife, my late wife Abbie, she died of a brain aneurysm two years ago.'

'Oh, I'm sorry to hear that.' Crystal's sympathy was immediate and heartfelt.

'What about you?'

'Testicles.' She said bluntly, to which Jason released a short laugh.

'My dad, he died of testicular cancer last year.' The sadness in her voice revealed that her grief was still raw, which made Jason feel ashamed of his instinctive laughter on hearing the word 'testicles'. He looked up at the drizzly London sky and wondered if this was indeed Abbie's idea of a joke, her way of reminding him that she was never far away.

'Terrible disease,' he said, clearing his throat.

'Yeah. You know, come to think of it, you look familiar,' Crystal mused. 'I think I've seen you before, on Reggie's socials. Did you guys host a fundraiser at a dog café or something?' she asked, tugging at her ponytail as she spoke, and Jason noted there was no wedding band on her finger.

'Yeah, that's him, Jason owns the place,' confirmed Reggie, who was enjoying watching them chat together.

'You own a dog café? Amazing. I love dogs!' Crystal cried.

'Well, the café was actually my wife's, now it's more my daughters venture,' Jason said, gesturing towards Ellie and Harry, trying to include them in the conversation. Always protective of their father, however, the pair stayed silent, merely nodding coolly as they sized Crystal up.

'I also own a car dealership, that's my main business,' Jason told her, drawing his attention back to Crystal.

'Well, I love cars too,' she said, gently touching his arm. It was only for a second, but in that moment, Jason felt a small flicker of something ignite inside him. He wasn't sure what it was exactly. Friendship? Physical attraction – chemistry, hope, maybe? But whatever it was, it felt exciting, if a little terrifying.

Over the past two years, he'd as good as written off any thoughts of a new relationship, convinced that no one could ever match the depth of the love that he'd felt for Abbie. But as Crystal laughed at his jokes and they chatted with ease, Jason Turner began to hope that a life of romantic solitude wasn't a foregone conclusion after all.

The End

SAMANTHA KAY

Thank you for taking the time to read
EIGHT MILLION MINUTES. If you
enjoyed reading this stroy, please leave a
review on Amazon or Good Reads.
Thank you.

BOOKS BY THIS AUTHOR

Found

When one-time teenage lovers Jack Lewis and Carly Hughes bump into one another, they don't expect to see each other again, but their fleeting encounter makes a lasting impression on them both. Jack and Carly each assume that, in the years they have spent apart, life has been kinder to the other than it has to themselves. An assumption that could not be further from the truth. While Jack is haunted by the tragedy that caused him to swap a successful career in journalism for teaching, dealing with yet another failed relationship and residing in his grandmother's spare room, Carly, having dropped out of university to care for her dying mother, has given up on her hopes and dreams and is slowly suffocating in a loveless relationship whilst feeling duty-bound to look after her boyfriend's ailing mother.

When Carly's hours at her place of work are

reduced due to budget cuts, she finds herself enrolling in an evening creative writing class, simply as a means of keeping out of the house. Little does she expect, though, that the teacher of the class will turn out to be one Jack Lewis.

With their paths unexpectedly crossing again comes the beginning of a friendship, with friendship soon blossoming into something more. However, with the realities of adult life now prevalent, will Jack and Carly be brave enough to start their lives over together, or will the demands and responsibilities of adulthood continue to hold them back?

Good People

Claire's life has fallen apart in the most spectacular way.

After her affair with a work colleague is exposed, Claire - a career driven mum, is banished from the family home, her contact with her young son reduced to scheduled weekend visits.

Having sought refuge with her sister Rachel, Claire is informed of a surprise birthday party taking place over the bank holiday weekend for their terminally ill Father.

Keen to keep up appearances and not wanting to burden her father with her recent relationship woes, Claire manages to convince her resentful ex; Mark, to join her for the weekend with their young son Dylan.

Built on a foundation of high tensions and strained interactions, Claire and Mark embark on a weekend in which they are forced to display a convincing act of harmony and unity, but could a weekend forced together finally help them overcome their issues?

You're A Dream To Me

After the suicide of her husband, Lydia Green's life is turned upside down.

In the aftermath of Steve's death, the secrets he kept begin to surface, resulting in Lydia having to say goodbye to her easy carefree lifestyle; and is forced to rebuild her whole life again from scratch.

Lydia is constantly haunted by the memory of Steve as she sleeps. The shame and anger Lydia feels surrounding her husband's death means she constantly experiences disturbing nightmares that she struggles to make sense of.

Embarrassed by Steve's choice to end his own life, Lydia is often quick to fabricate tales to others regarding the circumstances of his death.

During her journey home from a disastrous first day back at work, Lydia, quite literally, falls into the life of handsome rail engineer Scott.

Unable to come to terms with the unsettling facts of her past, while Lydia and Scott's budding romance begins to blossom, Lydia fabricates a fictitious tale surrounding the reasons behind her newfound widowhood.

With the help of her best friend Ruth and an unlikely bond found in her new boss Jon, can Lydia find the strength to eventually be honest with Scott, and finally put the ghosts of her past to rest?

Printed in Great Britain
by Amazon